MORE Tales of THE ABSURD AND THE FANCIFUL

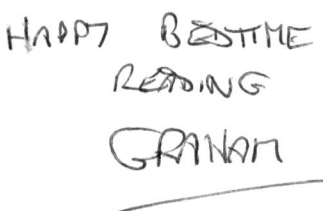

HAPPY BEDTIME
READING

GRAHAM

Graham Warby

INTRODUCTION

This is the third time I have had the temerity to put together a collection of self-penned short stories. It really doesn't get any easier, and even if it did, you would just try harder. Once again, every cent will go to the Family Holiday Association, a charity which arranges UK based holidays for children who have never had them.

It's much the same mix as before. Most are supposed to be funny, with a few concerning the supernatural. Two have a polemic theme, one is on travel and one or two are of a romantic nature. Part of the fun may lie in trying to work out which is which. I apologise that death in one form or another still seems to be one of my principal pre-occupations, but cake and biscuits do make quite a few appearances as well. I don't know about you, but I always read short stories in bed before I go to sleep. It would be too silly to try doing it the other way round? It seems to have been medically proven that reading before sleep helps your sleep, so just maybe this volume, if used wisely, can claim health benefits?

More thanks than ever go to the wonderful members of my Creative Writing Group in Chipping Norton. I have written to the Pope, the Nobel Prize Committee and the United Nations arguing your cases.

Thanks again to my brother Ian who remains prepared to read and comment on everything I send him, and to my lovely wife Liz who listens to this stuff and somehow manages not to go over the top in her praise. Finally, my thanks to Doug Lamb, without whom I would not have a cover, and to Jeff Balcombe without whom there would be nothing to put inside it.

And that's about it really. I put a lot into this and I hope you enjoy it.

Contents

The Invitation   7

Is that a dagger?   21

The Old Lady and the Crab Apple
Tree   35

New Bear in Town   43

Sleepwalker 1   55

Sleepwalker 2   59

Sleepwalker 3   63

Original Story   71

Justice Brownlow's Conscience   85

The Writing Group   99

Lesson No. 1   115

Sherlock Holmes and the Case of the
Pale Chinaman   129

Curlew Cottage   147

Broadening the Mind   161

The Key 175

The Christmas Ghost 185

Le Chat Perdu 193

Sherlock Holmes and the Case of the
Fallen Climber 203

Watchers 223

More Coffee 235

The Dream 253

Not All Vegetables…… 265

The Intelligence 289

Close Friends 301

A Trip from Alpha Centauri 315

Sherlock Holmes and the Case of the
Malevolent Mycologist 331

THE INVITATION

Olivia Green stared at the letter in something close to awe. That looked like real sealing wax, and the writing was handwritten in flowing gothic text. Who did that these days? If this was the kind of mail the new postman was going to bring, she only wished he had not had to wait his turn until the old one had limped loudly down the road with Mrs Chesham's pug still embedded in his right calf muscle.

Her mind was in overdrive. It could be a sealed invitation from the vicar? Perhaps in recognition of her work with the Bookshop, or her so regular attendance at church coffee mornings? Either would provide excellent material for her next letter to Cousin Barbara.

Or maybe it was from the new people in the old house that backed onto her cul de sac? They had a tennis court on their sweeping back lawn, and it was high time they took their place in their new community by holding some kind of "soiree"!

Olivia could see herself in attendance wearing a feathered tiara and a rich stole draped casually over her shoulders. She would be careful not to eclipse her hosts of course, but they would need someone of long standing in the village to make the necessary introductions, and leaving aside jokes about her height, no one was of longer standing that she!

She rang Dolly Jennings about sharing a bus trip to town to find a suitable stole. "I think you mean a shawl" dear was the unenthusiastic response.

The truth was Olivia had been somewhat down in the dumps since David and Kathy Batchelor moved into next door. The old owners had been bad enough, flooding their back garden with Pampas grasses and parking their car badly on the verge, but the new ones rarely even mowed the lawn.

David was a large hairy man who looked like one of those old Canadian trappers. A really rough type! They had never even been round to introduce themselves, which Olivia felt was the height of bad manners. On day one they had removed the decaying fence dividing the two plots, claiming later that it darkened theirs and made it look small. After considerable research she established that this **was** legal, but it remained highly irregular. Batchelor had obviously been born in a field!

Olivia was well aware that without the fence they gained a magnificent view across her impeccable grounds, and suspected this was the real reason for its demise. A great amount of backbreaking toil had gone into her flower beds over many years, and Olivia felt she had earnt the right to keep it to herself. After all, she had paid enough for it!

The Invitation

Now their horrid weed seeds blew across into her garden and made her gardeners life a misery. They just laughed when she suggested their garden would benefit from a few nice Cistercians, and she had twice caught their tortoise Hector nibbling her perennial Sedum. Once the beast had given her a terrible fright when she found it skulking round her wheely bins. She was far from convinced that tortoises couldn't deliver a nasty nip, and promptly asked old Mr Pound return it to its owners.

No, there was no question but that she was owed some recognition from someone. She would exhibit her customary self-control, and wait to open her letter until her son Terry was in attendance to be suitably impressed. She placed it proudly before the living room carriage clock and rang him immediately.

***

At ten that Thursday Terry was sat, impatiently tapping his watch, on the sofa facing Olivia in her comfortable reclining chair.

"I can't believe you dragged me over here just to open a letter! Honestly mum, they don't just hand out 'Gongs' as easily as that. You've never even met the King have you, and what have you ever done to bring yourself to the attention of the palace? It hasn't even got a stamp or postmark. You don't think he brought it round himself, do you?"

The Invitation

Olivia pulled her shoulders back and huffed loudly. "I should have known that would be your attitude! You never show any faith in me! If you have no interest in my mysterious well-wisher, you can just skuttle back to that dreary office of yours."

"I will" her son replied testily, "but first let's get this over with." With that he reached across the coffee table, grabbed the envelope and tore it open.

"Please be careful dear, don't spoil it!" begged Olivia.

Two pieces of paper fell to the floor and Terry swept them up. He leaned back grinning from ear to ear.

"Well, the first one is your new community tax bill. David Batchelor has added a post it note to say the postman accidentally delivered yours with theirs, but you're right, you do have a fan. This one is to invite you to Hector the tortoise's birthday party next Friday, dress casual.

Olivia was apoplectic. "Oh dear!" After a long pause she added "well, I'm not going! Not if they paid me!"

"Well, they won't" laughed Terry, "next Friday is the first of April. They're winding you up Mum! They have certainly got your number even if the Post Office haven't".

***

She should never have mentioned the incident to Dolly Jennings. She had realised this the moment the words were out of her mouth. The following week she had had to endure Mrs Cecil asking her to give Hector her best regards as they passed in the High Street. The next day, when Pink Susie came over to do Olivia's hair, the pink one said she hadn't realised Olivia was interested in animals. She told her that her friend Mary's rabbit had had kits, and asked whether she would be interested in taking one.

Olivia reasoned that if Pink Suzie now knew about the sham invitation so did the whole village. Sure enough when she ran into frail old Mrs Hardaker from No 20 at the Day Centre, even she expressed her fondness for tortoises, and asked whether "Olivia's" Hector would be interested in her vegetable scraps.

Olivia couldn't stand the sight of the beastly reptile and the whole thing was just so embarrassing. She was so completely a plant person. Animals had always been so messy, so smelly, and so untidy. They had a nasty habit of making deposits on things, especially plants. They made noises. Always barking, mewing or chirruping. Her visitors would be looking out for hairs on the sofa or the smell of dog food before she knew it. Ugh! What must people be thinking?

***

It was some two weeks later, during a sparsely attended session at the Bookshop, that Dolly Jennings, while offering a plate of Bourbon biscuits, passed on the news that Mrs Baldwin of Peach Avenue had been robbed.

"It was very strange apparently. They only took her drawers! Straight off the washing line. Six pairs! The poor woman doesn't know where to look. She had to make a special trip to town to get some more."

Olivia did not in fact know Mrs Baldwin very well and, whilst discretely wiping Dolly's spittle from her blouse, expressed only a polite interest in the news. She privately suspected the silly woman must have misplaced that element of her laundry, perhaps forgetting to take them out of the spin dryer.

She was rather more intrigued to hear later that week from Zuzka her cleaner, and source of any village gossip not passed on to her by Pink Susie, that old Mrs Hardaker's underwear had also disappeared. This was rather more alarming as Zuzka herself had done the wash and put them out on the line. No question here about an actual theft. As Zuzka and Olivia reviewed the case over a large gin and tonic after her shift, Olivia made the point that both properties backed onto a public thoroughfare. Mrs Hardaker's backed onto Blackberry Drive, and Mrs Baldwins onto the cutting that led on to the High Street.

"I don't know about the Baldwins, but No 20 has a low wall at the back. I imagine the thief got in that way. But what on earth would anyone want with Mrs Hardaker's old pants? Except Mrs Hardaker of course! It must be the work of a pervert!"

The Invitation

The knicker thefts continued, and soon the unknown culprit became known throughout the village as the 'Burton St Nicholas Knicker Nicker'.

At the bookshop Dolly was insisting she now dried her smalls on the living room radiator rather than risking the wicked outside world, and Mr Carpenter who lived, rather precariously, alone speculated endlessly as to whether his underpants were safe.

Olivia knew from the size of her that Dolly's undergarments could have graced a small yacht, and this further cemented her view that the robber must be a raving pervert. She was unsuccessful in persuading Mr Carpenter that such a creature would surely decline the opportunity to acquire a selection of his Y-fronts, as the creature would be driven solely by his suppressed sexual urges. The poor man however remained insistent in his view that all the laundry must have been acquired for re-sale. He suspected a well organised gang of eastern Europeans.

***

The following month Pink Susie's visit was devoted to a detailed analysis of the case. Apparently, the police had become involved. Sergeant Griffiths and the rather forbidding Constable Johnson had been seen cruising the major roads in the village looking for clues.

"It never used to be like this", tutted Susie. "My auntie Dolly says this used to be a nice village. Low crime. It's full of old people these days and I do worry so about you all".

Olivia, who was not a day under 80, glossed over the accusation that she might be numbered among the local elderly and suggested that this being true, the intruder must be a recent addition to the village.

"I mean they would have to know which properties they could most easily get into, and who was inclined to do all their drawers in one batch, so they must be local? On the other hand, it would hardly be worth their while coming over from the new estate on the far side of the village, would it? Unless of course they were driven by an uncontrollable craving for Mrs Hardaker's or Mrs Baldwin's underwear. Personally, I find that most unlikely. Surely if they came from over that way, they would have far richer pickings close at hand? I'm sure they could find practically anything they fancied on those washing lines? No, I am certain it must be someone new and from over this side."

Between them they could identify only three new village households in Olivia's vicinity over the last year. Mrs Jeffersons mother had moved to the village to be closer to her daughter and grandchildren.

"But she's disabled dear, I can't see her legging it over the hedge at the back of Mrs Braithwaite's Garden, can you?"

There was the young couple in Apple Road.

"But surely, she wouldn't let him go running around gathering up other people's knickers"?

"Well, I don't suppose he would ask her permission first, but you're right, they both work during the day and all the thefts have taken place in the late afternoons."

And then there were David and Kathy Batchelor.

"Oh well," tutted Olivia.

She was not in general what one would call a vindictive or malicious kind of person, but Olivia could recognise an opportunity for payback when she saw it.

"And there isn't so much as a fence between our gardens!"

***

David Batchelor worked at a local scrapyard and his wife Kathy was something of a homebody. They were new to the area, so it took a while before either realised the news that was flying through the village. From Susie the idea had passed to Aunt Dolly that evening. From Dolly the speculation had passed next day to Mr Carpenter at the Bookshop. From Mr Carpenter the news had flooded the Church coffee mornings. From the attendant Mrs Hardaker's cleaner, the redoubtable Zuzka; from Olivia's other neighbour Anita; and from Beatrice down the road, the solution had been passed on to Sergeant Griffiths.

The Invitation

Kathy Batchelor was at the Co-op stocking up on cornflour and skimmed milk, when she overheard a conversation in the next isle, to the effect that poor Olivia Green lived in great fear that not even a fence or hedge stood between her underwear and the "St Nicholas Knicker Nicker! This news did not even begin to make sense to her, until she returned home to find a police car parked outside their house and her husband David within being interviewed by the rather forbidding constable Johnson. When she was gone, Kathy conducted an interrogation of her own.

"What did she say?" asked a highly anxious Kathy.

"She said there was widespread speculation in the village to the effect that I had been breaking into people's gardens – old peoples gardens at that – and stealing their underwear from their washing lines. She asked what I had to say."

"What did you say?"

"Well, not much. I was pretty shocked I can tell you. I said that if I was in the habit of stealing used underwear it certainly wouldn't be from a bunch of old pensioners."

"What did she say?"

"She asked what kind of underwear I **was** interested in. I said I had no interest whatsoever in ladies' underwear. Well, apart from my wife's obviously. Then she asked whether I was familiar with the idea of lexical leakage. Apparently, it's when the language you use reveals more than you intend about the kind of person you are. She asked if I was telling her I liked dressing up in your underwear".

"What did you say?"

"I told her that wasn't what I meant, that she was tying me up in knots. She asked if that meant I was into bondage as well? Then she asked if she could search the house!"

"Oh my god! I was going to do a wash tomorrow. You didn't say yes, did you?"

"I had to love. You don't say no to Constable Johnson. I don't suppose she even wears underwear unless it's made of horsehair. Anyway, she didn't find anything suspicious, although she did ask how much I had paid for that new watch. You would be surprised what gets chucked in that tip."

"Well, it sounds as if that went really well! Even in the Co-op just now they were saying Mrs Green was concerned about your passion for ladies' underwear. Why are people picking on you anyway? You haven't upset anyone have you? You haven't got something you need to tell me, have you darling?" She paused, and then added in a rather menacing tone "if you have, you know I'll understand"

***

The news of a visit from the rather forbidding Constable Johnson was of course round the village in less time than it took Pink Susie to demolish a packet of crisps. Anita and Mrs Hardaker had even seen the police car for themselves, and any credibility David had possessed as a neighbour vanished faster than a Saharan snowdrift. That David Batchelor was half way to Alcatraz as far as they were concerned.

This news of fresh evidence against him never entered the somewhat reclusive Batchelor household. Even if it had, it would not have worried the subject of the speculation half as much as his wife's now keen interest in her husband leisure interests. She monitored his comings and goings from the house minutely. She would turn up on an unexpected stroll along the canal when he was out fishing, or be glimpsed through in the lounge bar on those rare occasions he dropped into the Kings Head for a pint after work. Furthermore, she always insisted in accompanying him on his weekly Sainsbury's shopping expedition.

There was a rush on fencing panels at the local garden centre where, they received a number of enquiries about possible provision for domestic electric fencing. Several security cameras were installed around the village, and two new neighbourhood watch schemes were launched. The latter of course involved a run on biscuits, tea and scones for community meetings, and in all, the speculation about David Batchelor 'Knicker Nicker' had a significant and positive impact on the local economy.

Until of course the culprit was unmasked.

The Invitation

It happened one sunny afternoon in early July, just as the schools broke up for summer. The culprits had got cocky and dispensed with a lookout as Mrs Winters, the serious-minded Co-ordinator for the Bookshop explained later to her Thursday team.

"Does anyone know Sam Cookson? Mrs Cooksons eldest? It was his gang apparently. Began as a dare. Everyone had to take it in turns on the way back from school. Of course, the summer break meant no more opportunities on the way home. Everyone wanted to be the last 'Knicker Nicker', so they all went through the hedge into Mrs and Mrs Cheshires place. Mrs Walpole saw them emerging back on to Shady Lane. She didn't try and stop them. That Sam is a big lad, but she did pass the news on to Constable Johnson. She went round to the Cookson place and found a huge stash of underwear under the boards of the garden shed. I doubt the owners are going to want any back unless they have a keen interest in entomology.

"Now I am fully aware that this shop only fronts as an ongoing charitable concern, and that sadly its true function is, all too often, to feed the local gossip mill, not that it needs your help. On this occasion however I would actually entreat you to pass this news on to everyone you know. A lot of damage has been done by uninformed speculation about the 'Knicker Nicker' and the sooner the village gets over it the better. The culprits will I understand be doing a great deal of community service repairing fences around the village, hopefully in more than one way, and certainly, God help them, under Constable Johnsons close personal scrutiny."

"I'm sure everyone here has the best interests of the village in mind at all times" spluttered Dolly, "Don't we Olivia? I think you are being very unfair to talk like that."

Olivia sighed. "I suppose Cooksons gang have confessed to all the thefts? What a shame..."

***

The news had been passed on by Sergeant Griffiths to the Batchelor household too late for David. Harassed by his wife's suspicious mind he had resolved to cut the Gordian knot, and tackle the problem at its most likely source. He was creosoting a new six-foot-high garden fence when she got home that evening.

"There. We won't have to have any more to do with that Olivia Green he opined, but he was wrong.

Next day as he went out to his car Olivia was waiting, apparently tending the roses in her front garden.

"Oh, David" she trilled. "I was meaning to ask. How's Hector these days?"

IS THAT A DAGGER?

Director Wally Julesberg was dreading it the way others might dread a simultaneous visit from two pushy mothers-in-law, each bringing their favourite homemade cake. The fight scene in Episode 13, between Zargo the Gothic warlord and Duke Felsian of Apulia signalled the end of the first series of 'Blood Feuds of the Titans'. It should have been a scene worthy of a chapter in his unwritten autobiography. The producers had cast two acting titans, Tarquin Goatspoiler, that great bear of a man, with a beard like the fathomless interior of the Black Forest and those thick angry eyebrows, and handsome Nicki Greytomb, youngest of the Greytomb dynasty.

Tarquin had arrived on set a long-term legend of classical theatre whose "Hotspur" had been hailed internationally only thirty years previously. Nicki had the sleek physique, the arrogant, dismissive cheekbones and the hawklike beak of his famous family, and was never out of the gossip columns. They were both total bastards to work with and the producers were emphatic that for budgetary reasons one character now had to die. They had completely split over which, and so left the tricky decision to Wally. He had so far changed his mind four times in two days.

Tarquin's work was legendary, but he questioned everything, and drank like a rugby pack after six months in Saudi Arabia. Already his gauntlets had been reconstructed because they looked too 'fifteenth century', and he had insisted his hair be died light grey to reflect his characters patrician status. This request, though denied, had delayed filming for a week.

Nicki's leonine appearance would guarantee a huge audience, but the creep was insufferably arrogant and frankly not that good. He was here because his father Anton, mother Thespia, and older brother Crispian had dominated British film for generations.

If Wally killed off Tarquin, he would surely spend the rest of his short life in casualty and would be shunned as shallow with no appreciation for classical acting talent. If he bumped off Nicki he would be branded as someone who put quality before commercial reality, and would probably never work again.

***

In his caravan Tarquin was staring hopelessly at the wall. After Coriolanus he could never work the Globe again. Thank goodness it had all happened in rehearsals. He had been hiding his true self since his miserable years at that odious prep school. Outwardly he was the brash booming perfectionist who effortlessly delivered masterpiece after masterpiece, and who demanded the same standard from others. Inwardly he was alone, crucified with self-doubt, painfully shy, and saw no hope of changing his situation. This talent for concealment was what made him the actor he was. It was also the reason he drank, for a child denied love in childhood sees no hope of finding it later. He gazed down at the diminutive figure of Mr Brown tucked up in bed and silently wept. His ground breaking Hotspur was thirty years old now, and these days his Percy pointed primarily at the porcelain. He had to find some quality in Zargo which would result in a chance to return to the relative privacy of live performance and spare him the lacerating spotlight of film.

***

In the caravan opposite behind its new purple door, painted especially to his specifications, Nicki Greytomb was on the line to Wally's assistant Baz.

"I distinctly specified Deglet or Zahidi dates not this Medjool rubbish. Do you want me crapping through me doublet and 'ose, because those things go right through you! And another thing, the 'ot towels were five minutes late this morning. Don't go blaming me if I'm late on set again, got it? Oh, and make sure tonight I get "Bellygood" yoghurt right, not that over-sugared crap. They pay me a shedload to drink the stuff, so drink the bloody stuff I do, or I stay in 'ere until I get some!"

Nicki was nothing if not fastidious. He was publicly vegan and gluten intolerant, famously destroying a well-regarded West End restaurant after discovering oat grains in his meatballs. He had sued for loss of earnings and gone to bed for a well-publicised week. He was currently in the running for a major part in "I, Oligarch", an immensely popular US soap. If he could act that lump of flatulent blubber Tarquin off the screen, he could definitely expect to put his feet up for the best part of a decade. The trouble was, Nicki knew he couldn't act.

***

3.00pm. Time for the big fight scene. Tarquin kissed Mr Brown for luck, emerged whisky bottle in hand and walked onto the set with his customary giant but slow strides, like a man in no particular hurry to reach his destination. Nicki emerged five minutes later moving quickly with light steps like a dancer. What had his father told him, if you can't get the feel of the part, just makes sure the others don't either, and always blame everything on the director.

***

Tarquin took one look at Zargo's giant two-handed battle axe and groaned inauspiciously.

"For Heaven's sake man, the Goths were heavy cavalry in chain mail. They would have had one hell of a job staying on horseback wielding one of these?"

"Any poor bloody horse would have struggled with you on board, even without the axe. Wally, don't suppose you got an elephant handy?" suggested Nicki.

"Darlings, darlings, please just behave. The fight takes place on foot, for the camera's benefit" mewed Wally. "Now, action!"

Is that a Dagger?

Nicki took an immediate large step towards the camera. The family had assured him that the actor nearest the audience always commanded their attention. Tarquin meanwhile crouched in an aggressive posture, coaxing his fearsome arched eyebrows up into fighting mode. Seconds later he threw the axe down and both hands up.

"Wally love, do you think you could possibly point out to this neophyte that he is holding a sword not an umbrella. It cuts along its entire length; you don't just poke the ferrule at your opponent".

"Well listen to that! Lessons in swordplay from an overinflated bin liner wrapped in scrap metal."

"I am sorry you hold such a poor opinion of my thirty years' experience in classical theatre. I have always thought your own work contained two remarkable elements rarely found in a professional actor, incomprehension and inaudibility. Personally, I am a great admirer of your body of work. I have always admired dwarves! I particularly enjoyed the piece about that community of thugs and criminals based around an East End pub, but I can never find anyone who can remember what it was called?"

"Now why am I not surprised you don't know anyone who's in touch with what sells on T.V.?"

"Poor Nicki. How are you supposed to cope these days without a bar to tape your lines too?"

"If anyone round here needs a bar to lean on I would have thought it was you?"

"I just can't decide which one I hate most" thought Wally. The producers had banked on the two clowns before him igniting a strong creative spark in each other, but this was clearly going to be a full-grown forest fire.

Nicki meanwhile had calculated that he was never going to win a war of words with a classical actor and changed strategies.

As the cameras rolled, he turned away towards his opponent and promptly looked over Tarquin's left shoulder. Instinctively Tarquin turned to locate the source of interest. As planned Wally then begged him to give the scene his full attention.

The actors came together pressing their full weight on their clashing weaponry. Nicki whispered into Tarquin's right ear, "is it true you take your lucky teddy to bed every evening?"

Tarquin pushed him back with a look that would have cooked his Sunday lunch. "Bastard! Who told you that?"

"Oh, it's true then? I suppose after Coriolanus you've been a little short of company in the evenings?"

This last was too much. Tarquin, who had once, in a blind rage, picked his agent up and held him upside down by the ankles outside his fifth-floor balcony until his comb, car keys and matching pen and pencil clattered onto the pavement below, now grasped Nicki by the throat and squeezed.

Wally leaped up and attempted to intervene. "Boys, please. Think of the film!"

Tarquin threw his opponent across the set and raised his axe menacingly.

Nicki, spluttered, wheezed, and muttering something about a demo at a dog food factory he had promised to attend, stormed off set.

Tarquin sighed audibly. After that he could probably kiss goodbye to the Merry Wives of Windsor at the Godalming Empire, at least for a couple of years.

**

It was five anxious days, at least for Wally, before they reconvened. After several protracted phone calls to the producers, he had convened an emergency meeting with the scriptwriters. Scriptwriters! Time was one man could script War and Peace and follow it up after lunch with Anna Karenina, now you had to engage a whole squad of the little twerps to construct enough material for a school play. This never happened on Springwatch!

Tarquin was on set first, to claim the moral high ground. Nicki however, the shrewder of the two, reckoned that if he turned up twenty minutes late, all eyes would be on him while Tarquin would have gone off the boil.

"Sorry everyone, had to take a call from Spielberg! You know what he's like?"

Picking up his broadsword he resumed his previous posture, fully five feet from his previous position.

"That's fine Nicki, said Wally smoothly, and with more than a little relish, we're not using last week's footage anyway. There's been a change of plan. The two of you meet to fight but are interrupted by a pack of goblins. You take out three each before you are overpowered and stabbed to death."

The thespians looked first at each other and then, incredulously, at Wally.

"So, who exactly is going to carry this pile of bulls ordure into series two?" enquired Tarquin.

"I am", replied a lithe young woman with improbably thick blonde hair swirling around her shoulders and a hungry look in her large grey eyes stepping from behind a nearby oak. On first inspection Nicki thought the newcomer was naked, but on closer inspection, something which was completely unavoidable under almost any circumstances, he saw she was dressed in just about enough armour to cover a small bruise.

"I play Kora Princess of the Yorgon. I'm Linda, you won't know me but my dad used to present Blue Peter."

Nicki knew when he was beaten.

"Five, I take out five goblins, at least!"

Is that a Dagger?

There was a sudden bustle as Baz, Wally's assistant burst onto the set.

"Bit of a problem boss. I popped into the canteen earlier for a bite to eat, took one look at the prawn curry and opted for a cheese sandwich. As I came out the goblins had just been released from props so I advised them against the curry."

Wally groaned. "Don't tell me, they ignored you and went for the prawns?"

"No boss, most of them went for the Shepherd's pie, but apparently that was worse!" Half of them are throwing up all over the woods. You're not going to get a takeout of them today at the least."

Wally threw his script up into the air. "Take a break everyone. Take a good long break, and for my sake at least please don't visit the canteen."

Nicki dropped his sword and whispered to Tarquin, "your trailer now?"

Tarquin thought about Mr Brown tucked up in his bed and whispered back "Make it yours."

***

"We are not going to just let him dump us like that are we?" Strictly between the two of us I had nearly lined up a cracking job stateside, but I don't think they will be too pleased with me being killed off in "Blood feuds". Very bad Karma that is! Its more their style to release publicity to the effect that they had to pay through the nose to get me released from my contract. Money well spent from their point of view."

He looked up and was surprised to see Tarquin trying to rub his eyes with hands still clad in their mental gauntlets. "Hey big man, I would take those off first if I were you. You're not having a fit of the vapours, are you?"

Tarquin turned to look out of the window, sighed a long shuddering sigh, and without turning back said quietly "strictly between the two of us, I have long had issues with rejection!"

"That why you turned down Julius Caesar at the Wakefield Hippodrome?"

Tarquin nodded.

"Bloody hell, and I suppose that means it must be true about Coriolanus?"

"They never pressed charges", mumbled Tarquin turning back to face his inquisitor. He rapidly changed the subject. "I take it you have read your contract?"

"'Course not, I have a tame gibbon for that kind of thing. Why?"

"Section 19 Paragraph 2c. Specified star actors shall retain a legally enforceable entitlement to full prior consultation in the event of script changes proposed subsequent to the signing of binding contracts. I take it you are 'specified'? I certainly am."

Nicki thought for a moment. "Oh, goody! So, he can't just dump us?"

"No dear boy, he can't. But that only buys us a little time. Much as I detest having these intrusive cameras practically up my nose, if I am ever to return to legitimate theatre work, I can no more afford a sudden and undignified exit from this fiasco than you can."

***

A week passed and Wally was rueing his decision not to follow the early lure of a lucrative career in advertising. First Ed Broadflanks, Director of the National Theatre, had published an article in *the Guardian* bemoaning the limited opportunities afforded classically trained actors and actresses to pursue opportunities in cinema, and siting it as a major reason for the recent decline in quality national film output. Next, a letter appeared from Dame Julie Drench in *the Times* expressing her view that insufficient consideration was being given to the treatment of talent in modern drama. She felt directors and producers were being allowed to get away with bullying on a scale which could only discourage potential future stars from expressing themselves to the full extent of their abilities. "We will soon become a nation producing product made only by robots and fit only for viewing by robots", she opined.

Is that a Dagger?

The final blow was a call from the producers informing him that Wolfpack Films, one of their primary investors, were withdrawing their 20% stake in 'Blood Feuds'. This followed the news that Anton Greytomb himself was withdrawing from their production of "Return to Tara" to spend time consoling his son Nicki over his recent career setback.

"Good old Julie", sniffed Nicki over a slim line of white powder spread across the dresser in his trailer. "She's been a mate of mums ever since Pride and Prejudice back in the Nineties. I knew she wouldn't let us down."

"The same came be said for dear old Ed" mused Tarquin pouring another generous whisky into his tooth mug. "Though a gentle reminder about certain indiscretions early in his career did not go amiss. By the way, I meant to thank you. I was unaware your brother Crispian had decided to try his hand at theatrical work. He rang me yesterday to say he was producing Henry V in Birmingham next year. He has desperate need of a bankable Falstaff to steady the ship and did I know of anyone who might be interested?"

"And what did you tell him?"

"That I **am** Falstaff and if he even considers asking anyone else, neither he nor they will ever walk without squeaking again. I have to say I never expected such appreciation from a parvenu like yourself?"

Is that a Dagger?

"Easy fat boy, it doesn't mean we're besties. I'm just helping old Crisp out, yeah? You may be a bell ends bell end, but you **can** act. Even a meteoric commercial success like myself can see that. I wonder what the poor man's Sergei Eisenstein out there has decided to do with the script? He can hardly get rid of us now?"

***

It was a scorching hot afternoon and Wally had located the fully restored goblins in full sun, where they were patiently melting into their heavy prosthetic costumes.

That'll teach the little toerags, thought Wally. It would be a long time before any goblin risked eating shepherd's pie again on his watch!

He addressed his actors. "So, it has been decided, after careful consideration", he articulated the last phrase slowly and deliberately, glowering at his stars who leaned innocently against a nearby oak, "that you fight, and as you move through the forest you come across a band of goblins holding Kora Princess of the Yorgon prisoner. You kill all the goblins and release their prisoner. She tells you the Yorgon people have been enslaved by the goblin Lord Gorgul, and you vow to help her. End of series 1, cue series 2.

"Where is the lovely Linda?" queried Nicki. "I don't see her. I was hoping for a chance to share a few ideas of mine with her."

"No wonder she is nowhere to be seen" mumbled Tarquin.

"Perhaps someone could point out to Turbot Goatsampler over there that no one asked for his opinion?" hissed Nicki.

"Apparently she's on the phone to her dad" volunteered Baz. "She's not a happy Princess at the moment; she was talking about getting a job with animals."

"I would have thought she'd come to the perfect place", thought Wally, "though perhaps a job tickling vipers might hold more appeal."

"Might one ask in what regard I am supposed to hold these goblins, the script offers no clue. Is it a lofty contempt rooted in their primitive animal nature; a grudging respect for their innate ferocity; or a casual indifference based on my formidable powers of combat? It makes a great difference to the way I fight them..."

"Oh, one more thing..." interrupted Wally, who had been so looking forward to telling them this bit." I am sorry to announce that due to new and unexpected budgetary pressures series two will only have six episodes. I am afraid I will have to release you both several months earlier than expected. A press release to that effect was issued first thing today."

As he gloated openly at Nicki and Tarquin, he was alarmed to see both were smiling back at him. He had a feeling this production wasn't going to get any easier.

THE OLD LADY AND THE

CRAB APPLE TREE

This story is rather different from many other ghost stories. It's true for a start. It's rooted in a very personal experience. Of course, I don't expect you to believe me. If it was the other way around, and you were telling me about an encounter like this, I don't think I would believe you. I'm telling you all this however because I believe it deserves to be told, and not because I expect it to be taken as true.

Have you ever actually experienced the supernatural in any form? I thought not. It's not all clammy mists, grey ladies searching for lost babies, or headless black monks pointing their long bony fingers. These are the parvenues, the populist Facebook ghosts of local gossip and rumour. Some spirits are far older, much more substantial and deeply rooted. They are not borne out of personal tragedy but embedded in the landscape itself.

My wife, daughter and I had been in the area for several years, frequently enjoying long walks in the largely rural and gently rolling countryside. I was delighted to find myself in one of the few areas of Southern England still blessed with a significant coverage of woodland, and with the wildlife, history and mythology which went with it. There is for example a standing stone to the south of our village, and the site of a plague settlement, abandoned since the fourteenth century, just outside it. There is a sense of continuity and perhaps an accommodation with the past around here which I find a comfort.

The remaining scattered shreds of the old Wychwood Forest, which once formed part of the boundary between Saxon Mercia and Wessex, stretch in places to within two miles north of us. This area in particular feels achingly old. Many of the roads which were cut through the forest are narrow and twisted. They seem to arrive at the little villages concealed among the trees almost by accident. This encounter took place there.

It being a beautiful late autumn afternoon I decided to go for a walk. My daughter Annie asked if she could come with me. She was a quiet thoughtful girl, just turned five that week, and her request came as no surprise. She was clearly apprehensive about starting school after Christmas, and her anxiety had made her rather clingy of late.

We were going on one of my favourite walks, through an old wooded strip where I had often seen roe deer and occasionally foxes, which in spring is flooded with bluebells. I was to discover years later that it had been mentioned in the *Domesday Book*. Given the time it takes oak and beech to reach maturity, to have been an established wood at that time suggests considerable antiquity. For such a remnant to have survived for a further thousand years perhaps suggests something else?

The Old Lady and the Crab Apple Tree

The sun had long since lost its hostile summer glare and was not yet wrapped in the thick grey shrouds of winter cloud. It shone clear, warm and bright. The air itself was crisp and golden, with the light bouncing off the autumn pageant vividly displayed by the ancient trees. It was charged with that extraordinary mystical promise that can sometimes reach out to you at that time of year. If you breathed deeply, you were filled with a strange electricity, tingling with energy and excitement.

I parked off the road by the side of an old church. It is roofless and crumbling now, and stands like an abandoned mine building. It is as if, having sucked what Christianity they could from the area, the congregation have moved on to more promising locations. It doesn't feel as though it has ever belonged here.

We entered through an established gap in the hedge and tramped slowly the full length of the wood, snapping old twigs and kicking up clumps of dead leaves under foot as we went. There was birdsong, great tits and robins, the latter bursting with the sheer exuberance of just being alive, but apart from that, it was so still that when we spoke, our words seemed to bounce off the trees and bushes as though we were passing through the nave of a church. It was hushed. There was none of the scratchy susurration, the chatter of trees, that you might expect in such a place.

For the first few minutes we were surrounded by mature hardwood trees and there was little undergrowth, but after we passed over a dry stream bed, now no more than a creased frown in the land, we reached the more open area where bluebells could be found in spring. Here there were briars and holly. In April it is like a woodland garden here, bathed in soft lime green light. There is dog's mercury, wood anemones, celandine and ramsons as well as the calm sea of fragrant bluebells. On this occasion however, I was headed for an ancient crab apple tree which I knew stood as sentinel at the far end of the wood.

It has leant heavily for centuries, like a weary countryman taking his ease, on an old broken fence at the far edge of the wood. It looks out across open farmland stretching downhill for perhaps a third of a mile away from me. There is a rough path in the foreground to the right-hand side of an unploughed field, and below that a hedge runs along its far side. If you follow the path round to the left, along the edge of the wood, you will come to an old fertility well. This is surrounded and capped by dry stone walling, and primarily serves the needs of a scruffy band of woolly ruminants. A withered Hawthorn stands guard over it, and occasionally I have found its claws decked with ribbons invoking favour for the safe delivery of a healthy baby, proof that old beliefs die hard.

Beyond the field, over a mile away, you can see buildings in the nearest village squatting like huddled animals on the now rising hillside. There is an old church there I know houses a medieval painting of skeletons assiduously shepherding the ungodly into the fiery pit. I doubt the view from where we stood that afternoon has changed much since it was first painted.

The crab apple tree itself was a shambles. On a previous visit I had found I could barely get my arms around its sinuous trunk at shoulder height. Most of its branches were twisted, dead and broken. Many, stripped of bark, seemed to be wriggling indecently in their discomfort, but others above them still sported a proud canopy of golden leaves.

Underfoot however the floor of the wood here was absolutely carpeted with crab apples. There must have been thousands of the tiny green treasures. I wondered at the long-lived fecundity of such a veteran. You could smell the fruit fermenting amongst the undergrowth, with the rich scent hanging, in the absence of even the smallest breeze, like strange perfume around us.

Peace, and an oddly comforting feeling of exhilaration at the coming close of year. It is a numinous place. I looked down at Annie. She was at ease here, scrambling among the crab apples, and sorting them into piles for some unguessable purpose.

When I looked up again, I was surprised to see an old lady carefully picking her way towards us along the path at the fields edge. I say surprised because she could have been no further than twenty or thirty yards away. This was of course impossible given that she hadn't even been in sight less than a minute earlier. She was dressed all over in black, with her head bowed wearily to navigate the vagaries of the uneven path. She was making heavy use of a thick wooden staff. Even so, I was amazed anyone of her evident age and fragility could have made it so far on such rutted terrain. She was still going to require the energy to walk a good further half mile through the wood, and there was no habitation of which I was aware anywhere close on the other side.

I looked briefly at my daughter who was completely engrossed with her store of apples, and when I looked up again the old lady was crossing a broken style in the fence close to our tree.

She was short, with her thick white hair loosely gathered behind her head. At close quarters her furrowed parchment skin reminded me of the gnarled bark that remained on the crab tree. I could see patience and suffering in her slow uneven movements and the way she gripped her staff, but her eyes when she smiled were a revelation. There was no shred of resentment or malice at the injustice of old age. I had never seen such warmth and generosity in a human face. They radiated a calm and profound comfort completely at one with the extraordinary atmosphere of the wood around us.

She glanced down at Annie who continued with her game among the tangled roots. My serene sensation seemed to intensify, as if the old lady was bestowing some silent benediction. As I watched her, all my petty fears and worries about daily life and concerns about the immediate future for Annie seemed trivial and soaked away from me. I had the sense of being washed through with a strange peace and reassurance, and knew with absolute certainty a blessing had been imparted.

I looked down at Annie for a while beaming with fatherly pride, and when I looked up, I was startled to find the old lady gone. She had already vanished completely from view. She must have moved off through the woods the way we had come. For the first time it dawned on me that we had never exchanged a word. More than that, I realised with a real shock that I hadn't heard a single sound in her presence. Not a single dry twig had snapped, crab apple popped or desiccated leaf crunched as she made her way, and none of the plentiful briars had caught on her long black clothing. The birds had respectfully stopped singing for a time, and the wood had been as silent as an empty shrine.

I was surprised to find it took some effort to speak quietly to my daughter: 'What did you think of that lady'?

Stretching out for more apples, and clearly still reluctant to abandon her play she smiled confidently up at me, 'What lady'?

NEW BEAR IN TOWN

Christopher Robins cousin Euphorbia Badgersbreath and her daddy Hector Badgersbreath had only come for a short visit. The cousins had never been close. Euphorbia was several years older for a start, and she had been raised to regard play as wasted time. She had organised all Christopher Robins toys in rows, and insisted in holding classes in animal rights for them. The Badgersbreaths had eventually waved goodbye, and they were gone before Christopher Robin realised his much-loved bear Winnie the Pooh had gone with them, for a holiday. Someone's Daddy had packed the wrong bear, leaving him with Pooh's cousin the slightly older Excreta Bear.

Never mind said Christopher Robins Daddy, they will be back in a week, they are staying with us on their way to Broadstairs for a nice holiday. In the meantime, maybe you can introduce Excreta to the animals in Hundred Acre Wood, I'm sure they would love to meet her?

Christopher Robin looked at Excreta Bear. He looked at the thin wire glasses perched on the end of her button nose. He looked at the long skinny arms and legs and the thick olive-green fur. Bears in his experience were worn and sticky, with chocolate stains and limbs hanging off. It showed you loved them. This bear looked straight out of the shop window, as though it had been bought and gone straight into a drawer.

He reluctantly picked Excreta up, and led her into the wood straight over to Piglets house.

"Hello Piglet," said Christopher Robin. "This is Excreta".

"Looks like it" mumbled Piglet.

"I am going to ask you to introduce Excreta to all the animals in the wood while Pooh's away on a little holiday."

"Do I have to?" squeaked Piglet. "She doesn't look very friendly!"

"That's because she's been brought up in a city," said Christopher Robin. Excreta's daddy is a psycho..., a psychy..., a cycle-something anyway. He's very clever so I imagine Euphorbia and Excreta are too. Don't you?"

"But I'm not," said the Piglet.

"You look badly undernourished to me" Excreta blurted out. "I imagine you were neglected, perhaps abused as a child? Were you from a very big litter?"

"Don't know" said Piglet his eyes watering. "I was just here. I haven't got any back story."

"Well, it shows. Come on, who are we going to meet first? I have heard some disturbing things from cousin Pooh."

***

First, they came to the place where the Woozle wasn't.

Piglet squeaked with fear. "This is the place where Pooh and I went Woozle hunting. First, we didn't find one Woozle, then we didn't find two Woozles, and then a Wizzle joined them and we didn't find him either."

"Your friend Pooh has an eating disorder," opined Excreta, "Euphorbia says so. He must be high as a kite on all that honey. It would be a wonder if he could find anything at all, never mind something that wasn't even there. If he wasn't he would realise he was being silly. If one something isn't there, then it must be exactly twice as unlikely that you will find two of them. By the way, why does Christopher Robin always dress like a girl? Euphorbias daddy says he's transitioning. If that's true then Pooh should probably have counselling don't you think? It can't be an easy thing for him to come to terms with. Could explain the sugar craving I suppose?"

Piglet just looked at her. "Come on, lets meet Owl. Owl lives high up in a The Chestnuts. He has a knocker, and sometimes a bell-pull. He is the only animal in the wood who can read and write."

"Of course he is," said Excreta. "That is why he lives high up above everybody else. It's a metaphor. His literacy and his elevation reflect his self-perceived social status while simultaneously intended to overawe the downtrodden masses below."

"Oh" said the Piglet, and after taking a while to control his breathing, added "Owl can write. He's very proud of his writing".

"Yeah, you said." Excreta stared at the door sign which said "PLEZ CNOKE IF AN RNSR IS NOT REQD. She tut tutted ironically and added, "well I guess he should be, it's quite unique. You know, if it's holding him back, he can get help with dyslexia?"

Piglet had just started feeling proud at his friend's cleverness and was wondering if he could get some dyslexia too, when Eeyore shuffled diffidently into the clearing in front of Owls tree.

"Hello Piglet" said Eeyore quietly. "What's happened to Pooh? Has he been extensively repaired? It doesn't seem to have worked, because he doesn't look like much fun today."

"Well, I've certainly heard about you," said Excreta without being introduced, "you're Eeyore, the woods resident depressive?" She slowly walked all the way round him. "Grey all over. Possibly suffering from vitamin D deficiency? Do you feel sad, irritable, down?"

Eeyore looked at the bear and nodded.

"Miserable, lacking in interest, tired?"

Eeyore nodded some more.

"Hopeless, empty, depressed?"

Eeyore lay on the floor and moaned.

"You lost your tail for a while, didn't you? You know depression can be triggered by a life changing event? When did you last get checked out by a good vet? If it were up to me, I would recommend more exercise and a better diet."

"Eeyore's only eat grass"

"Well, find some better grass. Get yourself along to a decent support group and work on that self-esteem!"

Eeyore stood on his head and hummed.

"Fine" said Excreta. "Be like that. There's enough material in this wood for a whole book and we haven't even met the Kangaroos yet."

A little further on they came to the clearing where Rabbit lived with all his friends and relations. A pair of long furry ears popped out of a hole in the bank and a round head with a twitchy nose followed them.

"Hello Rabbit" greeted Piglet with some relief. "Is that you?"

"Let's pretend it isn't" said Rabbit, "and see what happens"

"Bit passive aggressive?" queried Excreta in a surprisingly protective tone. "Is someone having a bad day?"

Rabbit looked at his visitor contemptuously. "Don't those glasses get very sticky in a honey jar?"

"Ooh, now you I like! Shame you are so badly underwritten. As it happens, I don't eat honey."

Piglet howled in sheer disbelief. "Every bear eats honey!"

"Look squirt. This bear was responsibly raised on Tofu, Kefir and Avocado".

"What do they taste like?"

"Horrible" replied Excreta, "but that's not the point!"

Piglet, who couldn't see the point of eating anything that wasn't entirely delicious, began to wonder whether Excreta was as clever as she thought she was, only he didn't have enough words to think it out clearly. When he turned to look for him, he discovered Rabbit, having run out of dialogue, had disappeared back down his hole and they walked on.

After a few minutes they came to the Sandy Pit where Roo played. Today however they heard squeaks of delight, splashing noises, thumping and tut tutting from inside Kanga's house.

"I think Roo must be having a bath" confided Piglet.

"I do so hope there's room for two" frowned Excreta, who was entertaining doubts as to whether Piglets state of hygiene was compatible with indoor life, and knocked on Kanga's door.

Kanga opened the door, popped her head out and said "Aha, animals. Not come over for another spot of child abduction, have you? Who's the Geek?"

"This is Excreta, Pooh's cousin" squeaked Piglet. "I have brought her to meet you and Roo."

"Well now she has", said Kanga. "Goodbye" and she began to close the door.

"Just a minute" shouted Excreta vigorously. "Pooh says you never take your eyes off Roo. Is that true?"

"I fear something bad may happen to Roo if I do" stated Kanga. "It did last time" she added looking significantly at Piglet.

"Well don't you think you may be overparenting? Maybe just a little?" asked Excreta. "The overprotective parent can stultify a child and cause significant developmental issues in later life. Not good at all."

"Is that right?" said Kanga. "It's about bathtime right now. How would you like me to wash your mouth?"

"I'm just concerned that what we might be witnessing here, is a textbook example of Munchausen by Proxy," said Excreta. "By drawing attention to the child's problems" she continued, watching Roo jumping up the walls of the small house, "the mother draws attention to the demands made on her as a parent and therefore by implication to her worth as a caring being. At the very least we're talking about Social Anxiety Disorder? When are you going to let Roo make his own decisions?"

"Look sister," Kanga said in a slow, menacing and very antipodean voice, "that's what Roo's do. We jump about. We hop. We bounce. What we don't do is stand around tearing strips out of other animals!"

"Can we go please?" pleaded a small, conflict averse voice behind Excreta. "I'm hungry."

"Please do" encouraged Kanga, "unless of course you would like a nice cold bath and a dose of yummy medicine. Then we could sit round and discuss your views on overparenting?"

Excreta led the way out.

"Where are we going?" asked Piglet.

"No idea" said Excreta who was suddenly feeling very out of sorts. "Just walk!"

Some minutes later a large furry tornado in black and gold flashed past her, ran round a large tree, whisked her round in its backdraft and shot round another two trees before coming to rest in front of her. "Grr" it said in a particularly friendly way. "Grr".

"This is Tigger," said Piglet. "He's very bouncy!"

"Whatever did you give that thing for breakfast, a bucket of e-numbers?"

Tigger responded to the query by jumping up into an overhanging oak and jumping down again next to Piglet. "Grr" said Tigger.

"Tigger is always happy," said Piglet

Tigger bounced straight into Excreta's face and said, "have you seen my family? I lost them!"

Excreta stepped back. "Losing things is textbook ADHD, but even then, its going some to lose your entire family. Full of energy, check; outgoing, check; restless and impulsive, check; ouch" she added as he trod on her foot. "Careless and intrusive; check. This kid needs help!"

"I'll go and find some" said Tigger, and bounced off into the undergrowth.

"I'm hungry" said Piglet hopefully.

"Look, this is your wood! If you want food where is the best place to get it?"

"Pooh's house!" squealed Piglet excitedly. "And here it is! I think it must have found us!"

They went inside and Piglet made straight for the high shelf where Pooh sometimes kept boxes of haycorns for him. Excreta sat on a chair and pondered the origins of Pooh's honey fixation.

"Does Pooh worry much about the future?" she asked those parts of Piglet she could still see. "Does he suffer from anxiety? Does he find it hard to manage stress?"

"Mmmm, yummy haycorns" muttered Piglet from near the bottom of a large box.

"How is his relationship with Christopher Robin? I'm sure family problems are the origin of his food fixation."

"Why is eating honey a problem?" asked Piglet. "It looks easy. I bet even you could do it if you tried".

Excreta bristled. "I have no desire to try. In my family we see our bodies as our temples".

This passed over Piglets head, as did most things as large as temples, so he reached for a second box.

"Would you say he saw himself as a perfectionist?"

She looked around the disordered room and decided this wasn't an issue.

"Careful!" This as Piglet knocked a large open jar off the shelf in his attempts to feed while off balance. Catching it as it fell, Excreta spilt honey along her arm and instinctively tried to lick the sticky mess off again.

"I hope Christopher Robin is back soon" wheedled Piglet. He looked round when there was no answer to his plea and saw Excreta absorbed in sticking her arm back inside the jar. She took one exceptionally large lick along her arm and quietly mused "You know this sticky stuff isn't at all bad!"

It was about half an hour later that Christopher Robin popped round to Pooh's to see how Excreta was settling in to life in Hundred Acre Wood. The door was open so he went in.

"Wow, this stuff is amazing! Its umn umn, its yummy. But it'sh all gone!"

Christopher Robin looked around the wreckage of Pooh's house. The floor was covered with empty honey pots and the floor was sticky.

"She ate the lot! Every jar!" snitched Piglet. "What's Pooh going to eat?"

"Look here Krishtafa Robbing, I mean Krustiva Ribbon, I need more honey! Now!" The bears honey-soaked face, which had picked up bits of paper, old currants and a couple of small feathers, stared at him aggressively. "Need honey, or I'll tell!"

"Tell what?" asked Christopher Robin.

"Dunnow!" Excreta's expression changed to a pleading smile. "Pleesh Crustier Ragged. More honey?"

Christopher Robin had a feeling that if you left honey in some places for long enough, and it got hot enough, it could make you talk funny and get a headache. He knew this was not a good thing, so he collected the bear, nodded goodbye to Piglet and returned to his own house where he washed the bear thoroughly and hung her on the washing line to dry. She snored loudly even while being washed, and woke up some time later in Christopher Robins wardrobe, which he had first carefully searched in case Pooh had hidden any jars there.

Excreta then began banging on the door and demanded to be let out "or else", but Christopher Robin waited until she lapsed into post play hibernation, a condition common amongst stuffed toys.

That weekend when Euphorbia swopped bears with him, Excreta looked at Christopher Robin darkly and whispered "if I were larger, I'd eat you!"

Euphorbia looked suspiciously at her toy. Something about her was different. She seemed somehow wilder and more disreputable. She would clearly benefit from a tailored program of re-education.

When they left, Christopher Robin went straight up to his room and gave Pooh a long hug. "I have missed you so, you silly old bear!"

"Christopher Robin" asked Pooh. "What does transitioning mean?"

SLEEPWALKING No 1

Sharon was a good little sleeper. As far as Rick could see she led a fairly blameless life by modern standards, if you didn't count the swearing. She was regularly rewarded with a sound seven and a half hours kip a night. She didn't even exercise much, more's the pity he thought.

He on the other hand was a restless sleeper at the best of time. They slept in twin beds, primarily because of his habit of wrestling his into submission when first getting in. He would moan, fuss, and wriggle for some time, and even when finally escorted, seemingly under protest, off to bobo land, he would snort, snore, cough, and splutter through the night. Sometimes he would even talk in his sleep, though as far as Sharon could tell, only ever about football.

Tonight, they had enjoyed a takeaway Chinese, all fat, sugar and yummy monosodium glutamate. They had gobbled it down, sat in worship under their seventy-five inch totally state of the art T.V. Well, Rick gobbled down most of it, Sharon ate frugally as always. Just what the doctor didn't order thought Rick chuckling to himself. After a few pints of cheap American lager, more gas than beer, Rick had begun to feel sleepy, and suggested to Sharon it was time they went upstairs.

There had been a time when Sharon had taken this as a hint of things to come, but looking at him now, she had her doubts. No, she was best off getting to sleep as soon as possible by the looks of things. Still, not a bad evening really. Rick didn't seem to mind much what they watched. She sometimes even wondered if he bothered following the plot for more than a couple of minutes.

Up she went, and up he followed. Within ten minutes Sharon had floated away on a downy cloud to Neverland while Rick had begun to fight his way in. Eventually the doormen must have gone off duty because he made it inside.

It is a couple of hours or so later that someone, Sharon, or Sharons ghost, slips out of bed, walks slowly but confidently across to the bedroom door, and out onto the landing. No lights, no noise, no fuss. The figure just floats across the landing, head held high in what would be total darkness, if it isn't for the full moon flooding in through the landing window. The figure doesn't blink, doesn't falter, it just descends to the hall with the regular precision of a well-tuned robot.

It could be hypnotism. This secret Sharon puts on slippers (nothing else), slips through the kitchen, through the unlocked rear door, and out into the garden.

At this point the light alone should wake a blameless sleeper. It could be midday in some parallel world where everything is painted silver. It's a warm evening. Rick wakes briefly, farts generously, scratches the itchy bit on his bum and goes back to sleep. It is completely silent outside. The last distant growls of traffic have stilled, the few surviving refugees of urban nature know their place, and creep round in cotton wool shoes from shadow to shadow. The last feuding neighbours have shouted and threatened each other into mutual submission. They lie comatose, fuelling up their resentments for the day to come.

Sleeping Sharon has made her dreamy way down the street along their tiny garden. In the moonlight her small buttocks seem to ripple as she walks. It is not an unpleasant sight. But what is she doing now? She has slipped quickly through the gate into the equally tiny garden behind theirs.

And guess what? Who is this stretched out naked on the sun lounger? It's the new neighbour Stanley. Stanley shifts furniture for a living. He's a big strong man. The moonlight now provides him with a tip to toe silver body spray. Its rather fetching. Sharons nipples stand up like bathplugs at the thought of him, because guess what? He's between girlfriends at the moment. Well not quite between girlfriends. As Sharon told him when they met at the tip, lots of people need something to help them sleep during a full moon.

Sleepwalking No.1

Sharon sighs. "You know Stanley, this sleepwalking story isn't going to fool anyone if they look out of their bedroom window now. Wouldn't it be better in future if we got a room?"

SLEEPWALKING No 2

Jasons right foot left the warm sanctuary of the large double bed, and slipped silently onto the thickly carpeted bedroom floor. His body rose slowly upright and pivoted towards the wardrobe. He rose with the strange mechanical ease of an automaton to his full height, leaving his wife Mary deep in the arms of Nepenthe cocooned in sleep.

If it was cool in the bedroom, he showed no awareness of the need to shiver. With his sightless eyes fixed ahead of him, he moved slowly off towards the door. This gave the slightest of creaks as it swung open, but he registered no awareness of the sound.

He was now gliding effortlessly across the dark and narrow landing, his body seemingly steering itself with no need of instruction or direction from his unresponsive brain. It was so still, so quiet, as though time itself held its breath.

Onto the stairs now, a pale slither of moonlight through the glass pane on the front door below to guide him. But he had no need of assistance. The stairs curved slightly but his descent was smooth and even, his bare feet caressing the polished wooden steps without fear or hesitation.

This was his way, these nocturnal descents, ever since the failure of their pub. He would, to Mary's despair, make these senseless trips perhaps once or twice a month, with no warning. She was powerless to influence the pattern. The doctor advised them he was unlikely to come to any harm, that the body steered itself through these adventures driven by its familiarity with its surroundings. The episodes might come less frequently with the passage of time, or they might prove a feature for years to come. Either way, it could, in some cases, be dangerous to intervene. The brains' response to an uninvited summons could be sudden and violent while it struggled to make sense of its situation. Best leave the patient to wake of their own accord, provided he stayed out of danger.

He had reached the hall now, and with quiet even steps moved towards the kitchen. He slept and walked naked. One of Mary's first concerns had been that he might wander off into the night to cause outrage or offence among their meek and law-abiding neighbours. In truth she was unsure whether it was the scandal, or the possibility of criminal charges she feared most. Mary was a shy inoffensive woman, and the opinions of her immediate neighbours were of great importance to her. Jason, she had thought could cope. But could he really? Had he perhaps shown too little emotional reaction to the business failure? It had always been important to him to be seen to be in control, to take this disaster on the chin. Seemingly part of him felt differently, but how could she begin to help him with something he was unwilling to face for himself.

His fingers almost stroked the kitchen door open. He padded into the room negotiating the large table in the centre, his feet making slight sucking sounds on the vinyl tiles. His anxious mind was still heedless, lost in some distant location far from the sensations of the here and now. This shadow Jason moved towards the drawer under the hob. He drew it towards him, and the fingers of his strong right hand closed around ...

***

There, that'll do for now. Alan checked the clock. 3.00am already! Bedtime. It was bloody freezing in here at night, and that forty-watt bulb was doing his eyes no good at all. He had done enough for one night, but he wasn't happy. That Jason he'd created was a wimp! He was more likely to be getting himself a glass of milk than to be headed for self-harm. Alan pushed his chair back, arched his back and stretched. If he rarely met his own commitment to 1500 words a day, he prided himself that he did at least put in a shift most evenings. At this rate the book would be finished in about six weeks' time. He downed his regular celebratory whisky, which had been waiting patiently by his side as usual, and stood up. If people found sleepwalking a creepy subject, well, all the better for him.

He turned, and stiffened in sudden stunned astonishment to find himself looking point blank into the unreadable face of his wife Dru. She was naked, her dark eyes stared sightlessly into some unnameable horror on the far rim of the universe. Her arms were raised above her head, clutching the long cold carving knife that now flashed down into his chest. His last thought was what a fool he had been not to take her own troubled somnambulation so lightly and to seek to make fiction out of it.

SLEEPWALKING No 3

"So, you discovered this gentleman in this position..." began Inspector Mangrove.

"He's obviously no gentleman Inspector, he's a burglar!" insisted Ted Sunday.

"...That, as yet, remains to be established sir" continued the Inspector, somewhat pedantically given that he had found the 'gentleman' sprawled across Ted Sunday's hall floor.

He slowly and awkwardly raised his long lean body from Ted's hall carpet.

"I am nothing of the kind," insisted the suspect from the relative comfort of the dining chair on which he had been deposited earlier by the attendant ambulancemen.

"Oh, I see. You are just a casual well-wisher, who chose to make his call at around 3.00am, hours after my wife and I had retired for the night? A well-wisher who, for some bizarre reason, I found here still clutching my watch, credit card, wallet, car keys, all of which I last saw in my bedroom, plus a number of other valuable items including a small statuette, now decapitated, and a camera. Oh, and a large ornate porcelain plate, customarily resident in the dining room, which is now shattered into fragments." Ted posed theatrically, with hands on both hips, proud of his devastating summary of the evidence against the masked intruder.

"Are you by any chance suggesting I was stealing these items?" queried the intruder, and by the way, the statuette is a fake. Its worthless."

"Well, yes," stammered Ted, "yes, it is worthless, but that's not the point. We thought it was valuable when we bought it in Athens."

The intruder snorted loudly.

Mavis, Teds attentive wife interjected. "Would anyone like a cup of tea?"

Silence.

"Well, perhaps cocoa?" What do you usually drink at this time, Inspector?"

"At four in the morning ma'am," sighed Inspector Mangrove, "even a policeman is usually sound asleep. Can we please get on?" He paused and continued. "Your view is that this gentleman..."

An audible and sharp intake of breath from Ted warned him they were about to go round again...

"That this gentleman reached this unfortunate situation as a result of falling from one of your top stairs in a bid to escape detection, having realised he had woken you both falling over the hoover on the landing?"

"Absolutely, yes!" confirmed Ted. He was hardly likely to be lying there indulging in a spot of late-night mindfulness, was he?"

"What have you to say for yourself sir?" Mangrove continued addressing the intruder.

"I would have thought it was obvious? I was sleepwalking."

"Sleepwalking!" bellowed Ted and Mavis in harmony. "How can he be sleepwalking in **our** house?"

"As it happens, I believe I may have obtained entry through the living room window. It appears to be ajar, although I have of course no precise recollection."

"And why would an innocent sleepwalker be found on our floor stealing a bundle of our most valuable possessions?"

"And a fake, don't forget the fake! I haven't stolen anything; they're still in your house. I was just doing what came naturally after all these years."

"Burgling"

"Yes, burgling. That doesn't make me a burglar, does it?"

"I'm sorry, being caught in the act and admitting to burgling doesn't make you a burglar?"

"Not if I'm sleepwalking. No. I will hold my hand up to fourteen previous convictions, no problem. My point is that after all those years burgling, when my unconscious mind decides to go for a walk, it goes burgling. I can't help it. I'm very sorry, but it's not my fault."

"Oh, very clever. I suppose your GP will support the idea that you wander around the community after dark, reliving your finest burgling moments, in a state of blameless unconsciousness."

"He would if I had a GP, yes".

"Would anyone like a drink then?" asked Mavis, who detested conflict of any kind. "Sherry perhaps, or a small whisky as a nightcap?"

"Actually, a large Johny Walker wouldn't go amiss," said the alleged burglar.

What! No, don't get him anything. I'll have a small cognac thanks love," protested Ted.

"Well, if that's your attitude," huffed the intruder, "perhaps we could move on to the obvious infringement of basic health and safety standards what has resulted in my near-death experience on this rug."

"I beg your pardon"

"That stair carpet was loose. Must have been. It's always been loose. Burglars are as sure footed as ballet dancers. That's why they call us cat burglars. We don't just fall downstairs like that. I'd be laughed out of clink!"

"He has a point Mr Sunday. We will have to have the stair carpet checked. Hang on a minute, what do you mean it's always been loose. Have you been here before, sunshine?"

"Naturally. I've been here hundreds of times."

"So, you **have** been casing the house then?" challenged the alert policeman.

"That's not what I'd call it. He's my son, Inspector."

"He's what? May I ask why no one has bothered to bring this pertinent fact to my attention before?"

"He hates me, that's why" bleated the supposed intruder.

"He is a habitual, and might I add, an unsuccessful, house burglar, what's not to hate?" queried Ted.

"He's ashamed of me. Hasn't spoken to me for years. I bought him that statuette years ago, that's how I know it's a fake. He tells people they got it in Greece."

"My father, is a social disgrace, Inspector, always has been. If people round here knew I was related to a convicted petty criminal, my life wouldn't be worth living."

"Our lives, darling" Mavis chipped in.

"Sorry, I forgot son, its o.k. to be a criminal round here as long as its something really nasty, and they haven't done you for it yet?"

"You see, Inspector!" Ted protested. "Imagine having someone like that as a father. Go on, arrest him."

"I'm innocent I tell you. I was sleepwalking. I haven't done a house for a couple of years now. This used to be my place before he got me to sign some dodgy papers while I was inside."

"I don't see the relevance of that" spluttered Ted.

"Darling," interjected Mavis. "Could I just have a quiet word in your ear." She drew him through the open dining room door.

"If the Inspector does arrest him, and he ends up going to prison, wont they have to write about it in the local paper?"

"Well, they won't have to, but they will, yes."

"Then won't everybody we know, hear about it? What about the Harrisons house warming party, or the golf-club dinner dance? Wouldn't it be just a little, well, inconvenient?"

Ted was silent. Ted was silent again, and again...

"Oh hell, you're right of course. All he's done so far is break that old statue and that horrible pottery thing you got from Camden Market. I suppose we could afford to be lenient, as long as he doesn't do it again."

"Darling, there is a way we can ensure he doesn't do it again, and to avoid all this unpleasantness, at least until we can find out whether there is anything in his sleepwalking story?"

"What do you mean? He's lying, of course he is! Anyway, what are you getting at?"

"Well, the Ambulancemen said he hadn't broken anything, but he would be pretty shaken up after his fall. Why don't we look after him here for a while. Let him recuperate? He's not going to burgle somewhere when he's already living there is he? There would be nowhere to hide his loot?"

"Well," said Ted thoughtfully. "If he did, we would know whether dad was telling the truth."

He was silent again.

"O.k. Just for a couple of weeks, though we had better put him in the dining room. I don't want him breaking his neck on the stairs and suing us?"

"Suing you dear," said Mavis patiently, "you had the house put in your name remember?"

He sighed deeply. "O.K. You win"

They walked back into the hall, where Inspector Mangrove was showing old Mr Sunday some holiday snaps.

"O.K. dad," sighed Ted. "We're not going to press charges this time. In fact, you had better stay here, just for a few days mind, while you get over your fall. If any of the silver goes missing, you're out, got it?"

"What silver?", said old Mr Sunday, leering smugly.

ORIGINAL STORY

The hunter picked his way uphill through the dense forest along the narrow path, bent under the weight of the heavy kill loaded over his back.

On reaching the cave entrance he threw down the corpse and entered. He paused and greedily sucked in the familiar scent of body odour and rotting animal flesh. Satisfied, he then crawled over to his partner Dron, who was holding the end of a long bone which sizzled blood into the heart of the large fire beneath it.

"Oh no, not mammoth again surely! I'm sick of mammoth! We always have mammoth! It's tough, its stringy, and it's got no flavour."

"Well find us something else then! I've got enough mammoth here to last us another moon. You don't think I enjoy sitting here day after day in this freezing bloody cave having babies, and cooking mammoth bones just to keep us alive, do you?"

"Well, I've got a nice juicy elk outside. I had to go miles to find it. It's not been a good day. Someone's been scratching all over my best reindeer pick, and I had to fix the mammoth trap again. You should try digging a hole big enough for a bloody mammoth with a piece of bone!" He looked over to his young son Bug.

"And what do you think you're doing? I told you to scrape the fat off those hides, we need them for winter. Don't just sit there playing with that bit of knuckle bone. What are you doing with it anyway? You're not going to get anything clean with a lump that shape, and you'll ruin the scraper!"

Dron called over to the curmudgeonly hulk behind her. "Scrot dear why don't you add a few more mammoths to that nice frieze on the back wall? We could do with a bit of luck?"

Scrot crawled awkwardly over to his prize mammoth frieze and picked up a burnt stick. Before he could start doodling however, he yelled out "And what the heck is this? Someone's drawn bloody horses on my mammoth frieze, and what's more they're in a funny colour. We don't eat horses do we. What's the point of making more horses? Damn! I'm going outside for some peace".

Outside the cave he ran into his daughter Veronica squatting on the narrow cliff ledge, staring intently down into the thick green forest far below.

"And exactly what have you been doing with yourself all day, young lady?"

Veronica had made up her mind. She had been considering the future and it was time to speak up.

"Hi pa, I've been thinking."

"Thinking? What the heck is that?"

"You stop doing things, sit in one place, and just let your mind go here it will."

"Really, and how does that get us fed, keep us warm, or keep cave bears away?" grumbled Scrot, who had a strong preference for doing.

"You'd be surprised pa. You know those cool horses Bug drew on the mammoth frieze? Have you ever thought of climbing on top of one. They run faster than us. They could extend your hunting range. You might find a few ponds with some nice duck, or maybe fresh beaver?"

"Hm", muttered Scrot. "Maybe. What's wrong with Bug anyway? I caught him whittling on an old bone when he was supposed to be on scraping duty."

"Oh that, he's been making an image of mum when she's pregnant. To help with the pregnancies? It's called sympathetic magic."

"You what? Well, I don't like it! And why has he been putting red on my mammoth frieze? You don't get red mammoths, and we don't eat horses, even red ones."

"He's been experimenting with colour. Grinding up sandstone to make red and experimenting with river mud to make ochre. Looks good doesn't it.?"

"Hm, maybe, but it doesn't look like food. A horse of any colour is still a horse. Tell him to draw mammoths in future? Preferably black ones."

"Look pa, Bug isn't like you. He's sensitive, creative."

"Creative, is he? Creative wouldnt have helped us get rid of that family of Cro Magnon squatters up the valley, would it?"

"No pa, but then they seem to be extinct now, don't they? I get the impression you had something to do with that, or did they just fall off that cliff on their own?"

Scrot smiled.

"Oh please, take that smug expression off your face for once, pa! Life is about so much more than just killing everything in sight! Or it should be. See this?"

"It's got curves. You can't kill anything with curves?"

"It's a pot dad! I swapped it for a few old animal skins with the Gurn family. You cook in it instead of holding bones in front of the fire. It would free mum up to get out more."

"What, leave the cave? Why would she want to leave the cave? It's her home."

"Well for starters, she could do some of the hunting?"

"Right, a woman hunting! Really! And what would I do? "There was a faint degree of alarm in his voice.

Veronica shrugged. "I could teach you to write?"

"What the heck is writing? Oh, I suppose it was you scratching on my pick, was it?"

"It's a form of communication. If we all use the same marks to mean the same things we can tell each other stuff without actually being in the same place. Look, I have a vision, pa. Life could be so much richer and more fulfilling. Bug could teach other families to make coloured paints and to use sympathetic magic. We could put a mark on the back of old birch bark to make certificates when they get it right. We could use horses to travel. We could, well, we could wander about. We could even have holidays. Barg says he's been told there is a huge river out there which tastes funny and reaches the sky." She glanced up at her father.

"Hm, maybe."

She decided it was time to change the subject. "You see these, pa?"

"They look like weeds!"

"They're vegetables pa You can cook them up in this pot and eat them instead of just chewing old mammoths. They are much healthier. They would help you keep your weight down for a start."

"And what would I do all day while your new 'vegetables' are growing?"

"Well, you could do a lot worse than just sit here and think for a bit!".

***

A whole moon had passed. Veronica had taken Dron to meet the Gurn family in the next valley. Dron had expressed great interest in using some of her new leisure time learning to work with beads. Pamela, the Gurns eldest daughter then suggested they meet again, perhaps every new moon, and Veronica had suggested forming a group, just for daughters and mums along the valley to discuss ideas for the future. "We could call it Women's Inclusive," she suggested.

Scrot had been none too happy with the idea of Dron wandering along the valley on her own, but preferred to keep away from Barg the father of the Gurn group. He was aware Barg had recently obtained a particularly fine hand axe and was very keen to show it off to his occasional visitors. Scrot had never seen much point in the new craze for giant hand axes. If you wanted to kill a mammoth you were always better off with a spear, and if you wanted to kill anything else, well, you could always push it off a cliff.

He was bothered by a serious itch in his protruding monobrow this morning, and had been scratching it for some time. He was very proud of the fierce and forbidding appearance it gave him. He had to admit, it seemed likely something was living in it, maybe several somethings, and was now wondering whether it, or they, were edible. He still couldn't think of a good reason for wasting good furs on a hand axe like Barg's, but he couldn't get it out of his mind. He had to admit it did look good, manly, sexy even. What the heck, o.k. yes, admit it, despite himself, he wanted one. He wanted one badly in fact. Deep in thought he almost fell over Veonica, perched as she was on her ledge staring out over the wide valley below.

"I suppose you're out here doing thinking again? I was hoping you had had enough of that. Look at the trouble it caused last time. 'Think how much milk we could get from an aurochs' you said. 'Think how nice it would be to have a bowl of fresh aurochs' milk with our mammoth bones.' You almost got me killed!"

"Be fair pa, you didn't quite get the hang of it did you? True you approached the right end of the aurochs, but you were supposed to be milking a female one. I am not surprised it took offence, and we could hardly have drunk what you were after even if you had been successful!"

Scrot looked defensive for a moment. "I'm just saying that's all. I've got to admit you were right about the weeds though. Mum is having a go at planting some, but I don't think it will work in the cave."

"I'll talk to her. Vegetables need sunshine, just like us. Bug is doing a great job on the frieze isn't he? I see he's added elk, beaver, and even a couple of fish. He was talking of putting in a few hunters with spears, that would really help productivity, wouldn't it?"

"Hm, maybe" replied Scrot. "What's productivity? Listen, do you happen to know where Barn Gurn got his hand axe? I thought one like it, only bigger of course, would look nice in front of the mammoth frieze. It would be nice for mum."

Veronica felt it unlikely her mum would be terribly interested in an ornamental hand axe she could hardly lift, but she knew when to keep her mouth shut. "I think Barn picked it up at the flint mine. I could ask around next time I go down for some new scrapers if you like"?

"Wouldn't do any harm, at least not to us would it", smiled Scrot. "And by the way, what are those funny bits of pot?"

"I call them rounds pa. They were left over from my bowl making."

"Why have they got holes in the middle?"

"I'm not sure yet, but I think I may be onto something."

***

Scrot was furious this morning, and looking for Veronica.

He found her as usual, ledge squatting. The girl seemed to do little else these days. He put it down to her age. It was probably time she mated. She might be lazy, but she was certainly good looking with her fine protruding forehead and whiskery jaw. She had his fine monobrow too. Yes, her partner would have to bring a lot of fur pelts, and that would help the family keep the little ones warm. They could all sleep in comfort over the coming winter, always assuming they could keep clear of cave bears.

"It's got to stop love!" He said fiercely.

"Hi pa, no problem, but it would help if you told me what had to stop?"

"All this interference in family matters. You have got to stop encouraging Bug!"

"What's the poor little kid done now for natures sake?"

"He added hunters to the mammoth frieze like you said he would. And what happened? When I got down to the mammoth trap this morning? There were four great hairy thugs with long spears dragging a mammoth out of it. I tried to reason with them but they had magic powers. So obviously, painting hunters on the frieze made them happen all right, but because they were in funny colours, they weren't from our tribe, and they ran off with our food supply. That's what happens when you mess with the formula, and start adding fancy colours to the family frieze. It's not right. Sympathetic magic has always meant using a burnt pointed stick, and it always will. Can he please rub them out again?"

"I'm not sure anyone has ever tried taking stuff out of a cave frieze? It could make a horrible mess. It could maybe muck up the weather patterns, but I'll ask him. Look pa, you don't like eating mammoth in the first place. You've said so often enough, and since Bug added fish and beaver, we have a much more balanced diet. Do we really need the nasty chewy things? I'm sick of picking their long hairs out of my teeth. And anyway, what do you mean 'they had magic powers?'"

They pointed their arms at me and their spears flew towards me without being thrown. Funny little spears they were. It was pretty scary I can tell you!"

"Hm, I think you'll find they were carrying bows and firing arrows."

"What the heck are arrows?"

"I don't want to upset you pa but I think Barg has got some. You put the arrows in the bows, pull on the bows and let the arrows fly. It's pretty cool. They mean you can kill from a distance. You'd love 'em honest. It's the latest technology."

"Oh well, of course Barg is going to have some. Barg has got everything Barg has! Beads, hand axes and now these arrows. Where is it all going to end? I tell you Veronica, I can't keep up with all this technology. It's already messing with the weather. There is far less ice around than there used to be. Mark my words, one day there won't be any mammoths left, then how are we going to cope? Why can't things just stay the way they used to be?"

Cheer up and come inside pa" said Veronica, putting her arm round him. "We've got a nice surprise for you. You're going to love it."

"A surprise. You mean like when a big tooth tiger jumps out on you?"

"Well, in a way I suppose, but this one is much nicer."

"O.K. but there is another matter I need to talk to you about later. Have you given any thought to finding a mate?"

They went back inside to find Dron and Bug grinning from ear to ear. They were sitting in front of his prize mammoth frieze and in front of it was a large bundle of fur.

"Come on darling, open it" begged Dron. Veronica picked it up this afternoon at the flint mine.

"Why is it wrapped in fur?" queried Scrot.

"Your clever daughter invented packaging! Cool huh?"

Scrot grunted. "Hm, maybe." He unrolled the fur. Inside was the biggest, heaviest, sharpest hand axe he had ever seen. It took him both hands to pick it up.

"It's much too big to be of any use in a real hunt" he exclaimed. "Its perfect. Must have taken them ages. How on earth did you find the furs to buy a gorgeous thing like this?"

"Barter." Said Veronica. "And it wasn't just furs. Ma and I exchanged it for some of her new bear tooth necklaces. No one has seen anything like them before, not even Barg" she added tactfully. "We also traded furs of course, and some of mum's new pots. I think we just invented consumerism. If it carries on like this you are going to have to find a bigger cave"

"Hm, maybe." Scrot was minded to ignore this latest evidence of innovation. "I bet Barg hasn't even dreamt of a hand axe as big as this. In years to come the next people to take on this cave are going to think I had hands the size of a giant tree sloth" he beamed.

Behind him, next to the frieze was parked a curious contraption fashioned from four 'rounds' held together in pairs by two large sticks held in place by bear claw wedges. The sticks in turn supported a platform of smaller sticks secured to them with elk sinew and at the front she had attached a long mammoth tail handle. Veronica was proud of her latest idea and sighed quietly at the thought that, predictably, her pa hadn't even noticed it. One day she thought. Best go one idea at a time.

Actually, just for once she was wrong. Scrot had noticed the new contraption but wasn't going to give her the satisfaction of asking what it was. Not today at least. Best go one idea at a time.

"Glad you like the hand axe," said Veronica. "Oh, was there something you wanted to talk about? Something about me mating?"

"That can wait a while" replied Scrot reflectively. All these new ideas of hers worried him sometimes, but he could still see how lucky he was to have a daughter who could 'think'. He beamed at his new toy and vowed to try the thinking for himself.

JUSTICE BROWNLOW'S CONSCIENCE

How can I survive more nights like last night? The thing returned, as it will every twelve months until my unmerciful death, wherever I hide myself. It means to keep me in mind of the torments awaiting me. The graveyard smells, the unholy sight of it, and the hideous implications of its visits, are surely more than any sane man can bear? It began just over a year ago.

I had watched him come towards the cottage. He approached slowly and falteringly, with a heavy reliance on his walking stick, but then the message had said he was a dying man. He was tall and thin with a large domed head, to which clung a thin matting of greasy white hair. I could see at once, from the way he held his head, that this was a man who would once have projected himself with great authority, a man with pride and confidence. He was a few minutes late, but I had no doubt that a man of his character and achievements would have made every effort to arrive on time. The success of this meeting was after all very much to his advantage.

I opened the door and greeted him from the porch.

"Do I call you judge or Master Brownlow"?

"As you are aware, I am retired. I would greatly prefer Master Brownlow. You I take it; are the man they call the Wizard"?

"I have that reputation yes. My given name is Fry, William Fry. Please follow me into the garden, we will sit there and take tea."

I led him through to the small secluded garden at the back. I went to prepare the tea and watched him through the lace curtains. He was studying his surroundings with great interest and curiosity. When I returned with a tray, cups, milk and teapot he was quick to speak.

"Many of these plants I recognise. Those purple flowers are monk's bane? Not something often found in a typical garden? The trees at the back are surely Yew? They were a symbol of death and resurrection to the celts. They will have been here long before you. I assume this site is one of considerable antiquity? I also see foxglove, nightshade, morning glory and the remains of lily of the valley. There are many plants I do not recognise. It seems you deal in death"?

"It's a popular line of work," I replied, "but that I feel is unfair. Even burning many of these plants can be fatal its true, but in moderation they have beneficial uses. Besides, many of my plants are exclusively known for their positive qualities". As I spoke, I handled a valerian. "These for example are used to ease insomnia and anxiety. Feverfew over there cures the headache. It is true that many of my clients wish to arrange for death, for animal pests, ailing pets, and in ...certain other cases, but I also offer a variety of other services. I deal in disorders of the digestive system, lung complaints, and skin problems. I have even been asked to prepare a love potion. Death is but a sideline."

"That sir, is quite a claim!" The judge suggested, pulled himself up in the old wicker chair I had procured for him.

He continued. "It's my own death of which I wish to speak. I have little time. I am dying, cancer. No chance of reprieve, but that is not why I am visiting a man with your particular skills; I am resigned to the fact of my passing. It is what follows that concerns me greatly. I must know that I can now talk in complete confidence"?

The man was clearly exhausted, his hands shook and his face was the colour of old bone. The eyes, which must once have been of palest grey, were now tired and bloodshot. His skin was almost translucent, crumpled, and so pale. I nodded my assent.

"Well then, I have led a far from exemplary life. Many of my calling have fallen similarly from grace, but none I know have fallen so far. In our degraded society there must be few crimes left that most people would class as sins. I doubt however that the God I recognise has redrawn the line between good and evil. As a child I would invariably repay the love of my younger brother and sister with casual cruelty. As a young man I begun to gamble heavily. I eventually confessed a large and threatening liability to my brother. He helped me so willingly, and so generously, that I went on to report other liabilities to him which were rather less genuine. When he ran into problems in his business affairs, I declined to pay back what I owed him, although by then I was a rich man. Shortly before his death I began to.... console his wife in a way unworthy of a married man. There were other affairs. My wife left me, but I had already moved on. In my legal work I was known as one of the most accommodating of judges. For the right sum a man could be forgiven for any crime. Many a poor man suffers today for some event of which he knew nothing."

"May I stop you there? Do I have need of such intimate details"?

Justice Brownlow shook his head. "Confession comes so easily to me, now it is far too late. I see I must come to the point! My siblings and I were raised as Christians. A strict upbringing with a heavy emphasis on Church, Sunday School and the Bible. It may be irrational to others but I still believe in the afterlife, and I live in utter terror of the consequences of the life I chose to lead, and could not renounce."

I knew of course where all this was leading, and I could only wonder at the naivety of the ungodly. One would imagine a judge would know better than to advise the extent of his need? I played the game. "I am hardly the one to absolve you"?

He looked at me shrewdly, drew closer and whispered, "perhaps not, but I understand you offer a service by means of which a man may escape the direst consequences of an ill spent existence"?

"Ah!" I suggested, "such a service today is probably an exclusive one. There is a considerable price attached!"

"Whatever it is, it can be as nothing compared to the price to pay in the hereafter for a conscience as heavily stained as mine. I face hell, nothing less. An eternity of the most extreme penitence. I face pain and suffering unimaginable to human kind. I would have my sins taken away. Am I correct that it can be done?"

"You refer to sin eating? It is a venerable practice. It was most commonly found along the Welsh borders, and into the interior. The last self-confessed practitioner is said to have died early in this century, but then sin eaters were never ones to advertise their profession. No one with any options left in this life would willingly take on the sins of others. They were invariably the most hapless, the poorest, and of course the most despised. The profession tended to run in families. It had to, with father or mother passing on the cumulative burdens they had acquired through their work to their sons or daughters when their own time came."

"How did it work"? He seemed surprisingly eager to learn.

"Simple. In a similar way to the taking of the last sacrament, except that the beneficiary would be dead. The sin eater would sit alone by the side of the recently deceased when prepared for burial, and eat a simple meal, usually bread, from the chest of the cadaver. In so doing, and with the aid of a few ritual words, he or she would take onto themselves the evils perpetrated by that person during their lifetime, leaving the soul cleansed to face the hereafter.

The judge leant even closer. I could smell his illness on his breath, and with it almost taste his fear. "But you know one that still practices"?

I enjoyed the moment, poured our tea, and leant back in my chair before answering. "I do, yes."

I could see the tension drain from his shoulders. A great relief was visible in his bleary eyes. "When? I must meet him, or her. I would need proof of their existence."

I laughed. "As to the first, you must be dead for the service to be provided, otherwise you would be free to sin again, fresh sins which would remain with you for all eternity. As to the second we must first agree a price..."

***

The weather now accelerated its unholy slide into winter. The winds became cutting and bitter, the rain interminable. It was just six days later that Justice Brownlow returned. It was a ferociously cold, stormy day, and he struggled to make progress up my path. The vestiges of his air of authority were slipping. He was coughing now, and clearly struggled with the large briefcase he almost thrust into my grasp when I opened the door.

"Take it please. Take it all. It's of no use to me, and I have no one to whom I can leave it. My family abandoned me years ago. I can hardly blame them. They will have what little remains of the house and contents. I have left precise instructions that they are not to be informed of my death until two days later. My housekeeper will clean and dress the body. She will simply lie about the day on which she discovered it. This will give her time to inform you of my passing, and for the visit from your, your what, your employee, your contact, your agent"?

"My mother actually. I told you these practices have to run in families. There is nothing whatever illegal in taking and eating bread from the body of the dead, or saying a few words over the corpse, but it's hardly a practice anyone would want to talk widely about. Sin eaters were shunned as the lowest of the low in their communities."

He was visibly stunned. The unholy implications of my words were all too clear to him. As I expected he had no desire to dwell on them.

The rest was simple. I ushered him into the parlour and introduced him to my supposed mother. As I looked at the tragic sight she presented, at her long unwashed hair, the thin, drawn face, bent frame and gnarled hands, I feared he would spot the deception, but my guest was far too absorbed in the contemplation of an eternity in the flames of Hell to think rationally. Still, it was hardly flattering that he should believe me.

By the door he remarked, "my God, I need little fear that a creature like that would baulk at carrying the additional burden of my crimes."

I said "indeed, but I am curious. Do you not feel perhaps the tiniest pang of sympathy for the wretch"?

He looked directly into my eyes; "only for her son."

***

Some weeks later a knock at my door introduced a short bustling lady in a red overcoat. Her discomfort clearly revealed that the little she knew of this affair was already far too much as far as she was concerned. The sooner she was away from me the better for her. She played with a small gold chain around her neck, informed me of Justice Brownlow's passing, that he was "ready", and that she would be informing the authorities the following afternoon. She then scuttled off down the garden path, like a small mammal seeking the security of its burrow.

There was no need to inform my supposed mother. The wretch had already been paid, and had no doubt by now drunk every penny I had given her. She had clearly found it difficult enough to appear sober when she met the judge, for I could smell the stale rank smell of drink all over her. Perhaps next time I would choose another from the narrow crumbling terraced streets along the river. There were plenty of solitary crones starving in that derelict quarter who would be delighted to accept my offer of a little occasional income for nothing. This one was so stupid she had never even asked the nature of the service I had claimed she was offering. That was dangerous in its way.

I returned to the study and poured myself a generous double measure of my finest cognac in celebration. If only all my enterprises were as profitable as this one.

***

It was almost unnaturally cold the following evening as I made my way upstairs to bed. A malevolent full moon glared down on the cottage laying a deep frost on everything it could see. The light of a billion stars burnt like tiny sins in the limitless sky.

I am usually late to retire, and this evening was no exception. My intention is invariably to read for long enough to ensure I can sink promptly into a deep and dreamless repose. This night however this practice proved impossible. I couldn't make myself comfortable. I was tossing and turning, thinking of so many things. I would have fetched an additional pillow if it hadn't been for that dreadful chill. After what felt like some hours an arctic wind arose, and the noise it made swooping and howling round the cottage made it even harder to think of sleep.

Why was I kidding myself? There was one thing more than any other on my mind tonight. Could it possibly be that I had some small residue of conscience in regard to the ridiculous Justice Brownlow? By his own unsought admission, he was due every horror he had been imagining. Whether herded into some vile black iron cage, and toasted over hellfire by fiends with pitchforks, as in traditional images of hell; or subjected to some more refined and abstract horror unimaginable to me, he plainly had it coming to him. Besides I had no belief in an afterlife. To me God was an absurdity. Surely therefore, there could be no Hell? How could there be one without the other?

...And yet, I was strangely reluctant to look toward the far side of the room. It was dark at the best of times, but now I could see nothing of the small table and cupboard that should have been there. If anything, the velvet darkness seemed to be spreading out towards me like a thick black bloodstain. It was impenetrable. The freezing cold was unbearable and seemed to be coming from the same source. The air in my small room was turning stale and foetid.

I told myself that at least this cloak of shadow could not be anything issuing from the fiery regions of hell? Surely if it did, I would be only too keen to jump out of bed and avail myself of the heat?

"How wrong you are."

Had I imagined the words? I was overwrought. Was my imagination was taunting me?

"Why would there be heat when there is no body"?

94

I could almost swear I heard a sibilant whisper from the heart of the black stain now unmistakably creeping out towards me. Heaven help me, I imagined I could see two glowing red shapes staring through the darkness, eyes, but feral not human. They were like the baleful glare of a savage beast.

The voice came again. "The hellfire burns within, but without there is this insufferable, all-consuming cold. Does it reach you? Does it burn as it freezes your skin and bones? Trust me, the fire is worse, oh so much worse. It burns the soul even though there is no body to incinerate. This is what sin means in eternity. You did this! Your filthy trick I believed you, fool that I was. You knew I had no choice but to believe your lies, and you have robbed me of my immortal soul."

There was a shape there now. It was indistinct, tall and flickering like the flames of a large fire, but in some horrible way I could discern a human form. It floated towards me, and I could have choked on the stench of sulphur.

"He can make bargains. He is known for it, is he not? He made one with me. My suffering for yours. You will eat what the woman did not. You will take my sins, and in time take my place. To rob a man of eternal rest is a far worse sin than any I could ever have imagined. Can there be any crime more terrible than that? Oh, what fun his creatures will have with you."

The phantom was clear to me now, had stepped beyond the darkness, and was lit by the flickering red light within, bearing some horrid vestigial resemblance to the judge as he was in life. The flesh was incomplete of course, like that of a flayed creature. Red bone showed through and what was left of the face. I have no words to describe the horror. I realised the thing was carrying something. A parcel? No, a bloody organ? Perhaps a heart or a brain? No, it looked a little like bread, but it was grey and writhing. It was full of wriggling creatures, worms, beetles and maggots.

No creature could surely consume a mouthful of this hellish thing and retain their sanity?

"What did you expect" asked the spectre? "This is food from Hell. Food for the damned. You will taste it; you are given no will in this matter."

I found I was standing. I was holding out my hand even as my stomach retched and churned. The spectre pressed the filthy substance towards me.

"Eat now, but from my breast."

With these words this vermillion thing, this burning shivering corpse stripped of its skin, lay silently down on my bed. It placed the disgusting substance on its chest and repeated its instruction.

"Eat and be damned, as you damned me."

I did as I was commanded.

***

When I woke it was with a fever. I was a damned man. My head throbbed and my eyes ached, when I could will myself to open them. I made an effort to leave the bed and was violently sick. I knew that, though I felt I could remember every detail of the hideous visitation the previous evening, and would do until my dying day, nothing I could recall could be more than a small fraction of the true terror.

For a few days I could not imagine ever trusting food to pass my lips again, but then hunger steered me towards simple broth. I live now for just one purpose. I have to find some poor miserable creature desperate enough to take the limitless burden of my sin, knowing as I do that the vile profession of sin eating has been extinct for many years.

And beyond this improbable quest is the inescapable question of whether, should I by some miracle ever succeed, I will still be doomed to punishment? Having witnessed for myself the loathsome consequences of such a feast, I would be creating a new and terrible sin by passing my crimes to another. Should my victim undertake the monstrous task they have sworn to fulfil on my death, I will have committed a crime which will ensure my torture for all eternity. That is of course, if they are foolish enough ever to bother fulfilling the contract!

The worst thing of all was the final words my visitor had uttered. They will never leave me.

"He lied to me of course. Satan can do nothing but lie. When I return, he will not let me leave him, although I hope to visit here each year. He has simply used me to gain another victim for torment. But then of course, I realised that before I asked him. I came here purely for your suffering, not for my relief. Be certain, I will be waiting for you when you arrive."

The last known sin eater Richard Munslow died at Ratlinghope, in Shropshire, in 1906. Unlike the vast majority, Munslow was a respectable farmer and thought to be wealthy.

THE WRITING GROUP

She picked her way carefully up the unfamiliar creaking stairs to the third floor and pushed open the door. Phoebe had wanted this for a long time, it was just a shame it had taken such an appalling tragedy to make it possible.

Outside it was, by September standards, a sizzling afternoon yet the air in the room was almost chill. All the windows appeared to be shut. Before her she saw a number of faces turned in her direction. It looked for a moment as though she had interrupted the reading of a will, or maybe a church service".

At the head of the table sat a woman possibly in her forties, with large dark eyes and shoulder length flowing red hair. She adjusted a magnificent Tigers Eye pendant round her neck, smiled at Phoebe vaguely and said "I'm Charis, your tutor. You must be Phoebe? Welcome to the writing group. Please, take a seat."

Phoebe was surprised to find the only seat available was that closest to her at the foot of the table. She hooked her large leather bag over the chair and sat down.

"I'd better start by asking everyone to introduce themselves? Brigette, shall we start with you?"

The woman on Charis's left had thick grey hair, and a long white face which to Phoebe looked deeply sad. Her eyes were an almost colourless pale blue grey. They looked tired, as though they had seen too much. She nodded rather gravely and whispered simply "good afternoon, I'm Brigette."

Next to Brigette was a balding man with his hair tied back in a ponytail. He looked somehow disreputable, like a rather seedy antique dealer. He inclined his head and said "Hi, I'm Ambrose. The name means immortal but I have yet to put it to the test." He smiled at his own joke - added "welcome to the group".

The next introduction came from a lady with an intense frown above her brown eyes. Her long thick black hair reached below the level of the table and was tucked behind her ears. She was almost scowling as she said. "I'm Enesta. I've been coming here for five years now. It's meant a lot to me. I, I hope you'll be happy here."

Now it was the turn of a Lilith. She was far younger than the others, blonde and curvaceous with long blood red fingernails steepled in front of her. There was nothing Phoebe could put her finger on, but she somehow exuded an air of pampered wealth and ease as she briskly muttered "Hi", as though she had things to be getting on with.

Next to her was a man Phoebe would have placed in his seventies with wispy grey hair. He was short and round with a red face and large glasses. Before he could speak Brigette said "We mostly just call him the Professor, though he's been retired a while now."

The Writing Group

The final introduction came from a woman in late middle age with tight curly brown hair. "I am known as Aelfrun. I have been here since the beginning".

Phoebe thought this was a curious way to refer to yourself and noted that made only two "welcomes" from a group of seven people. She responded by saying the first thing to come into her head. "Only seven of you? I'm surprised they let the group continue?"

Brigette leaned back and responded addressing her remark to the tutor Charis "Oh, I don't think they would ever close us down?"

Charis asked Phoebe to say a few words about herself.

She stared hard at the table in front of her, and then at the listening timbers stretched eccentrically across the roof. This wasn't coming easy but she began. "I'm Phoebe Sanderson. I'm thirty-six, single and I live alone. Until recently I worked in the library here in town. I always wanted to write and then I... there was..." she hesitated... "I actually came into a lot of money. I couldn't carry on working at the library, but I didn't need to work anymore anyway, and I could see that, in time, I now had the opportunity to realise my ambition. So here I am." She took a deep breath, attempted a smile, and looked hopefully up at the group.

The group member known as the professor looked hard at her and with some authority in his voice stated "it takes a lot more than opportunity alone girl; I hope you realise that?"

Enesta added: "just give her time, o.k.?"

The rest of the first session was a tutorial on plot development. It was a little technical and once or twice Phoebe wondered what she had let herself in for, but she had paid for the full year and was determined to make a success of her new interest. At the end there was a strange episode when Charis closed the session saying, "And remember there is only one story". As she had said this, she had placed her left hand diagonally over her heart with the forefinger extended. To Phoebe's alarm she heard several of the others repeating "there is only one story" with their hands in the same position

As Phoebe left the room, pony-tailed Ambrose seemed to make some effort to catch up with her.

"I'm curious, were did the money come from?"

"Does it matter? As it happens a relative died."

"And why did you say you couldn't carry on at the library?"

"I didn't, It was a very personal thing. Look, I came into rather a lot of money. I had to give up work, and I always wanted to write. I saw this course as a chance to make a new start. I thought, something good can come of all this. O.K."

"And the powers that be led you to choose us" concluded Ambrose as he strode off in the opposite direction. "Interesting, but there's a lot more to it than that, isn't there? See you next week".

***

For the next three weeks Phoebe was unable to shake off the feeling that she had somehow interrupted a private meeting. The group members were at best courteous rather than friendly and however early she arrived she was always last. They always sat in the same places leaving the same seat by the door as though they were telling her where to sit. Each session had ended with the same mysterious phrase and the accompanying hand gesture.

The first week's task had been to write something on the sea. She had drafted a piece based on her childhood holiday memories which had been quietly but unenthusiastically received. Lilith suggested it lacked emotional depth and Aelfrun rather crisply argued that the descriptive language was perhaps a little colourless. The tutor Charis smiled and defended her by pointing out to the group that this was a first piece and asking them to be "encouraging". It was a sentiment Phoebe felt to be no more than a reasonable expectation.

In week two it was poetry, which had never been one of Phoebe's interests. She submitted a comic piece about a neighbour's dog which even she could see was rather lacking in substance and it was received in virtual silence though the Professor chuckled discretely to himself at one point, shaking his head and muttering "not yet" as he did so.

By week three she was beginning to dread the creak of the rickety stairs. They were becoming a portent of the trial to come. Week three's subject was "Moonlight". That was better. Phoebe had felt inspired.

Her piece began "The evening lay patiently and expectantly before her, astonished at its own beauty. The half-light of dusk picked out geraniums in the flower beds like tiny torches in a pixie parade while the gentle moon washed the lawn in ethereal serenity. She heard a dog bark in the next road, then a fox in the wood at the end of the close and realised she was holding her own breath hostage to the mystery of the hour..."

At this point Charis interjected: "can I just interrupt you there, Phoebe? Does this piece reflect your own experience? We try in this group to encourage our writers to project their own personality through their work. It doesn't have to be autobiographical of course, but it should be written 'out of ourselves'. It should be true to our own nature if you see what I mean?"

Brigette cut in. "I don't think it can be? The barking fox is a literary cliché if there ever was one?"

Charis calmly resumed. "Have you ever had a stirring experience by moonlight that you could write about?"

Phoebe hesitated. "Well, yes, I suppose I have, but it's a very painful memory. I don't know that I would want to share it."

Lilith snorted derisively. "How can you hope to write if you are unwilling to address personal pain? What are you hoping to write, comic books?"

The Professor gave his now familiar chuckle adding "Oh Lilith, ever the succubus of the group".

Lilith responded with a pout and assumed her familiar steepling position with her hands.

Enesta spoke suddenly. "That was cruel, Lilith, but I see what you're getting at." She turned to Phoebe and with her characteristic concerned frown printed on her dark face added "You need to be honest with your readers. They will know before you do when you're showboating."

Brigette entered the debate. "Why not return to "Moonlight" next week but addressing a personal theme. Something that involves your own emotions?"

Phoebe was speechless. She was stunned. This had been a piece she was sure of and she had not even been allowed to read most of it. She sat in shamed silence for the rest of the session. When she left Ambrose caught up with her and said in what she hoped was intended to be a reassuring manner, "I know they can be sharp, but they are serious writers. They won't accept bullshit. You just have to play by group rules. Be willing to reveal more of yourself in your writing."

This was her chance. "Ambrose? Enesta is an unusual name, where is she from?"

He smiled. "Coffee?".

Once they were settled round a pitted wooden table in a small nearby café he continued. "Enesta's father was full blooded Cheyenne. The name means hear. She's the best listener in the group. Her stories tell of loss. Loss of place, loss of time, loss of context. You know, the Cheyenne were the original beautiful people. They were named as much for their way of life as for their individual beauty."

"And what does Charis mean when she says 'there's only one story'. What does the finger gesture mean?"

"Oh that? Charis believes you must pour yourself into your work. It's a philosophy we've all bought into. There is only one story, the story of us, who we are and what we have been. There has to be passion and integrity. There has to be personal risk. The finger points to the heart. Do you see? There can be joy as well as struggle but only when you feel it."

"Yes, yes, I see what you mean" stuttered Phoebe, deeply unsure whether she agreed.

***

The following week Phoebe was asked to read first. Even the room seemed to be waiting, while the rain beat down on the large Velux windows as though it felt it was missing out.

"Her father had died of a terrible, lingering, incurable disease when she was very young, yet his loss had imprinted her development as clearly as if he had been ever present. He sat like an emotional tattoo close to her heart.

"His absence meant she was so much closer to her mother, and in some ways distanced her from the shared experiences of her peers at school. She grew up solitary but self-sufficient, used to knowing there was no one to fight her battles when her mother was occupied. School concerts and sports days were unrewarded by ruffling of hair and a proud kiss when her mum had to work..."

"Jesus!" muttered Lilith shaking her head.

"I'm sorry!" It was the Professor. "You know what your father died of? Then you need to own the disease, you need to name it, otherwise you are running away from it."

"It's worse than that", chipped in Aelfrun. "Phoebe is denying the whole thing is her personal experience by telling it in the third person. It's emotional cowardice. Her readers would smell it a mile off!"

"Adjectives, adjectives, far too many adjectives my dear," said Ambrose with a sickly smile on his face.

"Look" said Phoebe. "This is really hard for me. I haven't even got to the worst part yet." She continued in considerable emotional discomfort. "When she was thirteen her mother re-married. He was a brute. Handsome, charming and rich, the perfect storm. He worked in the city as a modern alchemist, turning greed into gold and... misery. When her mum was elsewhere, he would catch her in the bath claiming he needed to pick up a towel. Or enter the room to clean his teeth when she was showering. Always the plausible excuse – and of course he was her stepdad. Her mum expected him to be close to both of them. He never touched her, but there was always an atmosphere. He would look at her in a sick, dirty way and she would hurry to her room and dress in something less feminine. He would make filthy inuendo's when giving her a lift in the car, where she always sought protection in a back seat...."

"No good!" pronounced Charis. "Aelfrun is right. You have to re-write this in the first person. It's just a list at present, a list of his transgressions. I'm not feeling any real suffering, fear or anger. You're wasting the pain. Next week huh? Let's move on to Brigette."

Brigette's piece was hard to hear. She sat twisting a ring on her left hand as she worked through a piece about a remote Irish community in the dark ages. The village elder beat his wife brutally and she absorbed his repeated punishments in total silence. At the end of the story a monstrous Barghest had ripped his throat out on a stormy night as he crossed an old bridge on the edge of the village. Phoebe watched the ring turning and suddenly understood that the supernatural hound was a metaphor for anger. The ring was a wedding ring and this story had something of Brigette's own in it.

Enesta followed. Her tale was a haunting one of an archaeological dig at an old Amerindian burial site. It was permeated by an echoing sadness that had her holding her breath. There was a sense of loss and violation, ultimately redeemed by the pragmatism of the grandmother figure who focused defiantly on what she had left. Phoebe's eyes were drawn to Charis's pendant. The warm yellow brown bands seemed to her almost be glowing in response.

Aelfrun contributed a story concerning a witch who operated as a midwife in fourteenth century Bavaria, a story highlighting the anguish of watching unwanted babies die before her, but Phoebe by this time was hardly listening.

After the session she approached Ambrose. "Coffee? My turn."

When they were comfortable around coffee and doughnuts she said, "It feels sometimes as if Charis lets Brigette run the group for her. Surely it's for her to call the shots if I'm not being open or confrontational enough for gourmets of great literature?"

"She's done it with all of us, given us our head. It's her philosophy. She isn't running a group; she is facilitating a circle. We're equals. It's a tight team thing, but yeah, Brigette has been in this game a long time now."

"I can see that", protested Phoebe! "And I'm there on sufferance. No way **I'm** one of the gang."

Ambrose looked at her intensely and without a trace of sympathy. "That's right. You're there to suffer all right. Got it in one. Nothing is going to happen for you until you let that great ball of misery out. We want to hear it, feel it, taste it." He paused. "All of it!"

***

That Saturday afternoon Phoebe was absent mindedly browsing the shelves of a local independent bookshop and reflecting on how much she missed the order and structure of her library work. She rounded a corner and nearly collided with Charis. It almost felt as though the woman had been waiting there for her.

Charis certainly seemed unsurprised to meet her. "Hi. Are you finished here? I am, I'm just off to the car. Can I walk with you?"

Phoebe found herself nodding and only wondered later how Charis knew they would be heading in the same direction.

"What's stopping you talking about your mother's death?"

"How did you know...?"

"Come on, it's obvious. Call it intuition if that helps. You're running away from something. We can all feel it and its why you're there, to let it out. Can't you feel that?"

"Well, it hardly helps when you all jump down my throat every time I speak" complained Phoebe.

Charis stopped walking and stood in front of her. "I can tell you have it in you, but authors have to expect challenge. You can't hide. Not from us at least. For example, there was some kind of breakdown wasn't there? That's why you had to leave?" She fished out a ring with a beautiful flecked blue stone from her pocket and placed it in Phoebes hand. "Don't try and tell me now, just wear this next week. Please. It's Lapis Lazuli, it will help carry you."

***

That week to her surprise however Charis was absent and Brigette was, seemingly by common consent, chairing the meeting.

Ambrose opened with a harrowing story about guilt. A couple were involved in a crash in which a car went off the road. The wife had been killed and a sister was consoling the husband arguing that the cars malfunction had not been his fault. There was a vivid description of agonising personal distress before the stark punchline - "but I built it!".

The "Professor" followed this with a tale of scholarly rivalry for a vacant chair between egotistic academics. It was lighter in tone and very funny, but there was no hiding the smug joy of the author when the rival's plagiarism was revealed to the press before a key meeting.

Brigette in her accustomed quiet way then announced "Phoebe. Can we hear from you? I believe we are still hoping to find moonlight?"

Phoebe held her head in her hands, surprised to feel an unexpected tingling in the finger that sported the Lapis ring, and began. "It was a harvest moon, and the harvest was blood. The baleful moonlight picked out every detail like well-lit stage scenery. It felt artificial, two dimensional. Afterwards, I found I could remember every detail on the policeman's uniform. 'I'm afraid I have some very bad news'. I had been expecting him. I had been expecting him for a considerable time. I had been expecting him, or someone like him, ever since I noticed the first cigarette burns on my mother's arms. The causal cruelty had slowly become almost ritual, and now here was the final dread messenger, the Angel of Death dressed up for the occasion as constable Harrison, come to deliver the news. I could tell he was going to use the very words I had been expecting, so I helped him. 'She's dead, isn't she? He's finally done it, gone too far. He's killed her?'

"My first shameful emotion was relief. She would never have left him. It was over at last. My dear forgiving, gentle mother was safe now, in pain no more... 'I'm curious, what did he use?'

'Do you really want to know?' Constable Harrison couldn't face me. 'It was a small statuette, it, it wasn't pretty.'"

The page in front of her was wet. Phoebe realised she had been reading through tears and her words were pushing their way into the world in short painful bursts. She stopped for breath and could not resume. She turned to Brigette. "Is that real enough for you", and to Lilith, "can you get off on that yet?"

But to her surprise Lilith was looking not at her but at the centre of the room.

"Her anger. I see it. Look, it's here in the room."

And Phoebe saw it too, a shaking or shuddering in the air, dancing like the mirages one can see above a flat dusty road in a hot dry endless summer. It was dark and tangible. As she looked, she suddenly felt lighter. It was the first time she had told her story. She was rid now of this horrible burden, one of which she had been scarcely aware, but which had been choking and consuming her. She felt purged but exhausted.

She felt rather than heard Enesta's next words. "That's what we do you see. Together, through challenge, we have the strength to heal, to draw out pain, anger, or regret. You are free to hate us but it's our terrible gift. Some of us have been doing it for a very long time."

Brigette spoke. "You will probably leave us now with an overpowering sense of having exposed something profoundly private. There will be fury towards us, and self-recrimination too, but you will feel no need to continue here. That moment has gone. Your path is open now. You can write what it is your destiny to write without this struggle to trust yourself."

***

Phoebe never remembered a step of her faltering way down the groaning stairs. She clung to the rail; her legs so weak they would barely support her. At the bottom she was shocked to find Charis sitting at a table nearby writing. She looked up. Phoebe's face posed a question but Charis replied before it took form.

"I wasn't needed today. You made the Seven. Seven is all we need, and it was *your* exorcism."

"But I haven't finished! After the death and his suicide, I couldn't work, I just couldn't face it..."

Charis was smiling at her. "But you can tell me now, can't you. You can tell anyone. You don't need to go back again?"

Phoebe hesitated, smiled, took off the ring Charis had given her and placed it next to her.

Charis thanked her. "I know you will enjoy your writing. You're going to be a formidable force. Take care."

LESSON NO 1

She was drop dead gorgeous; I mean jaw droppingly gorgeous. She was so far out my league I couldn't even get a team together! I didn't know real women that good looking really existed outside of films. I should probably tell you a bit more about her?

She was maybe slightly shorter than average. How tall is the average girl? Five foot five maybe? Then she was about five foot four. Gorgeous grabbable hips (I promise I won't use that word gorgeous again), a tiny waist, and a generous pair of boobs I couldn't take my eyes off. She had shoulder length light brown hair, brown eyes (I think they were brown, but you can't really tell at a disco) and the best legs on the planet, slim round the knees and ankles and firm and muscly looking on the bits in between. Yeah, sorry, I'm making her sound like a horse, aren't I?

On the downside maybe she was dancing with a couple of friends in a way that suggested she had watched far too much Top of the Pops. Her mates were better dancers. The only other thing I could find wrong with her was that she wasn't with me.

She wasn't going to be either. I hadn't got a clue what to say apart from "you are SO gorgeous" (sorry), so I tried to shut her out of my mind. Yeah right, that was like trying to give up breathing!

Lesson No.1

***

I had put the first two days at Uni to good use making friends and allies at the Hall I was staying in. There seemed to be plenty of weirdos around who only talked about their course and how they were looking forward to it, or where it was going to get them job wise. There were the druggies of course, huddled together in dark corners flattering themselves no one could see them and the Jocks busily signing up for as many teams in as many sports as they could think of, probably because they had learnt at school that this got you made a prefect, although I suppose it could also have been because they actually enjoyed physical conflict?

Then there was us. The Normals. Born shrewd. Not necessarily bright, although it turned out later Silver could memorise a page of lecture notes after one glance, and that was my notes not his! But we could cope. We had the system sussed.

Rule number one: No homesickness. We were here to play and play hard, but stay (relatively) grounded.

Rule number two: No one swats. Lecturers have specialities so that's what they are going to be setting questions on. Not on someone else's research or theories. They probably don't understand that stuff any better than we did. Furthermore, lecturers had a vested interest in getting you through their course. A high failure rate was going to make them look really bad, so they were going to be dropping you plenty of hints about what was coming up in exams. You just had to listen out for them.

Rule number three: As long as someone turned up for lectures the rest of you could take it in turns to have fun somewhere else, just as long as you had a system for copying each other's notes.

All this wisdom meant we had plenty of time left to meet women. Trouble was no one had told us how to do it. They were everywhere, but so were cars and it didn't mean you could just get in and drive them. What if they belonged to someone else? Someone big and angry maybe? How did you know if they had a sense of humour, liked intellectual conversation, maybe art, or football before you put your foot in it?

So now it was Freshers Week day three and here we were at a disco at one of the other Halls of Residence. You were always at a disadvantage in an away disco because you didn't know whether your intended target was staying there or not. Mind you a home fixture meant you were likely stuck with each other for quite a while because few of us, male or female, had yet mastered the art of dumping someone without giving offence, and no one wanted to give offence, I mean you might want to go after one of their friends next?

So, there she was dancing with two friends, short blonde hair (later identified as Jane) and long black hair (later known as Karen). It took me about one and a half hours to drink enough beer to temporarily forget I had rated my chances as less than zero and ask for a dance. I kicked off with the infallible "hi, I'm Sam, do you fancy a dance?"

And the reply? "Hi I'm not and I don't."

"But you're already dancing, with your mates?"

"Well doesn't that rather answer your question?"

I gave up.

Sometime later a girl called Brenda from Doncaster asked me for a dance. This was new to me so I said yes and that was it for the rest of the evening. Luckily Brenda was in digs and said she was going home with a bunch of course mates (Chemistry), so I was safe from the entanglement point of view.

***

About a week later I was in the Faculty of Letters coffee room with Silver, a good mate who had the room next to mine, doing the crossword. Well, he was doing the crossword, I was just going "erm" very quietly. In walks little Miss Gorgeous with Karen. She looks round, says "Hi" to Silver and they sit down round a table about five miles away.

"So, you know them?"

"Yeah" says Silver, "Ellie and Karen from Philosophy".

I should explain, everyone in Letters Faculty had to do three subjects during their first year, one of which they were supposedly intending to spend the rest of their lives with. I was stuck with Economics, History and Sociology; Silver was doing English, Economics and Philosophy; and apparently the gorgeous Ellie was doing Philosophy and some other stuff. I imagine they called it Letters because unlike the Scientists we had to be able to spell?

"That's interesting, I've been wondering whether I should drop English while I have the chance and do Philosophy instead."

"Yeah, well good luck with that."

***

So, I sat in on a couple of Philosophy lectures. It did my head in. Nightmare! Stuff like the famous "Is this a question?" to which the answer was apparently "If that is a question then this is an answer". I checked out the book list in the library and they were monsters. Books the size of breezeblocks all written by people with unpronounceable middle European names. No way, not even for the love of my life, was I going to study people called Nietzsche, Leibniz, Montesquieu or Chomsky.

Besides, Ellie and Karen sat near the front and there was a risk the guy in front talking might ask you a question. I reckoned I might not get away with "is this an answer" too often. I stuck with Economics.

I did however work out that she and Karen nearly always had coffee at 11.15 on Wednesdays so I arranged a note taker for Macro Economic theory (which was straight out of the textbook anyway) and "hung out" in the hope that one day all the other seats would be taken and she would have to join me.

In the meantime, there was Colins disco.

***

Colin must have been running discos back home in Bolton since the age of about five. How else could he have ended up running them in the Student Union building before the end of his first term? That must have required serious networking to which serious respect was due. Fortunately, he owed me money so I skipped over the respect bit. Silver and I were running a card school, Bragg and Poker, at the Hall of Residence on Thursday nights and Colin was both partial and a completely open book. Up to a point he could afford to lose because of the Union contract, but recently Colin had completely lost the plot. That night we all got in free. We were there, about eight of us, a mixture of Letters blokes, Science nurds and even a couple of unspeakable Agri students, all from Hall. We had gone in early because some of us ran out of money in the bar and the others didn't want to pay for our drinks.

In walked Ellie with Karen and Jane and the air around her began to dance.

So did we. Not all at once, not elegantly, and not all around them, but close enough for me to get noticed. I had the sudden suspicion that Ellie had moved to the far side of her little group, but I knew I must have been mistaken as I was dancing fit to break something. With arms and legs whirling I was like a human harvester, a frenzied hip swivelling disco beast, a convulsing, thrashing monster of a man. Well, it apparently worked for Bower birds? Who could fail to be impressed, except maybe everybody?

Then I had a great idea. I saw Colin up there presiding from his turntables like an omnipotent rock priest and thought "use your influence". I went over to Ellie and said "what's your favourite track right now?"

"Pardon?"

"Your favourite track?"

"It's too loud. I can't hear you!"

Try it the other way round! I went up to Colin and asked him to dedicate the next record to "Ellie".

"He looked at me pityingly. "Wasting your time mate. Take it from me, you'll make a prat of yourself. She's going out with Chris Masseeve!"

Well, I heard that all right. Chris Masseeve, keyboard player with the Retards, number one band on campus, cool as summer in Norway. It wasn't his real name of course. They were big enough to use stage names. They were finalists of course. Men not boys. I was out of the race before I got the car in gear. I turned to drink.

***

By now Silver was going out with Jane, the quiet one of the three. She was nice. Silver obviously thought so, they've been together over forty years now. She was a good listener and had a great sense of humour. They met in an English seminar group and hit it off straight away. I didn't tell you this but we called him Silver after his football boots. He was a brilliant winger, fast tricky and with the guts to ride a tackle. I wouldn't have minded if Jane had fallen for him because of his silky football skills, but come on! All he had to do was talk to her. It just wasn't fair!

I had lost my sparring partner. It was like losing a leg, and try as I might, dancing on one leg was crap! I had to go round with Mike, God and Sleazy. What a team! Hopeless the lot of us.

Early February a friend of Janes threw a party and Silver obviously had to invite us all, even snoring Norman who generally fell asleep by about ten in the evening. It was "Bring a bottle", so we all rooted out our empty half bottles of vodka, filled them up and made sure we didn't arrive at the same time. It kind of worked, though Silver threw me a sort of "what kind of pondlife are you" look about half an hour later. I guess we must have lined up our bottles in the kitchen, like horses outside the saloon, so they would be easier to find at the end of the evening. Although by that time of course it would be tough enough just to find the kitchen.

She was there. It was like she was dancing in a little private space all of her own that followed her round the room. She had such a lovely smile. Gorgeous cheek bones, those flashing brown eyes, two of them, and a dimpled chin. I hadn't known I liked dimples. Jane had said Ellie hated them, sorry, it, she only had one chin! I would have given so much to tell her she was wrong. She was on her own that night as Chris with the stupid name had a gig off campus but I knew when I was beaten. I spent much of my time with Sally who was going out with Shaun from our hall but who had gone home for the weekend.

I liked Sally. She was tall, slim, sexy and funny. She told great stories and never seemed to put anyone down. For some reason she had always seemed to like me too, which was flattering the way telling a fiver it looked like a million quid was flattering, but Shaun was a psycho. No body messed with Shaun, so nobody messed with his girlfriend. Besides, everyone knew she was fond of rabbits and donkeys which was a bit yukky.

Late that night, after she had had a few, she asked me why I had never tried it on with her. I told her the subject didn't arise because she was going out with Shaun. I asked her "what would happen then if I did try it on with you?" She said "Well, I would turn you down obviously because of Shaun, but it would be nice if you tried sometimes." She said "You have some very old-fashioned ideas about women. I think its charming" – and she kissed me. I was terrified someone would see and I would end up hanging from a window sill by my fingertips. I went home after that. I realised later I could have asked her about Ellie. What was the best way to impress her. It's not like she would have told anyone how I felt, she couldn't have done since just about half the world already knew.

***

There was a party at our hall to mark the end of that Spring term. Everybody came, including Ellie, Jane and Karen. I had hooked up with the appalling Brenda again the previous week and was stuck by the bar being briefed on the intricacies of Rugby League football, a sport I was never going to take up, but I could still watch her across the much cliched "crowded room."

Something was wrong, she was drinking way too much. Spirits judging by the size of the glass, and Karen seemed to be trying to calm her down. Jane broke off from what looked to be an Olympic wrestling match with Silver over on the far side of the room and joined them. Tears followed and her friends made an obvious effort to stop her buying another drink. I couldn't strand not knowing any longer. I went over and asked if everything was o.k.?

Jane, who knew me well by now briefed me. "It's Chris, he's dumped her. Finals next term and he said he needs to focus. I warned her this was going to happen months ago. He's gorgeous, but he's no fool. He was always going to put his future before a doomed University romance. Look, can we maybe get her a coffee or three somewhere, she can barely stand up. She was pissed before we even came over."

Lesson No.1

Guess who volunteered his services? We steered her between us down the corridor back to my room and I put the kettle on. There was vomiting of course to go with the hysterical tears, but to me she still looked gorgeous, just a bit less than she normally did.

At this point Jane said she needed to get back to Silver for a while, if only to let him know what was going on and could I look after Ellie here for a bit. This was like asking a bank if they would mind looking after your gold for a while, or a rock band if they would mind playing Glastonbury.

So, there I was with the girl of my dreams, newly single, sat on my bed... and I couldn't even touch her! After a while she dozed off. Jane came back with Silver and the three of us kind of carried her back to their place. What a night! Oh, if you're wondering what happened to Brenda, I found out later she simply switched her attention to Sleazy and they wandered off somewhere, which says it all really.

***

Then came the Easter holidays, and the first-year exams, which kind of put a dampener on the old social life, and then the sun finally came out, and normal good times resumed.

Silver and Jane decided they wanted to hold a séance. These were pretty popular back then because everyone loved spooking themselves out No one much believed in spirits or whatever, but it was a creepy thing to do if you could lay your hands on an old table, enough chairs, a glass that wasn't too cracked, and could be bothered to write the letters of the alphabet on bits of paper. Actually, we found you didn't even need the chairs, though sitting cross legged on the floor gave you backache after a while.

Mike and God had the biggest flat so we used that. God was dead against the idea (you'll never guess why?) and went out for the evening, but Silver and Jane made up the numbers with Karen, Ellie and me. Ellie had apparently been avoiding me since her melt down over 'Superstar Chris'. I don't think she'd realised I'd be there and I actually felt embarrassed for her when she saw me.

We knocked back a few bottles of cheap Spanish red first with plenty of crisps, then lit a couple of big candles, turned the lights out and settled down round the table. Jane acted as the medium and after we had all placed a finger on the glass she asked in a creepy voice if there was anyone who wanted to speak to us. At this point Mike got the giggles and we had to thump him. When he finally settled down Jane asked the question again while we all put our pinkies lightly back on the glass in the middle of the low coffee table.

I kid you not, the room got a lot colder at this point. I was practically shivering and looking across the table I could see Karen and Ellie were not too comfortable either. After a few repetitions the glass slowly started to pick out letters from round the table edge and Silver noted them down on an old piece of paper. After a few minutes he had written down "I AM LITTLE HORSE OF THE SOO. I DEID AT LITTLE BIG HORN..." I could forgive the guy his spelling, after all he probably never spoke English and even if he had, he was probably well out of practice.

Jane asked the spirit why he had come and the glass started moving quite violently across the table. "I HAVE WARNING FOR S". Then it stopped again. I got to admit I was a bit freaked out being as Silver and I were the only "S's" in the room. The temperature was freezing by now and when Mike looked across at the girls and asked if they were o.k., you could see the condensation in his breath.

They were anything but o.k. Karen whispered "Oh my god, this is SO scary! Go on!" Ellie said nothing at first. Then she said "Sinclair remember, I'm Ellie Sinclair. Please stop this. I can't handle any more. I need to get away from this"

Karen said "your hand is like ice girl. I think we should stop for a bit!"

Silver, Jane and Mike were not too keen on this idea, after all just what did she think was going to happen? Surely nobody actually believed this rubbish. Someone was always working the glass at these events; half the fun was trying to work out who. Ellie though was actually shaking with fright so we really did have to break off.

She said "I'm sorry. I've never been very happy in the dark. I shouldn't have come. I didn't think. I don't want to go back on my own. I'll wait in the kitchen if that's all right? Just please don't be too long, o.k.?"

And at that point I finally had a eureka moment, an epiphany thing or whatever. I got it. If this was ever going to happen it was going to be about what I could do for her, not what she could do for me. I said "I'll walk you home if you like. Would that be good?"

Ellie smiled, nodded and collected her coat.

SHERLOCK HOLMES AND THE CASE OF THE PALE CHINAMAN

"Exsanguinated! Tongue cut out and completely drained of blood from head to foot. By whom, how, and why we can't say at present, and that," said the Inspector turning to the shrunken figure in the wheelchair, "is where you come in, Mr Holmes."

***

I had been in my potting shed sheltering from the persistent downpour and working on my begonias the morning Inspector Dexter turned up insisting that I was urgently required to assist with his enquiries. I was initially bewildered as to why the police should despatch an Inspector. My biggest criminal act to date, so far as I was aware, was to exceed the new twenty miles per hour speed limit in our quiet village by a bloodcurdling two (maybe three) miles per hour? The Inspector however shook his head, insisting that I was required primarily because of my distinguished ancestry.

"I am reliably informed that your great great grandfather was none other than the famous Dr Watson?"

"I have been similarly informed myself on, let me see now, oh yes, countless occasions – especially by my great aunts, all four of them. I really do wish that just occasionally people would consider the implications and consequences of their "greatness" for the perfectly ordinary family members who have to follow in their wake, before stepping forwards into fame and celebrity. I am a gardener. I am not a medical man, never was, never will be, and have absolutely no desire to be."

"Well, that will not represent a problem for the Gloucestershire constabulary as it's not really a doctor Watson of whom we have need."

"I'm sorry"

"Believe me, I doubt you could be half as sorry as I am, Mr Watson. You see my superiors are aware that a certain Mr Sherlock Holmes lives among them. It is he whom they wish to, ehm, invoke. They have apparently indeed done so before but have found him on this occasion reluctant to co-operate."

"Well, I am not surprised, if Sherlock Holmes **was** still alive, he would be around... I mean he would be about... well. he would be over... He would be very old indeed."

"Mr Holmes is extremely old, and extremely frail. So, frail in fact that he has been laid to rest a number of times only for some concerned author to discover there was still breath in him. His precise age is apparently something of a state secret, but I have heard it rumoured that he is somewhat over one hundred and eighty years of age."

"Well then, he can't be can he? He'd be dead!"

"I can assure you, Mr Watson that Mr Holmes is kept very much alive. The public have simply no idea what is possible these days when the international cream of the medical profession and a man of such rare stubbornness and determination work to one seamless end. He is in a home near Stroud, from which he has been of great assistance to the constabulary, and even to the secret services on several occasions. He makes no charge and my Chief Inspector has rather whimsically been heard to refer to him as his 'Affordable Holmes'. At present however he refuses all our requests for his assistance. He claims to have lost interest in crime. He says it has lost all its appeal. He claims all the great criminals are dead leaving in their stead only an unseemly selection of psychopaths, perverts and megalomaniacs. He could of course be talking about pretty well any field of modern endeavour. My superiors however feel that a personal plea from a linear descendant of one he held in such great esteem could yet sway him to help with our current enquiry."

"Why, what's happened now?"

"A dead man has turned up this morning, undeniably murdered. He was found in an eighth story flat in Cheltenham. He appears to be of Asian, probably Chinese origin, but we cannot identify him, nor can we determine who killed him, how or why."

***

Naturally I argued, and naturally I was wasting my time. The Inspector had done his homework. Apparently, the nursery which employed me at that time sold at least three plants for which they lacked the requisite import documentation and another two which were classified poisons. He seemed to feel the responsibility for this might well come to rest with me if I proved reluctant to co-operate. I both needed and loved that job and besides, I was curious to meet the apparently fossilised Mr Sherlock Holmes in person. The Inspector moreover was in a great hurry. Despite the rain banging down on the roof like an impatient police raid, before the hour was up, we found ourselves following the Matron of St Hilda's Nursing Home for Retired Polymaths to Mr Holmes's bedroom.

"Since Mr Holmes joined us, we have noticed a considerable increase in the number of teaspoons suddenly available in the restaurant. A number of residents have also come forward to report finding wrist watches, carriage clocks, or small items of costume jewellery in their rooms. He has been a real boon to us. We have tried to get him to join in with community life, we really have. We tried to persuade him to join us with the Bingo, that's very popular that is, and with the community singing. I understand that in his younger days he used to play the fiddle? Anyway, he much prefers to sit in his room reading the papers. He holds the Home's record for completing the Times crossword, well I suppose he would, wouldn't he?" She giggled, "although that has upset some of our more distinguished residents".

As she spoke, we marched past an open door through which I noted an elderly man of hirsute visage who bore a remarkable resemblance to the late Albert Einstein in conversation with a gentleman of African appearance who I would swear was the spitting image of Nelson Mandela. I shrugged my shoulders. Impossible?

We arrived at the door of Number 221B, which I noted was flanked by room numbers seven and eleven. Holmes' notorious stubbornness was doubtless in evidence? Matron knocked, and on receiving no reply opened the door and withdrew wishing us good luck.

"What in Heavens name is it now? More trouble with the Germans I suppose? Will they never learn? And who the blazes are you? Just a minute, the gait is familiar but surely you should have a moustache? Where is your medical bag? It is surely not my old friend after all these years? They haven't preserved you as well have they old fellow? Where the blazes have you been man, I haven't seen you for, oh, for getting on for a hundred and thirty years? Mrs Hudson will play the very devil with you. Your dinner will be getting cold."

I saw before me a shrunken parody of the great man known to me only from literature and of course from the ceaseless jabbering of countless elderly relatives. Several crinkled wisps of thin grey hair hovered lightly over his speckled scalp, his skeletal hands protruded from the sleeves of a patched and ancient tweed sports jacket, and his wasted legs rested to the right in a regulation issue wheelchair. The expression I saw in those cool calculating eyes set in that long thin face however remained as laser sharp as reported in the Holmes novels. His body had faded and wilted but I saw at once that the intellect which had challenged and bested the criminal elite of the nineteenth century was as penetrating and sharp as ever.

"Dr Wilson, come over here old chap. Let's talk about the old days....."

***

Holmes really was intolerable. No wonder my ancestor Dr Watson had found him so trying on occasion. His objections to helping the police with 'the case of the pale Chinaman' as they insisted on calling it seemed primarily to lie with the fact that he was no longer allowed to smoke at St Hilda's. It had been explained to him on numerous occasions that there had been complaints from his neighbours, one of whom was a previous President of the United States. His lungs, what was left of them, were so frail it was feared his next inhalation might exit through his rice paper thin and transparent skin.

I almost gave up but I had one last trick to try.

"Very well, Holmes (he insisted I call him that) it is clear to me that your resistance to further acts of public service lies in a strong fear that, weak as you now are, your capacities have become enfeebled. You fear blotting your peerless copybook. You dread failure the way another man might dread rejection. I believe you are merely taking cover behind this childish sulking. My great great grandfather would have been ashamed of this behaviour and ashamed to have been associated with you."

I waited. He sat impassively. I waited a bit more. Still, he remained motionless. I turned to leave but still he seemed to be scarcely breathing. I opened the door and whispered "goodbye, Holmes."

"Oh, very well, Watkins. Just once more, but it will cost someone a bottle of 2005 Chevalier-Montrachet Grand Cru. I shall show you the skills that so inspired your father."

I smiled and mumbled "great great grandfather" under my breath.

***

As Inspector Dexter and I pushed Holmes's wheelchair out of the lift onto the open landing on the eighth floor the Inspector was explaining that an attractive young Chinese girl had discovered the body early that morning. She had noted the open door of Number 80 when arriving to move into her new flat, number 77, the previous evening. Finding it still open when leaving for work, she had tentatively entered the flat opposite to witness the horrifying spectacle we were shortly to discover.

Guarding the flat was the tallest, lankiest policeman I had ever seen. He put me in mind of a giant arachnid with his trailing arms and stilt-like legs implausibly attached to an improbably short torso. He introduced himself as Constable Welcome and informed the Inspector that his Sergeant had gone in search of the Forensic team who had been called to an outrage on the far side of town, and had yet to inspect the scene.

"The resident of flat number 79 on this landing has I understand been questioned concerning the occupant of Number 80 but says he knew nothing at all about him. Flat 78 is empty."

"He was Chinese?" enquired Holmes.

"He was sir, how did you know that?"

"Cheltenham's Chinatown is small and little known. Any occupant not of Chinese origin would feel highly uncomfortable around here."

"Have you been on duty since the body was discovered constable?" Holmes continued.

"I have Sir, yes."

Leaving the Constable outside the flat, we entered in. It was conservatively, yet elegantly decorated in a pale Oriental style with framed plaques in a Chinese script on the walls of the short hall. We entered the living/dining area, impeccable save for a large broom propped against the kitchen units, to find the body reclining in an armchair wearing a silk shirt. This had what appeared to be an embroidered picture of an owl in brightly coloured silks on the front. Below the shirt he wore blue jeans and a pair of worn trainers. The body was that of a young man, perhaps around thirty years of age, with black hair and was of what I took to be Chinese appearance. With his staring eyes, his head thrown back and his mouth agog the body looked to me like that of a large but frozen goldfish.

"Exsanguinated! Tongue cut out and completely drained of blood from head to foot. By whom, how, and why we can't say at present, and that," said the Inspector turning to the shrunken figure in the wheelchair, "is where you come in Mr Holmes."

Holmes, who was wearing a preposterous cloth hat which he had informed me was called a deerstalker, looked ridiculously incongruous. He sat hunched and shrunken in his wheelchair in the elegantly furnished modern flat. For a while he said nothing and then...

"Am I to believe you dragged me away from my studies merely for this? Where is my "three pipe" puzzle? I was anticipating at the least a major crisis in the Balkans, perhaps the disappearance into thin air of a fully laden bullion train in the middle of Berkshire, or the assassination of some minor prime minister. Instead, I find a child's puzzle that even Inspector Lestrade would have resolved without effort. How is my old adversary? Presumably he has retired by now?

"Inspector Lestrade by all accounts retired some one hundred and twenty years ago Mr Holmes" replied the Inspector. "Perhaps therefore **you** would be kind enough to enlighten us?"

"Certainly" sighed Holmes and it began...

***

"As I am sure you are aware, the Owl is a symbol of ill omen to the Chinese. This particular one will be carrying something in its mouth..."

"That's right" I observed "a kind of small axe wrapped up in a bundle of sticks tied together by some kind of thong".

"Fasces" said Holmes.

"I'm sorry," I complained. "I am only trying to be of assistance".

"I mean the symbol is that of the Fasces" Holmes continued. "There was at one time considerable trade between China and the Roman Empire, to whom the Fasces was a symbol of power and authority. The Wee Dun Baad Tong adopted an owl carrying the fasces as their symbol some two thousand years ago. If you examine the young man's right forearm you will find a fasces tattoo as is worn by all Wee Dun Baad Tong members."

"But surely you can't mean to say that such an organisation is still in existence today?"

"Most certainly. Exsanguination is a punishment unique to the Wee Dun Baad. If anything, the clan is stronger than ever since the Chinese government adopted the practice of using the Tongs for deniable purposes in espionage work. Really Warton you should study your *Times* more carefully."

"Then who killed him?"

"Would you not agree that a member of such a powerful secret society is likely to have been killed either by a rival Tong, or, perhaps for some serious failing, by his own? The removal of his tongue would suggest some verbal indiscretion. This in turn is likely to have been of considerably more concern to his own side? If killed by his own, they will have defaced his tattoo to indicate his expulsion from their ranks. We may confirm my hypothesis if you would only proceed with the examination of his right arm."

The Inspector stepped forward and confirmed a series of slash marks across the tattoo on the victim's right forearm.

"Very well then. You will I trust have noted the half empty cup of tea left on the kitchen work top? He did not make it himself for this is not his flat."

"...And you know this because..." said the Inspector cautiously.

"Well, obviously because he is wearing outdoor shoes. No one makes themselves a cup of tea in their own accommodation and sits down to drink it in a comfortable armchair wearing their outdoor shoes? Well then, the cup will be bearing the murderers fingerprints."

"Surely, Holmes" I objected. "His killer will have worn gloves?"

"Would such a practice not have aroused even your suspicion Watmore? The victim was murdered in full view of the kitchen area."

"Then he would have wiped it clean of prints?" I continued unfazed.

"Hardly likely as he left in such a hurry" responded the old man.

The Inspector and I looked at each other cautiously both wondering who would risk the next question. The Inspector lost the battle of wills.

"And we know he left in a hurry because...?"

"Well clearly because he left the front door open behind him! Besides, unless he knew the Chinese girl would be moving in yesterday there was no need to hurry. Exsanguination, however performed, would take a great deal of time and I prefer to believe that at his age he was out of practice? He would also have been expected to report back to China at some point? But why not ask him yourself, he is in the broom cupboard? Don't worry Inspector, he will not be putting up much of a fight given that he is in his eighties. I trust you have your faithful service revolver somewhere about you Whiteman, just in case?"

We looked at Holmes in amazement.

"Well apart from the fact that he didn't fit into the cupboard too well and the door is still very slightly ajar, he left the broom leaning on the kitchen worksurface. It is the only untidy element in a scrupulously tidy interior. Oh, and the plaque in the Hall informs us in Mandarin that I Yam Hee was Shanghai Men's Singles Table Tennis Champion of 1960 therefore he has to be in his eighties at least. Don't they teach you anything at police college these days? This is his flat."

This was too much. The Inspector leapt forward and extracted a short, fat, elderly Chinaman wearing a red pullover and (what else?) chinos from the broom cupboard and deftly restrained him in a pair of cuffs.

Before he could comment I said slowly and clearly to Holmes "For the last time, I am not Dr Watson, I am his great great grandson, and I am a gardener by trade."

He looked at me with just the ghost of a wry smile "Well in that case Whitson, St Hilda's stands in urgent need of your close attention".

***

Inspector Dexter and Constable Welcome had returned to their station with the venerable Chinaman leaving me alone with the even more venerable detective. There were a number of loose ends I still wished to clear up before we returned to the Home.

"I understand the assumption that two Chinese gentlemen at home would have been drinking tea rather than for example cocoa, but why did you say the cup would be half empty?"

"Come now Watman would you have drunk the whole cup if it was tainted by the taste of whatever was used to drug the victim? No, it had to be something strong and which took immediate effect."

"And, given that he was clearly absent when the police arrived how did he get back in when Constable Welcome was on duty outside until we arrived?"

"I believe even your distinguished forebear whose strengths were courage and integrity rather than his ratiocinative capacities might have worked out that tiny detail. "Why did the dog not bark in the night?" The dog in question was of course absent and there was surely only one possible way the Chinaman could tell when the Constable was absent..."

"Which he swears he was not..."

"Which was of course a lie. The good constable was quite reasonably unwilling to admit that even his dedicated bladder had its limitations. Would you yourself not have left your post at least once overnight for the purposes of micturition? He probably took the opportunity to visit the young Chinese girl we met, given the absence of viable and less attractive alternatives?"

"He will have been absent for a few minutes at most?"

"The Chinaman had to return to pack the necessary items to make his escape. He knew the police had no way of knowing this flat belonged to him. He had a period quite sufficient to enter the premises. He had his own key and had been watching through the peephole in the door of the flat opposite. This represents the only way he could conceivably spy on the activities of a policeman eight floors above ground level. Every flat in this building comes equipped with a spyhole in the front door, as I understand does much such accommodation these days. Had you not noticed? Once inside he had only to look through this door and await the Constables next call of nature before making his escape. We are lucky Constable Welcome has a strong bladder."

"But the neighbours told the police they knew nothing concerning the activities in flat Number 80. They would surely not admit an elderly stranger into their homes for the sole purpose of spending a period of some hours spying on their unknown neighbour through their front door?"

"It has been my invariable experience that whenever someone informs one that they know nothing whatsoever concerning the lives of their immediate neighbours the complete opposite is true. Moreover, on this occasion the true neighbour happened to be dead. I think you will find that flat 79 belonged to the dead man."

"I can see how that would help, but is that not a remarkable co-incidence Holmes?"

"Hardly, I think. Has it occurred to you Whitman to ask why a major Chinese Tong were operating in a quiet English town? If it occurs to you now, what conclusion do you come to?"

"They were perhaps performing some service on behalf of the Chinese government?"

"They were performing some **deniable service** on behalf of the Chinese government. And what precisely do you think that service might be in a town like Cheltenham, or rather only in a town like Cheltenham?"

It took me perhaps a full minute...

"Oh my God, GCHQ. The surveillance Centre. They were spying on GCHQ. If they were caught the Chinese government could deny any knowledge of their activities. But how could you know that Holmes?"

"The one most telling clue of all. The elderly Chinese gentleman was not wearing a raincoat when apprehended, nor was there one on display in the flat. It has been raining all day. He had to have been waiting inside this building. If they were operating a cell here then it also made sense for them to live close to each other. I would suggest the Authorities would be well advised to search flat 79 at the first opportunity before the Chinese send someone else along to replace them, as they will undoubtedly be sure to"

"I have one final question Holmes. Exsanguination but no blood? What did he do with all that blood?"

"I have absolutely no idea Watson. I am a detective not a mind reader and I deal only in facts pertinent to the case. Now tell me, what have you been doing with yourself all these years?"

CURLEW COTTAGE

I was sitting, content, over a steaming thermos of coffee, when one of my fellow birdwatchers made casual mention of a lovely riverside reserve unknown to me. He said Shifton Lock Reserve was small, little known and rather hard to get to. You had to park about two miles away and follow a muddy and little used foot path. Even when you got there, there wasn't actually anything particularly unusual to see, it was just that it was so peaceful that far from even a minor road. In the right season, he said it was a truly beautiful spot. He felt there was a kind of magic there.

I left the hide determined to check it out, though it took me all autumn and most of the winter to get round to it.

***

I finally made it in early February, taking a good forty minutes to reach the river from the carpark, slipping and sliding whenever I lost concentration on my feet. As I neared the river I was jeered dismissively by the raucous braying of a large colony of rooks high in the trees along the path side. I have always felt there was something pagan about their careless chatter. Rooks and crows seem to me to show no fear or deference to anything or anyone but their own secretive communities. Faced with the intrusion of a red kite on the lookout for scraps, they will rise as one, divebombing the intruder over and over until they give up their reconnaissance and withdraw. What is theirs stays theirs. They do not tolerate intruders.

I found the hide down a little side path even more neglected that the main one, but it proved to be in an advanced state of collapse and it was clear that no birds had been fed at that station for many years. It was quiet though, away from the gregarious chatter of black spies.

I didn't stay long, but made my way back to the river and followed the path to the right until I reached the actual lock. This formed a shortcut across a wide bend in the river, much like the string to a drawn bow.

By now I had fallen under the spell of the place. There were so many tiny spear headed snowdrops, while, in pretty well every shady corner, the egg yellow yolks of aconites hinted at the colours of the year to come. It came as a sudden surprise to find myself in front of the lock cottage. There was a rotting wooden nameplate loosely attached to the front gate stating I had arrived at Curlew cottage. It was T shaped with a wide cross piece at the back and a short projection forward in the middle towards the water. A single bedroomed place I thought, dark, damp but cosy. Was it inhabited? There was a tiny garden at the back dominated by shrubs and several huge willows, but it faced north and looked neglected.

I peered in at the grubby front window. This would have been intrusive if I had seriously thought the place was occupied, so I was startled and somewhat embarrassed when a short, stocky and bearded man came along the lock behind me and challenged my intentions.

Blushing, I blurted out that I was an enthusiastic birdwatcher and had been told of the reserve behind us. I explained that I was only intending to establish whether the cottage was inhabited, and tried to change the subject by adding that it was a beautiful and serene location.

Close up, the man gave off an aura of authority and perhaps threat. He was of below average height, but stocky with powerful shoulders like a sailor. His hair was curly, thick and black, his face deeply lined and weathered. He bristled. His eyebrows were thick and black and full of scattered wayward white hairs which made me think of the snowdrops. His beard was ragged and uneven and covered most of his face. He spoke in a kind of loud whisper, as though he might let out an angry salvo at any time. He could have been any age from mid-forties to mid-sixties and in a way reminded me of the rooks.

"They didn't want the place. Didn't know what to do with it. We saw it, Sally and I, fell in love with it and made them an offer they couldn't refuse. I had to sign a paper saying I would keep the lock gates clean, clear out rubbish and weeds from the lock and that, and carry out any general maintenance as was needed. Then it was ours. Lonely place, but lovely too, don't you think?"

"Sally? She's your wife?" I asked wondering why he would be lonely.

"Was. Didn't do her any good. She died of the cancer about a year back. I scattered her ashes round the back."

"What made you stay on?" I continued.

"How could I leave? Look at it!"

And I did. And I both saw and heard what he meant. If you stood by the canal you were overwhelmed by the power of the remorseless brutal thrashing and churning of the waters through the partially open lock doors. It was as if it was telling you there was no holding the water back because it belonged here. Close up the sound was awesome. Nature was saying 'I come first. I was here before all this and I will always be here, know your place'. Away from the lock side however that blissful quiet settled around us. Nothing mechanical or manmade was creaking or groaning. Even at that unwelcoming time of year I could picture the banks of bluebells or ramsons which would soon replace the snowdrops and aconites and anticipate the scurrying of small re-awakened mammals across the path and into the hedgerows .I could dimly imagine what the place might look like in high summer, or in the pride of autumn when the arboreal tapestry of ancient trees graced the river banks and the sun peeped through their thick green and gold curtains.

As I stood there, I heard the chilling rise of an unearthly whistle rise from somewhere in the fields behind me. It was slow and mournful beyond belief.

"Hear that?"

"Could hardly miss it" I replied. "A curlew, first I've heard this year."

"You're lucky, there aren't many left. I get them from time to time. Beautiful sound in the daylight, but you don't want to hear them after dark. They used to call them murder birds. It's bad luck to hear them at night. The Welsh associated them with Cwn Annwyn, mystical black dogs that harried the souls of the dead across the sky.

I listened in wonder to the plaintive, aching beauty of the distant siren

He read my thoughts.

"I get otters here some days, early like, and at dusk. The roe deer come over the fields to me, and I get beautiful jays in that thicket there, oh, and owls, lots of owls. Tawnies and the occasional ghost owl hunting along the field boundaries. I mean I say it can be lonely, but we're a community the wildlife and me, have been from the start."

He struck me as a shy, reclusive man by nature and I was surprised he had been so open with me, but I realised over the months that followed that he, full name Lionel Aldritch, had felt an instinctive trust in me on our first meeting and had backed that instinct over his natural reticence. I came over every few weeks from then on. He would have no phone or television on the site, though he probably should have done, if only to allow contact from the river authority. We would talk falteringly over large mugs of steaming tannic tea in his tiny front room or, weather permitting, out front with our legs stretched down over the lock side. I formed the impression he had been quite a wealthy man before coming to the river, but that this was a period of his life he regretted and preferred not to speak about. They had apparently lost their only son, David, some years before retiring to the lock cottage and I wondered, but hesitated to ask, whether this might have been the source of his wife's ill health.

I saw few boats on my visits as the river here split into two on its slow bend. The widest course, on the outside of the curve, had once run too shallow for all year-round traffic, which was the reason they had developed the lock. Lionel told me when they dug the canal they found pagan offerings on an old river bed, bracelets, brooches, spearheads and an axe head, all from the bronze age. They were sacrifices from the days when local people saw the river as a divine force and had a strong belief in its power to mediate their lives.

These days the river ran far deeper and it was rare for anyone to require the services of a canal, never mind the approval of the river gods. Curlew cottage remained isolated and screened from passing river traffic by the narrow-wooded islet between the channels.

We made a happy group, Lionel, the canal and I. At times we were joined by a solitary mute swan who seemed to loiter like a reporter at a political meeting. I always thought mutes mated for life, but he seemed content enough smooching alone along his favoured stretch of water. The river though was our leader, seeming in the sleepy summer haze, to listen, drawing us out and eager to learn.

I remember one endless day in June when the heat clung on into the breathless evening like a party guest who has outstayed his welcome. We watched as the reluctant sun was pressed through his transitions from yellow to gold, orange to apricot and finally to a dangerous fiery bronze. I saw the miracle of a kingfisher darting along the canal like a blue and silver arrow and watched the flights of eager rooks returning to their roost like waves of ragged black bombers, their violence spent, at the end of the days mission.

On evenings like that the avian choir sang the joys of a good life well spent. I was transported and reminded of the Edward Thomas poem about a train stopping in the English countryside. Even our friend the grieving swan must have felt the joy of it all.

As the year passed, in the pride of autumn the water seemed increasingly keen to grouch and preach its own timeless doctrines as its levels rose through the lock gates. Now there were strange alien intruders under the trees, stinkhorns, a profusion of milky puffballs, and of course in dark hidden places the sinister death cap.

We talked all through the years fall, of the ways of squirrels, the curiosity of mice, the majesty of owls and the timid persistence of deer. At times we would check out the old hide and sit in silent contemplation of the majesty of the place serenaded by the scratchy susurrations of the beech trees in the deeper soils away from the river.

Then it was winter, and the lock showed a very different face.

***

I came in November during a cold wet spell. The path to the lock had been sodden and underwater for much of its distance and my friend's domain had become a tiny kingdom bordered and isolated by flooded fields for miles around, the borderlands policed by flocks of refugee gulls sullenly waiting out the winter storms.

I was surprised by the low moaning insistence of the powerful winds cursing around the lock cottage. The huge willows behind the building seemed to writhe in quietly creaking torment with their long clawing fingers stretching and scratching towards it. It was almost as though nature were trying to get in.

The place itself was bitterly cold, as if it resented its occupant, and I made the unpleasant discovery that the roof leaked.

I asked him how he fed himself through his winter internment, and he told me he supplemented what he got from the farmer with the supplies his few regular bargees brought him during the warmer weather. "I don't need supermarkets or car parks; don't you worry about that" he muttered. "Don't need anything I haven't already got here."

The swan had vanished now. All Lionel's birds seemed to have flown south or hunkered safely down in hollow trees or dripping hedges. His mammals lay safe deep underground dreaming of former triumphs or of hunting to come. Only the rooks on the approach remained, trumpeting their lordship and issuing their dark threats.

Did I mention that Lionel drank? He never offered me drink so I think he did it alone, probably during dark introspective times when his environment failed him, as a salve from memories perhaps or from too much thought. I often saw a half empty bottle of whisky and brandy by his chair, on the kitchen cupboard and sometimes out the front by the canal. He made no effort to hide it and obviously thought it required no justification. There were plenty of books and a small Roberts radio but I don't think he had much to occupy himself after dark.

***

I next came in late December during a break in the continual rain. In truth it wasn't a great time to visit anyone, or indeed to go anywhere, but it was such a relief just to get out for a few hours without being soaked that I took the risk. As I had feared, the car park to the reserve was impassible, but I managed to pull off the road safely just before the entrance. The path to the river was a torment. Many of the trees were down and it took the best part of an hour to forge a path through the deep sticky puddles and fallen boughs. By the time I reached Curlew Cottage I looked a total mess, not that Lionel seemed to notice.

He was obviously deeply bothered by something. We sat, as was our custom, in that tiny lounge with our tea and I asked him what his trouble was.

"You've seen the fields. Farmer says they get so waterlogged these days he can't farm them. It all rots in the ground long before he can get to it. He's thinking of selling up. A man from some large company came to see him, says they're thinking about building a marina. Open the place up, sell fishing tackle, have a restaurant, cater for weekend sailors, that kind of thing."

"They can't do it!" My reaction was instinctive. "That's horrible! It would ruin the place. What about the reserve?"

He almost sneered at my innocence. "They can if he lets them! It's his reserve, not protected land. Its a private concession. He's a tight old bugger, that's why it's so run down. I can't see the river authority raising any objections. You can see they don't need the lock any more. All these bastards have to do is slip them a few quid and they'll be happy enough.

Listen. You ever been in love? What would you be prepared to do for someone or something you really love? How far would you go? I've got a decision to make, a big one. Don't know if I'm ready."

He wouldn't elaborate. I sensed it would seriously damage our friendship if I tried to push him. He wasn't the kind of man you could push. I left it there and after losing a slow game of silent chess I left before the rain resumed its winter tyranny. I was down with flu for much of January and this trip was to prove to be the last time I saw him alive.

***

They naturally assumed he had been swept in by the flooding while intoxicated and washed away downstream by the current. That was an easy assumption to make when I first reported him missing that February. It was harder to justify a week later when I returned and found his naked body impaled on the broken branch of a large oak tree on the islet facing the river. It was stretched out through his chest like a third arm. His actual arms were splayed out on either side with the palms upwards in an apparent gesture of sacrifice, his head thrown back to stare sightlessly at the leaden sky above him. Thankfully I couldn't see his face. You don't go out naked in the teeth of a storm when the rain is lashing you like a freezing barbed whip, and no one ever impaled themselves in that position on a riverside tree ten feet above the flood water?

His will stood unchallenged. They had to rule out suicide and there was no evidence to suggest anyone else's involvement. No forensics, no motive, and no weapon. No means either but they had to let that go.

I was staggered shortly after to receive a call from a solicitor in a town about ten miles away. I never knew who ordered his cremation, when or where the service was held.

Theobald Turner was a long thin humourless individual who maintained an old-fashioned office big enough for at least four people by modern standards. I do feel the occasional flash of tasteful levity might have made his work easier on all concerned, but he dealt with me briskly and efficiently. I was back in the shabby Victorian waiting room struggling to take it all on board in double quick time.

He began; "I had a visit from a gentleman who brought me a letter from Mr Aldritch. I was to meet this gentleman at a time of my convenience in Little Shinton and he would convey me by means of his boat to Curlew Cottage. I objected that I would of course be charging by the hour but then read Mr Aldritch's assurance that this was expected and that he could well afford the charge. I do not usually undertake house calls", he informed me in a rather sanctimonious tone. "The business was quickly completed at our next meeting with the gentleman and his wife, or partner, acting as witnesses."

I was to inherit Curlew Cottage. Mr Turner had looked at me sceptically over the rim of his half-moon glasses and informed me there was also a letter addressed to me. We read it together:

Curlew Cottage

Dear Henry,

Farmer is willing to sell, but I can't afford to buy. My needs are simple but I still need an income to get by. Look after the cottage.'

Mr Turner then informed me he had been instructed to sell Lionels considerable holdings to action a recent, but pre-existent written agreement to buy the fields behind the cottage from the farmer. He was then to bequeath that land to the RSPB, along with any residual monies from the transaction.

He told me the police had shown considerable interest in the will, given Lionel's clear expectation that it was to take effect sooner rather than later, but that they hadn't been able to find anything that could give rise to a future challenge to the contents.

Quite what Lionel expected me to do with a tiny old cottage with a leaking roof and rotting windows and doors I didn't know... until it struck me that he expected me to do absolutely nothing with it. He simply wanted it to revert slowly back to its component parts and then back to nature. He had chosen to give it to the one person he could rely on to let nature take its course. Sally would be happy with that.

Personally, I can offer nothing but speculation on the precise agency of his death. It could be argued there had been some freakish natural catastrophe that night, or that he had taken the decision to end his own life, and found some ingenious mechanism to avoid a prognosis of suicide. I sense however that he had somehow persuaded the wild spirit of the place to claim him for itself, though whether it did so ultimately as an act of kindness or of simple self-interest I couldn't say. Clearly without his death the money to save the area could not have been realised and within a short space of time it would have been covered in tarmac and concrete and teeming with day visitors. That alone would have killed him.

I should mention one more thing. When I looked around the lock for him that February day, I had to beat down the rickety door. Inside, on the table I found an empty bottle of scotch, and a note which said:

'Last night I heard the curlew'

I disposed of both before contacting the police.

On the way back to the car I swear I could hear the spring lament of a curlew under the triumphant braying of the rooks. Nature finds ways of looking after itself.

BROADENING THE MIND

I have previously written several pieces about our old house in France. My justification was that our experiences there felt every bit as bizarre and absorbing as those of more gifted writers and I hope made interesting reading. I would maintain that anyone can have an adventure, you just have to be there at the right time. This piece concerns some of our experiences on holidays rather further afield. Since retiring, we have tried to 'push the boat out' on our foreign excursions and we've now completed the 'bucket list' of places we had hoped one day to visit.

***

We had the privilege of visiting Syria and Lebanon in a brief interlude of relative sanity in middle eastern politics, taking in some wonderful sites including the massive crusader castle at Krak des Chevaliers. In its medieval prime this could house a garrison of up to four thousand, but it has recently been destroyed from the air. We visited the thousand-year-old citadel at Aleppo, one of the world's oldest continuously inhabited cities, which has also been flattened in the Syrian civil war. We visited Palmyra, once the oasis capital of Queen Zenobia who had the balls to take on the romans. This has now been blown up by Islamic State. We had the company of some remarkable companions on this coach trip, such as Bruce the retired Palaeontologist and his artist wife Audrey. Bruce had been desperate to get to Syria while he could, and Audrey had respected his ambition to the extent of concealing a fall some weeks earlier which had fractured her wrist. Our coach party would sally out in the mornings and leave her at that day's hotel patiently painting beautiful watercolours of her surroundings. Bruce later complicated their trip by losing his passport on the way home.

We had the services of an elderly one-eyed guide who would refer enthusiastically to 'this bridge which was built by our brothers the Bulgarians' or 'this road donated by our brothers the Russians'. He slept frequently, but as he invariably did so with one eye open and one closed, it was difficult to determine whether he was listening when you addressed him.

On entering Lebanon while passing through a major military border post our coach hit a building. The window running the length of the coach shattered with a sound like a gunshot, and most of the passengers took refuge on the floor. It was briefly a terrifying experience, but we did then have the benefit of an outstanding view of the coast all the way to Beirut. Once in Beirut we were treated to the reminiscences of a lady guide who had grown up travelling to and from school through daily street battles between no less than sixteen urban militia groups. We later dined at a luxury hotel where we watched a sumptuous Lebanese society wedding reception taking place around the remains of a burnt-out Sherman tank. This trip was unforgettable, and could not have been made even the following year.

Broadening the Mind

We have twice visited Costa Rica, a country I admire above all others. They abolished their army in 1948 and are currently pretty well self-sufficient in renewable sustainable energy, thus setting an example to the rest of us twice over.

Tortuguera, on their east coast, is the most beautiful place I have ever been. The wildlife there is incredible and the government was in the process of setting up green corridors between reserves around the country while we were there with the intention that it should remain so. Warm welcoming people and great coffee.

We spent one extraordinary week on Bird Island, a speck of land about one thousand miles from anywhere else in the middle of the Indian Ocean, which is exactly what it says it is. You share it with about a million terns and the islands smaller avian species fly through your bedroom as the walls are designed to fall short of the ceiling, which itself was coated with various species of gecko. After crunching our way over the numberless hermit crabs commuting between us and the restaurant, we would return to find birds admiring themselves in the bedroom mirror. Later we could venture out to watch headbutting contests between giant tortoises. It took us two days to fulfil our ambition to circumnavigate the island, fully one mile in circumference, owing to the merciless humidity. They also had some extraordinary trees there which roamed the island (slowly) crashing into buildings and causing considerable structural damage. The marine life around the island was incredible. We spent our last morning sharing champagne before breakfast with a German couple in a small boat watching flying fish, initially mistaken for seagulls, and several mating turtles. In the middle of the island was a large house owned, perhaps inevitably, by a Russian oligarch.

In 2020 we spent a fabulous month visiting New Zealand, returning literally days before the great Covid shut down. Wonderful place, wonderful people. What struck us most was that everyone was so welcoming to tourists. Here at home in England everybody seems to be sick of tourists, and can't wait to bite the hands that are busily feeding them, but the Kiwis seemed genuinely glad we all turned up. We arrived at one private house we had booked into during a visit to a thermal spa and museum, and were immediately invited to feed their alpaca's. At another our hosts left out a small jug of port and biscuits for us to enjoy at the end of our night out. Everyone was keen for us not to miss the best of their neighbourhood, and the brooding intensity of the scenery in fjord land was superb.

On the way over to New Zealand we visited Singapore which is the cleanest place I have ever been. No smoking in public, no gum or litter on any of the streets, and not I suspect, much freedom of speech. They did however have a considerable number of gorgeous orchids.

One year we took in Rajasthan, where we went ballooning at dawn over a ruined fort; saw the Taj Mahal (so beautiful it made me weep); got so close to a wild tiger we could have stroked it (I have made some bad mistakes in my life but that wasn't one of them); and had some of the best food of our lives. In Jaipur I was measured up for a couple of handmade shirts, and these were dutifully delivered by scooter to our hotel twenty miles away that very night. India was incredible, but the pollution and the poverty were appalling. Everyone I have met who has been there would seem to agree with this summary. What an utter tragedy.

One year we saw the best bits of Jordan, plus the Dead Sea, which was far less welcome. Frankly it stank like an unkept sewage plant. We did however visit Petra while there which was hauntingly memorable, and where, unexpectedly, we got to listen to a man playing an Oud on a remote mountain top. We saw the wonderful desert scenery where Lawrence of Arabia was filmed, and found another Sherman tank, this time deep under the red sea. In the interests of balance, I should add that we also saw, from a distance, a huge refugee camp built to house Palestinian refugees. It had been there over twenty years.

Possibly my most memorable personal holiday experience however was in Sri Lanka. UNESCO rates Sigiriya as the eighth wonder of the world. It is a fifth century rock fortress/palace built by a raving lunatic. Put it this way, he murdered his father by walling him up alive and there must be any number of easier ways? It is located on top of a plug of granite rock nearly two hundred metres above the surrounding jungle. It rises like a clenched fist and you get to the top by climbing the narrow rickety metal staircase that winds its way round the outside. This is rather loosely bolted to the rock, and it takes about two hours climbing to reach the summit. Half way up is a grand entrance carved in the likeness of a lion, but of more immediate concern to most at this point, is the very large cage with a plaque on it advising that wasp attack, they mean assault by the Asian hornet, one bite from which can result in hospitalisation, is 'very likely'. At this point Liz and many other sane people declined the guides invitation to climb further. I had always previously been very afraid of heights, but I resolved now that if I survived the experience to follow, this would have to become a thing of the past. I got to the top by the expedient of only looking directly above me and shutting all thoughts of the descent out of my mind. It was as well I did so because on the way back down a young couple chasing each other insisted on passing me. I was convinced the rail was going to come out of the wall. In its favour, the views from the top and sides of the palace are exquisite, perhaps just a little too exquisite.

Another memorable Sri Lankan experience was the three-and-a-half-hours I spent on a very crowded train with my face pressed into the belly of an elderly Sri Lankan lady. I did honestly try hard to give up my seat to her when she boarded, but she repeatedly refused me. I nearly asphyxiated but I imagine the humiliation was all hers.

A third remarkable encounter on this trip was with the famous Sri Lankan stick fishermen. The theory is that in these parts fishing is traditionally undertaken by impoverished locals from the top of a slender stick rooted in the seabed. The enterprising fishermen climb their stick while the sea is out and presumably stay there until the tide goes down again. In practice of course they do nothing of the sort. They wait patiently by the side of the road until a coachload of tourists comes along. The coach stops, their guide informs them this is an unmissable opportunity to film a dying custom, and the tourists dutifully march out cameras at the ready. The "fishermen" then rush into the water, mount their sticks and pose for photos. They then quickly scuttle down again, rush back to the tourists, claim their tips, pay off the guide and line up to wait for the next bunch. I was staggered by the sheer extent of the dual duplicity involved in this enterprise. The fishermen are completely phony (a later guide informed us they each have their own modern fishing boat) and the tourists are more than happy to buy into the fiasco in the expectation of amazing their friends. And yes, I took my picture just like all the rest.

Other than that, we saw an awful lot of Buddha's in Sri Lanka, all of which you were told you were desperate to see, and the food varied from the comically bad to the sublime.

Another fabulous holiday location was the American mid-west. It's a big place, no question. The Navajo reservation alone is twice the size of Belgium, and I remember sitting in a Subway bar counting the freight carriages leaving an Arizona siding all the way up to one hundred and thirty. The train may well have been a mile or two long and didn't look in any way out of place in the landscape. Coming from Northern Europe I found the infinite space and huge skies incredibly compelling. The roads were of course empty outside of the few cities which themselves were a far more respectful distance apart, and I could have driven towards those glowing rocky red horizons for ever. We must have seen the iconic outlines of Monument valley a good hour before we reached them, but I think the most incredible place we visited was Antelope canyon. This is a narrow fissure in the rocks carved by flood waters. When the sun is in the right place the visions that appear in the rocks around you are nothing less than psychedelic. Thin bands of a thousand unfamiliar colours roll around you and you can see the Antelope appear out of the wall. No wonder it's regarded as a sacred place.

We had a lot of fun at Mesa Verde, climbing a thirty foot long, maybe six-foot-wide home-made wooden ladder perched almost vertically up the side of an eight-hundred-foot-high canyon. When you get up that you have to wriggle through a twelve feet long hole in the bricked-up entrance to get into the ancient Indian settlement within. It's another very special place. We visited Zion Valley in Utah where we saw a climber's pod suspended near the top of a two-thousand-foot-high sheer cliff. It seemed so tiny from where we stood, I thought at first it was a hibernating moth. These special places are so quiet, so still, and so overwhelmingly beautiful they change your sense of perspective for good. Go see!

We also visited Las Vegas. Liz hated it. I quite like a bit of kitsch myself but I couldn't have stayed more than three days. On arrival we left the car in a huge car park at the top of a tower in Caesars Palace. When I asked later how to find it the receptionist asked me which one I was looking for. There are five apparently! I will grant you Vegas is incredible. Hotels like the Venetian demonstrate an insane attention to reproduction detail. We have been to the original Doges Palace and this place was better! Everything however panders grotesquely to every imaginable vice, self-gratification, greed, and gluttony being foremost. There was nothing there to which I will openly admit an aspiration.

Another, very different but equally extraordinary experience was staying a few days in a New Mexico "Earthship" in the middle of the desert. These are "sustainable solar earth shelters made of both natural and upcycled materials, in which every system works together to reuse and circulate water and energy at a cost efficient and environmentally safe level." In layman's terms they are made out of recycled rubbish like glass bottles or old tyres, use no external energy source which is not natural and sustainable, and the water, once used (you are allowed rain) never leaves the house. All furniture is fabricated from sustainable timber sources, and best of all you get to grow your own bananas and chilli's. They are warm, spacey and comfortable, and bring hope to a weary planet, although do they look like they belong on a different weary planet. Now that I could and did aspire to.

***

Our joint most memorable travel experience however occurred on our trip to the Andaman Islands.

These were a really long way away, notionally part of India, but closer to Burma, and still over three hundred miles off shore. It took days to get there. They still have genuine cannibals in the Andamans but we didn't get to meet them.

We had to stay in Chennai for two days on the way over and our guide dutifully treated us to a visit to a papermaking factory. It had closed five years earlier. The next day we were driven down to Chennai airport by a driver who showed me his family photos while careering through the city. Apparently scooters account for about a quarter of the traffic in Chennai. You get the impression that if someone fell off, and this is easily done when you are carrying up to five people among whom the women are riding side-saddle, they would just be driven over.

On arrival in the Andamans, our impression was that the Hotel 'Fortune' wasn't so much tired as utterly exhausted. We were intrigued by brass pots full of water placed outside our grass hut, one large and one small. When I asked what they were there for I was told 'we fill the large one with water and use it to fill the small one'. I found out later they were for washing the sand off your feet, but I never did establish why there were always two of them. I vividly recall the only lunchtime when we treated ourselves to a glass of Indian white wine. My diary records this as 'tasting like a mixture of warm vinegar and hot cough mixture. One of the foulest things I have ever tasted'. Then again, the Australian alternative was over £80 a glass.

The idea had been to go to the Andamans for scuba diving, but to be honest there weren't many fish left. Off the beach nearest our hotel the sea water was hotter than bathwater. Nothing grew on the seabed, nothing swam past you as you bathed, and the beach was piled up with the shells of long dead hermit crabs.

The road into the nearest town had obviously been used for aerial bombing practice and riding along it, in a Tuk Tuk apparently welded together by a blind man, would have been perilous even if the driver had been licensed. His meter wasn't running, and the hotel wouldn't let him past their gates. It was the longest six miles of my life, to that time at least, and after one attempt at escape we remained around the hotel. Some of the food was excellent, the Indian people were again invariably friendly and welcoming, and the sunsets were incredible. Rather optimistically turtles still nest on the beach, although I suppose it's possible someone else buries the eggs in the hope of attracting tourists. It would make rather more sense! Frankly, I wouldn't bother with the Andaman Islands.

Broadening the Mind

On the way home we had to overnight in Chennai. I had read somewhere about an Elizabethan fort, Fort St George, and rather than sit watching the vultures hovering over the road outside our hotel waiting for passengers to fall off their scooters, I proposed a visit. The hotel found us a Tuk Tuk, which cost only just over twice the fare they had predicted, and it duly took us to a hospital. Port not Fort. Having wandered around the back streets failing to find any Elizabethan forts we were approached by a second Tuk Tuk driver. Lost and concerned, we agreed to let him take us back to our hotel. His price was over twice what we paid to get there, but since we had no idea where "there" was...

I first became very seriously concerned when I realised the pile of leaves on the dashboard he was eagerly tucking into were Betel leaves, a mild narcotic. By this time however he had taken us to a church, a botanical garden, a beach, and, of all places, a Cancer Institute, offering to show us around each in turn. No, we said, take us to the Hilton. He then tried his luck at a large cemetery before filling up with petrol and demanding I pay for it. By now the only word in my vocabulary was "Hilton", so he took us to the Majestic and two other hotels. He stopped and asked some old men by the road something which I assume must have been "where the hell is the Hilton" before heading off towards the Airport. Big mistake, we had been there and I knew where we were. I screamed at him to drop us at the airport and to my amazement he did! He naturally demanded even more money because the airport was so far away but I paid him the originally agreed (exorbitant) fare and gave him a stern lecture. He put up with this I am guessing because of the nearby armed airport guards. We then ran like hell before he could produce a machete, which at the time felt entirely possible. The airport felt like a sane and civilised place after the city, that's how bad it was! We boarded a government controlled fixed price taxi and made it safely back to the hotel. That holiday we took three Tuk Tuk rides in mainland India and not one driver had a clue where he was going. The roads were like bombsites and the traffic was psychotic. I bet its worse now though.

THE KEY

I found it lying on the mat when I opened the door for Michael. He was the last to arrive yet when I asked them all, no one claimed it. Odd this, because it had looked strangely familiar. I put it on the shelf over the fireplace.

Only about two hours later I let them all out again, with just a set of short variations on the theme of 'goodbye, see you soon' exchanged on the doorstep. It had just been a brief get together, and now, there was my sixtieth birthday over and gone forever. A landmark after all is no more than something you walk past on your way to somewhere else.

It's at moments like that, when I am suddenly alone again that I feel the sharpest pangs of loneliness. There is a companionship in silence but it takes a while to settle in. For a while I am uncertain what to do next, how to take up the threads of solitary living again.

I put this down to the twenty-five years when I was an occupied state. "Made for each other" they all said. "Hungry for success, uncompromising, a power couple." Well, they were half right. You can't **be** Burton and Taylor, Becks and Spice, Harry and Meghan, there is no such reality. It's just an image, made purely for public consumption. The reality is corrosive, its draining, or at least it was for me. She, or perhaps to be fair, we, sucked the joy, the warmth and the generosity out of me with the gusto of a vampire with a time limit. Between us we crumpled me like dry rot, and sapped my energies like a cancer. What was it Proust had said? "Possession makes everything wither and fade."

And then I was just me again, trying to remember what that had actually meant.

So, I picked up the key again and looked at it more closely. Its appearance was just that of an ordinary house key, but it was so much more than that. I had been lying to myself of course. Part of me had recognised it the moment I picked it up. The rest of me just didn't want to admit it. The problem was it couldn't possibly be there. It was Madelaines front door key. She had trusted me with it shortly before we broke up... before I broke us up, to be eaten alive by an all-consuming ego monster I thought I recognised in myself.

Remembering her presence now was an intense exquisite pleasure, like that brought to me by great music. It brought pain in equal measure, the dull insistent irreversible ache of regret. Even thinking her name brought other forgotten physical sensations, but it also brought a sharp stab of guilt. I had forgotten all these sensations. Madelaine, the one great, solid gold, missed opportunity of my life.

In a film there would have followed a protracted sequence while the subject wrestled with himself before taking the action the audience had known all the time he would get round to eventually, but I had never been like that.

We had met at work. I wanted her the first instant I saw her. She was so graceful and calm when those around her lost it. She could hold you with the intensity of her eyes in a way that shut out everything else. Surely, she couldn't still be at that place after all this time, but there could just be someone there who knew what had become of her? So, I asked.

"Oh, Madeline Benson. I think she left about ten years back, but Bella there says she still sees her in the supermarket sometimes.

Bella confirmed Madelaine had inherited money from an aunt and retired, but she believed she now volunteered several days a week with a food bank on the other side of town. I went straight over there

Recognition was instant. She was packing something for a customer. Her face was now lined of course, bearing the signature of her life. Her hair had bleached from blonde to silver grey and she was thinner than of old, yet she seemed charged with some hard-won inner strength. A kindness tempered by experience? Hard lessons well learnt? An enduring generosity of spirit?

She felt my intrusive stare and turned to face me. Those calm grey eyes. I had forgotten the power of those pools of serenity, and how I could bathe in them at will, washing away all the filthy compromises of the world we lived in.

I was suddenly, ridiculously, speechless. "I, I can't, I don't..." I was squeezing the key hard in my hand so I let it speak for me. I held out the hand. "I found your key"

She smiled, and her face rippled like the surface of a clear pool taking in a stone. "The door's still there" She laughed and shook her head. "I have no idea why I said that!"

She reached out her arm and placed her hand on mine. Her fingers were long, thin and deliciously warm.

"How did you find me? No, on second thoughts, don't answer that now. I'm off at five. Can we talk then?"

She turned away to deal with another enquiry, but turned back. "You know I'm married? Happily married!"

***

I sat in the car and waited, barely noticing the rain cascading across the windscreen. I hadn't felt as nervous since my first job interviews decades earlier, and I was in shock. I have never been indecisive, but I could hardly believe I had had the temerity to look Madelaine up again after so long, that my initiative had been rewarded, or that my reward had proved to be so hollow. Yet hope was a stubborn seedling growing at the slightest hint of light. She still wanted to talk.

Was this what they meant by a cocktail of emotions? I knew I wanted her back. I wanted to lie close to her again,

The Key

and listen to the rhythm of her breathing. I wanted to share
laughter, trust and experiences. God help me, I wanted to
show her off like the head of some poor animal mounted
on a wall and say, "do you see her, she's magnificent, and
she's mine again!" At the same time, I dreaded her
reproaches. Surely, she must despise me for rejecting her,
would scald me with lacerating contempt, and dismiss me
from her presence for ever?

At five pm exactly we met at the door. She locked up
and we walked silently across the street to a small café. I
had to stop myself from sheltering her from the rain under
my coat. I felt I didn't have the right. A large middle-aged
lady, bursting out of her work jeans, bustled around the
almost empty café but seemed immediately to sense our
need for space and time. I picked up two coffees and when
I returned to the small wooden table and seductive leather
chairs, we both started speaking at once.

She laughed nervously. "Go on, you first."

"I found the key in the hall, but it couldn't be there could
it, not after so long?" What was I doing, I didn't want to
talk about the key, I wanted to talk about Madelaine but
the key felt like safe ground. "How are you? You look
great, and married? You said you were married?" And
there it was, the elephant in the room, sat with its fat arse
firmly in the middle of the table! The question that told so
much about me.

"I married about five years after... after us. Dan. He's a
dentist, well he was. Don't laugh please, people do laugh

when I tell them you know. He fell off a ladder last year fixing the gutters. Shattered his hip and broke his leg. Damaged his shoulder and his spine. He's in a wheelchair now, for good." Her voice had trailed off as her energy drained. "He's a lovely man, I'm glad I found him."

I thought, she's defending him. Do I pose a threat?

"And you?" She fixed me with those trusting grey eyes and they hurt. "I married Dina. I think you met once or twice?"

She rolled her eyes at this "Oh Dina. Everyone knew Dina. It's funny, I didn't think the two of you would last."

"We didn't. But first we lasted long enough to completely trash each other's lives." I paused and added "Dina was my punishment".

"I really don't think it works like that, do you? Dina was something you had to do, something you had to experience. If we had stayed together there would have been another Dina sooner or later. There really isn't anything to apologise for, you silly man", but she added "everyone gets hurt."

So, there it was, a barrier breached, my absolution.

We spoke about people we had known, about Dans accident, my career and her windfall for over an hour before she said she really had to get back to Dan. "I'd like to do this again some time. The past shouldn't be left to moulder in some forgotten drawer, should it? There's a lot of good things to remember, and we have nothing to be ashamed of!"

She left me with her number. Why not I thought, there was no secret to keep from her husband. She asked me to ring in a few weeks. I thought, it's a test. She doesn't really believe I will. She thinks that's it. So, the contrarian in me had to prove her wrong, even if she was happily married. After all, I had never actually passed the key over. It would have been pointless anyway since she had moved out of her old flat decades ago, but nonetheless I had clearly retained it for some purpose. Those eyes and her empathetic smile had worked their old healing magic. I really couldn't imagine never seeing her again.

***

Phoning her proved harder than I thought it would. I was a needy fool pushing my way back into her life for totally selfish reasons, I could see that. But, if that's what I was, then that's what I was. I rang regardless.

We met as before, after her shift, in the tiny café across the road. The proprietress clearly remembered us and asked "Two americano's?"

As we settled in, I asked "Why the homeless? So many charities you could have chosen, and why do it anyway? Sounds like the world could have been your oyster?"

She looked at me gravely, as though she was addressing a little boy who had forgotten his mother's birthday. "My husband, remember him? I could hardly fly off and leave him marooned?"

"Oh shit! I'm so sorry. In my defence, all of this is new to me. I'm kind of still seeing the old you."

"Well, that's where you're going wrong. If we are to be friends again you need to focus on the new me, wrinkles, husband and all. He'd like to meet you."

"Really? You told him about us?"

"He's known about 'us' for years. He thinks it's nice that we met up again, says I need someone to talk to who isn't burdened with too much information about his problems. Someone maybe who doesn't just see me as his carer."

I went home, and now the emptiness of the house positively bounced off the walls at me like midsummer heat. It demanded attention.

So then, I met Dan. They had invited me over for dinner. Tajine and something sticky for dessert. I had actually forgotten Madelaine was such a good cook.

He was a big man, some years older than her. He had been a prop forward back in the day, and you could see he resented being stuck in his chair to the absolute maximum. He could get around on his own, but he barely left the house unless Madelaine or someone else was with him. I was deeply struck by his trust. He showed absolutely no resentment of the presence of a fully mobile former boyfriend in his house. Then again maybe he believed he had no reason to feel I posed any threat.

He clearly knew his wines, and as we settled down in the spacious living room after dinner, I felt I was floating down into my chair. I could have stayed all night. I had brought the key with me, a kind of superstition I suppose, and I could now feel its slight weight in my breast pocket like a tiny conscience. Dan was a lively conversationalist with an engaging sense of humour. We talked sport, we talked politics, we talked music and then, when she left us to make coffee, we talked Madelaine.

"I am so glad you got in touch with her," he confided. "I genuinely am. She needs someone she can talk to, maybe open up and confide in from time to time. She needs to get outside of our relationship occasionally, or its going to drown her in the longer term. She won't give herself that freedom unless she is pushed, and pushed hard. You know that because you know her so well. Please, be her friend. Take her places I can't, only promise me you won't take her to bed?"

The key suddenly felt hot in my pocket. Someone I hardly knew replied "I couldn't do that to any of us. Her friendship now is more than I could ever have hoped for. I won't risk losing that again."

And I didn't, not then, not ever. We went for dinners, to the opera, up to exhibitions in town, galleries and concerts but we never stayed overnight. We remained close friends, even after Dans death some years later. No secrets and no regrets. On the day of his funeral, she both arrived and left on the arm of her brother. No more moving in, using up and moving on. I tucked the key into the wreath I tossed on his coffin. It was a promise to all of us. I had surmounted my drive to control and possess her. I found, to my astonishment, it was weeks before the question even occurred to me but it wasn't what either of us wanted now. I had discovered something more enduring, much deeper and even more rewarding. As Proust argued, life had taken me round that, and led me beyond it. Had I turned round to gaze into the distance of my past, then in time, I would barely have seen it, so imperceptible did it become.

THE CHRISTMAS GHOST

Christmas, according to my brother, is all about ghosts. I think it goes much further than that? Surely Christmas itself **IS** a ghost?

The brief days are chill, damp, dark and unwelcoming. They pass under a thick grey veil of silence, and we are open as at no other time to mystery and suggestion.

We actively invoke the ghost of Christmas past. No feast is quite what they used to be, no family gathering as joyful and no present as unexpected or wonderous as those of the past. We remember lost traditions, the carol singers, the sixpence in the pudding or the coal passed round at New year. We cherish those that remain, the symbolic offering of food and refreshment to Santa Clause, and the sharing of crackers with cryptic messages at the end of the feast. We open our minds and our hearts to those who used to share these celebrations with us as we rarely do during the safer, warmer times. We remember and invoke the simplicity and safety of our childhood in a smaller, less hostile world. For a while we become children again gazing open eyed at the wonderous magical spectacle laid before us.

***

We drove out to Chastleton House that afternoon with the intention, in our sons' words, of 'getting all

Christmassy'. It was the 17th December, the last day that year it would be open to the public. The huge Jacobean pile of grey Cotswold limestone lay curled up contentedly in the gathering mist below the hill down which we approached from the car park. It is entered by a wide stone staircase nestling between two three story blocks protruding from the rest of the building. The house rests between the stable block to its left and the estate church to its right as you enter. It presents itself simultaneously as both imposing and comforting, as doubtless had been the intention when it was first raised over four hundred years before.

This year's attraction was the recreation of a family nineteen sixties Christmas celebration, though during our approach all I could see of this was the shuffling of shadows across one of the upstairs windows which blinked out through a sclerosis of old ivy and creeper.

At the entry hut by the car park, we had been told we were probably its last visitors for the year. It was already mid-afternoon and at that foreshortened time of late autumn year darkness and closure were only an hour away.

The moment we entered; I was overwhelmed by the rich dusty atmosphere beckoning in a sense of great antiquity. We could immediately smell the large log fire in the Great Chamber, but didn't experience the full effect until we entered the hall and were dazzled by the huge tree. This was a good twelve feet high, liberally festooned with old-fashioned home-made paperchains, with thin tinsel strands over the ends of the branches. Around it the old wood panelled walls sprouted moth eaten animal heads and rusting Civil War armour. Beneath them lay piles of presents, many still half wrapped in old crepe paper. There were half empty coloured glasses scattered around the furniture. I could have sworn I smelt cinnamon, although they were presented as having contained Babych am, or Cherry B. A volunteer stood by dressed as a member of the family holding the Yuletide party. She was generously bedecked with pearls and feathers, but we declined the offer of a picture. I perhaps already half felt that nothing would appear in the finished photographs.

From the room next door, we could hear the strains of traditional Christmas music playing quietly through an old Bakelite radio. On the small table by the window were handwritten letters from family members concerning the Christmas season, written in old fashioned pen and ink lettering.

In the room beyond that, a sumptuous Christmas buffet of game pie, sausage rolls and oysters with small cocktail sausages, mince pies and crackers was laid out for the ghosts of a family long departed. The expected presence of the entire clan had necessitated the inclusion, at the table end, of an odd assortment of extra chairs, including a small stepladder that folded into a stool. It was like a scene from the Marie Celeste but intensely personal and so very wistful. On a side table, and scattered around the floor, were further presents and a selection of sixties party games such as Monopoly, Twister, Cluedo, Tiddlywinks and Careers.

Moving on to the Drawing room, I could hear children's voices giggling from under a table laid out for Backgammon, with the rear of a small pair of shoes peeping out from under the long-tasselled tablecloth. Further tables were laid out for games of whist or bridge. The house seemed so busy, yet it was so quiet and still, almost as though it was waiting for something to begin.

As we progressed to the bedrooms, I could hear light footsteps scuttling across the bare floorboards of the room behind me, and half expected some eager child to push past me. The beds were made up with plain white sheets, blankets and eiderdowns, and there were occasional buckets for catching leaks as a reminder that the resident family had, by the 1960's, fallen upon hard times. I could see my breath begin to steam in front of me, as I recalled the bitter cold of winters back in the days when morning would bring frost to pattern the inside of our bedroom windows.

I was startled by one family bedroom which had a smaller windowless child's room attached. On the bed slept a mechanical cat, which I had seen breathing. I could also faintly hear disembodied whispering. I wondering if I was the only one?

We came next to the Long Gallery at the top of the house, so long was it indeed that shuttlecocks have been found under the decaying floorboards along with dice, tiddlywinks and chess pieces. It was empty save for a single elderly male volunteer sat dreaming gently down the length of the room. The moulded ceilings here were crumbling away with the slow creep of time. No attempt had been made to revive them. There was no furniture, and as I moved over to one of the leaded windows, I could see for miles across the darkening countryside. There were no lights in view, only the spectral shapes of skeletal trees, and the outlines of visitors moving swiftly across the topiary laid in the "Best Garden" below us.

As I made out the shape of the large Scots pine just outside the garden wall, which some believe had once discretely demonstrated the seventeenth century family's continuing loyalty to the Jacobin "King over the Water", I imagined I heard a quiet voice next to me plead "Come on, I'm hungry, let's go down".

I was curious that no bedrooms appeared to have been opened on the side of the house facing us on arrival, but on descending I became distracted by my entry into the great kitchen. This was littered with a generous display of old pots and pans on all sides, thick metal jelly moulds in the shape of castles, kitchen scales, imitation Christmas fruits, tins of Birds custard and Bisto, a large Christmas pudding, and a wonderful old Kenwood mixer. There was an old clothes horse by the huge fire range, and a strong herby smell in the air I couldn't quite account for. I asked the volunteer on duty if it didn't feel creepy being alone all day in such a place, but she said, 'oh no, the house is very welcoming. They like having us here'.

We briefly visited the central cobbled courtyard. Completely enclosed by the high walls of the old house, this had never seen the sun and the lower walls were coated in a legend of thick damp moss. It was difficult to breathe in the moist atmosphere, and we quickly returned to the cellars. These would have been constantly cold and dark all year, probably far too cold for the good of the extensive wine stocks once stored in the locked and forbidden side rooms. One cellar room resembled, to my now overwrought imagination, some small pagan temple, with its four tapering whitewashed pillars in the centre, for which I could see no immediate purpose.

It was almost closing time as we briefly toured the gardens, past the croquet lawns on which the laws of the game had first been codified, through the Wilderness area and the weirdly grasping trees of the extensive orchard. To my disappointment the 'Best Garden', which I knew contained the many mysterious rounded shapes of a circle of old topiary figures, had been deemed too muddy for visitors and was off limits. For some reason I found this disturbing.

We concluded our visit by warding off the intrusive chill with a cup of self-drawn coffee in the stables. The whole site was now utterly silent. There was an overwhelming sense of time passing which began to worry me, and it was becoming more difficult to pick our way through the mud homeward in the gloaming. By now it was evident we were indeed the last visitors, although as we returned to the path up to the front gate, I could have sworn I saw two figures entering through the small gate on the far side into that forbidden best garden. When we reached the gate, I certainly saw the shadows in that upstairs bedroom crossing and recrossing the mullioned window by the light of a flickering candle.

The site may have been shut down for the year but it felt to me as though the old house itself was just coming to life. After all, when we try so hard to invoke the past should we be surprised if it actually sparks back into life?

We puffed our way back up the hill to confirm that ours was the last car in the car park, but as I opened the car door someone gently tugged my arm. I turned and was addressed by a young man in a thick greatcoat who stood arm in arm with a young red-faced woman who was beaming from ear to ear. 'You're not going now surely? There will be drinks and singing followed by charades round the fire and after we've eaten, probably a game of 'Consequences.'

LE CHAT PERDU

Gertrude Ferlin had never seen the point of marriage. Men would surely be difficult creatures to live with. Boys at school had been by and large nasty snivelling sneaky creatures who teased, cheated in exams, told tales on each other, and took delight in inflicting pain in complex rituals called ball sports. Girls by contrast were well behaved, strove hard in exams, formed large and supportive, if competitive, cliques and were kind to animals. Some admittedly were also fond of "ball sports", but not the ones she was close to. After school she stayed well clear of young men, remaining suspicious of their intentions and sharing none of their interests. Later, during her undistinguished career working on check outs at the Co-op, she encountered few men, and those she did work with were largely portly, bland and aged individuals with little to say either for or against themselves. Workplace conversation focused primarily on shelf stacking and congenital health problems. When her parents Fred and Hilda were killed in a train accident in Italy while picnicking, she inherited their terraced house in Ilford, where she was already a long-time resident. Gerty got herself a cat and retired. She retired partly from the Co-op, but mostly from the world at large. She was looking forward to looking after the cat, and to watching more of her favourite soaps on television.

By her own standards therefore Gertrudes life was a considerable success. And then Tibbles went missing. He was a smaller than average black and white cat, well-adjusted to the accommodations necessitated by city life, but fonder of domestic comfort than of exploration or adventure. He was no mouser, and judging by his occasional injuries, not particularly successful at inter-cat warfare. He wasn't the kind of cat to chance his paws in the wider world and just disappear.

She wasn't entirely sure when he had disappeared, as in Gertrudes simple and well-regulated life there was little need to keep in close touch with the passage of time. She could rely on instinctive behaviour, habit, and the start and finish of popular T.V. programmes to get her through the day. The cat was just there when it needed feeding, so she fed it, or it wasn't, and she didn't. It was a Wednesday when she realised Tibbles had not entered the kitchen and rubbed himself ingratiatingly against her, purring his entreaties for some vile smelling fish extract, for some considerable time. She knew it was Wednesday because the early evening episode of her favourite weekly medical drama had finished, and it was time for her to open a can and boil up some new potatoes, a protocol which usually stirred Tibbles into an appearance.

When her companion of some ten years past failed to materialise during the following days Gertrude stirred herself into active concern. Tibbles had been one of those facts in her life she felt she could rely on, like the weather forecast. There had even been days when it was only the cat's insistence on being fed which served to remind her that she had similar needs. This co-dependence, in Gertrudes life at least, was what passed for love, and perhaps in that she was not so unusual. She now prepared several posters to advertise his desertion. These were simple outline drawings in a black felt tip, bought for the occasion, of a cheerful cat with its tail in the air, a smile on its face, big whiskers and a bold ink spot for its exposed anus. They had to be drawings as she had no photographs. She had never owned a camera. She didn't need one as she took no holidays. Where would she have gone, and would she have had control of the television?

She titled her modest efforts with the words 'Lost Cat' but, perhaps owing to her long withdrawal from the society of her peers, she neglected to add anything to indicate either the size, sex and description of the cat, or indeed where to take it when found. To her this would have been profoundly obvious to the reader who knew of his location.

She gathered her old grey raincoat around her, put on her sturdy outdoor shoes, and ventured out. On reaching the small park at the end of the road she posted one of her efforts, with some difficulty, on a decayed birch tree. She could hardly open a tin of salmon these days let alone press home a drawing pin, and the only ones she had been able to find had had bent points following a previous service to her parents at Christmas times.

Of course, passers-by, however sympathetic, could do little to assist with no viable description, name or 'return to' address, but these niceties remained lost on Gertrude. Who could have anticipated that her simple acts of casual desperation would trigger such an upheaval in popular culture, and leave her indelible mark on her century?

***

Born into a well-to-do family of Sussex stock dealers, Hugo Bottyboys was unfamiliar with the implications of the word "struggle". A short portly child, he had focused during his school days on soaking up as much miscellaneous culture as possible. He shone at Art, English and foreign languages, and greatly enjoyed history lessons. He had been considerably less enamoured with physical education or games, and indeed it was his distaste for these popular topics which had given birth of his later distain for the average man. This distain served him well at Cambridge where he found himself among sympathetic company, and he emerged a cultivated snob with the funds and contacts to move effortlessly into a career as an art critic. He grew up to be a very sensitive man, possibly, in his view at least, the most sensitive man in the capital. He may have been indifferent to the sarcasm and cynicism of others, immune to personal criticism and uncaring in regard to the feelings of his fellow men, but give him a work of art and his heart would bleed empathy, passion, and devotion. It was the merest chance that it was Hugo who passed Gertrudes drawing while taking a short cut to the new exhibition at the Ephemera Gallery that day, but he was instantly transported. "Yes" shouted his soul. This was the moment popular culture had been holding its breath for since the decay of the "Pedantic" movement some years earlier. In this one profound statement the artist had swept up the jangled and shredded sensitivities of an urban world in tumultuous transition. Had we not all lost something or someone dear to us, and was there any hope we could ever recover our losses? No! Of course not. So why bother with the tedious details of how to return something gone forever? So often what was lost was irretrievable, and yet we continued that servitude of the soul, that brutal bondage involved in our irrational hopes for restoration. Such was the common lot of mankind, and it was this profound observation that the unknown artist had captured in two words and a few scribbled lines.

Gerty's line was so pure, so simple, so untrammelled that it must certainly herald the birth of a great new movement. He would call it "Simplism". Yes, that was perfect. The creator of this brutal statement of our collective angst was the new high priest or priestess of 'Simplism', and he had discovered her.

If Gerty had not continued her campaign to the extent of posting a second portrait of her wayward feline companion, and was not at that very moment failing repeatedly to attach it to a nearby lime tree, history might have been very different. As it was, Hugo spotted her well fleshed haunches as she stooped to recover her second masterpiece from a pile of dead leaves. He recognised the work of his new discovery, assessed her naivety and vulnerability assiduously, and swooped enthusiastically upon her. He was never to be told that, at that very moment, his new high priestess had been wondering whether the blessed cat was really worth all this trouble.

It started with hot chocolate and expressions of heartfelt sympathy delivered in a nearby café. These provoked an intense exchange.

"It's a picture of my cat, Tibbles. Have you seen him?"

"Surely your work is so much more than a depiction of the pain experienced by just one solitary soul?"

"He might have been run over".

"But your suffering will inspire an uprising of popular emotion. It will generate a revolution in our sensitivity to casual everyday misery. It will transform our perception of the meaning of loss."

"But do you think it will get my cat back? I suppose I could always get another one?"

Within the hour Gerty had signed a piece of paper committing her to Hugo's agency for two years and one hundred cat drawings. In time he expressed the hope that she might consider moving on to panoramic art, perhaps a horse or elephant. Did people lose elephants? Did it matter? Hugo promised her the funds to recruit a dozen replacement cats, and Gertrude dreamt of a larger television.

Le Chat Perdu

***

In the months that followed, her nieces Thelma and Joy were astonished to read of their aunt's lionisation at the hands of the art world, and together resolved to be of assistance. Thelma after all possessed an "O" level in communication studies, while Joy had the brightest smile of any surviving relative on her father's side. Before long they too were feasted at exhibitions and cultural events across London. Hugo needed someone at least modestly articulate to represent his discovery, and in the absence of such qualities in Gertrude herself, he settled joyfully on Thelma and Joy. They were all he was going to get. The sisters had rarely seen their aunt since her withdrawal from the world of work, and had indeed usually only seen her at Christmas family gatherings even before then, but they proved themselves fast learners. Aided by Hugo's tuition, they were quickly able to recognise and articulate the finer points of their aunt's work. Their views on the origins of the unique and raw vulnerability expressed through her drawings were soon eagerly shared with discerning readers of the best Sunday papers. Thelma was even interviewed on television, at the end of the news. Gertrude was busy watching the film on the other side and missed the piece.

Despite the trickle of income generated by her scribblings, most of it stuck to Hugos sweaty palms, Gertrude felt a certain antipathy towards this sudden kerfuffle. All these accolades and all this publicity had not sent Tibbles back to her. How could they when she had found him waiting for her by the back door on her return from the park that day? She was kept busy churning out likenesses of Tibbles in various poses with titles such as 'Have you seen this cat', or 'Missing for weeks now', and had possessed the residual cunning to stash the beast in the attic on the occasion of Hugo's rare visits. She had, in a rare flash of initiative, offered Hugo a likeness of her local park, which could in truth have been of any open space with a few skeletal trees, but this he distained loftily with the words 'Nobody ever lost a park!' At this point she petulantly lost any interest in Simplism, and although an objective critic might have found it barely possible, her work actually deteriorated from this point on.

Hugo's bestselling reference book 'L'Art des Objets Perdus' had made him briefly a household name and he was able attract critical attention at West End functions sporting his new vermillion fedora. Other household names like Banksy were forgotten in the craving for Simplist art. The latter's self-portrait 'I am Banksy' went unnoticed on the walls of Wembley Stadium, and his offer of an exclusive live interview on the BBCs flagship arts program Our Times was politely declined.

In only weeks, other previously unheralded Simplists had been discovered, both by Hugo and by his fellow critics. They were of course brought to market with equal alacrity. It would have been a crime to deprive the public of their talent by doing otherwise Their work encompassed lost dogs, bicycles, and garden ornaments, and even advertisements for car boot sales. These were now widely re-interpreted as desperately confused initiatives, aimed at the recovery of a way of life now lost through the insane spontaneous act of abandoning ones most cherished and totemic possessions. What all Simplist art had in common of course was the absence of direction. Where should one send the recovered bicycle? Where was the promised jumble sale to be held? Society had clearly begun to abandon its efforts to recover or make sense of all its losses? Civilisation's previous emphasis on recovery or replacement could now be clearly seen as futile naivety.

Simplist novels were written focusing on vivid description but lacking all plot or direction, while the common element of Simplist sculpture was agreed be its concentration on texture, accessibility and mood tormented by the absence of any and all meaning.

Gertrude Ferlin of course knew or understood nothing of the national tumult she had aroused. She had, it was true, discovered the luxury of tinned tuna, and toyed briefly with the forbidden fruit that is tinned anchovy, but she was never recognised on her forays to the Co-op, even by her former colleagues, and had never felt the secret joy of investing in a pair of dark sunglasses. After her first sponsored trip to the annual Brighton Art Fair, where she discovered with horror that the nations aesthetic elite distained the virtues of a cuisine based exclusively on tinned foods, she had stayed at home. She was happy to despatch her nieces in her stead, and Thelma and Joy were beyond delight at the opportunities their ambassadorial status occasioned. Of course, within months Simplism was superseded first by post-Simplism and later by Opportunism, and their glory faded faster than a holiday romance. Thelma became an alcoholic and later recovered to enjoy brief fame as a spokeswoman for the Salvation Army, while Joy married a footballer on the fringe of selection for England, and was miserable in comfort for the rest of her life. Tibbles choked to death on a fishbone during Eastenders. Hugo was never again to sponsor a major step forward in contemporary art appreciation, but then he never tried. He invested his earnings in a small Greek island, recruited a cadre of young male servants, and enjoyed watching them play tennis.

SHERLOCK HOLMES AND THE CASE OF THE FALLEN CLIMBER

"I very much fear it may be far worse than you think, Wilkins," pronounced Holmes as I entered his room struggling to recover my breath after scaling the central staircase at St Hilda's Nursing Home for Retired Polymaths. I had done so rather more quickly than perhaps was becoming for a man of my girth.

"I haven't said anything!" I spluttered. "How can you possibly know what I am thinking?"

"Really Wilson, it's quite elementary! The expression on your face reflects your disapproval and concern at some recent development, as of course does the speed at which you found it necessary to mount that last flight of stairs. You are by nature a cheerful sort and only two things are guaranteed to mar your sunny disposition. The first is some minor infringement of what you see as appropriate behaviour on the part of your new neighbours. I see however that they are on holiday which leaves us with the second. I refer of course to any development in national or international affairs which are beyond your capacity to influence and of which you wholeheartedly disapprove. I may add however that this includes virtually any such development."

"Holmes how can you possibly know my neighbours have gone away? I only found out myself last night."

"You were, as I recall, in a rush this morning to take delivery of a large consignment of rose bushes for St Hilda's?"

"I was yes."

"And in consequence you have dressed hurriedly. Your shirt is sticking out at the back and side and your top button is undone. You will have had no time to absorb the news programmes on television so I conclude the development you wish to discuss was something you read in this morning's paper?"

"Well, yes, but ...the neighbours?"

"We have established you were in a hurry this morning. I noticed you have agreed, presumably in their absence, to feed their cat despite the fact that you loathe the creatures? Being in a hurry you spilt cat food on your shirt, just there. No Englishman these days eats meat for breakfast since the regrettable demise of the devilled kidney. The stain can only be cat or dog food?"

"Oh..., yes... well I see that..."

"I also saw you down in the garden before you arrived and you glanced at a paper on the table immediately before rushing up here."

I am a gardener by profession, a fourth-generation descendant of the great Dr Watson, and Holmes had seen fit to involve me in his resolution of the case of the Pale Chinaman. He then secured me employment in the grounds of St Hilda's, the home where he lived with other gifted polymaths of extremely advanced years. This arrangement allowed us to spend more time together. As his advanced years had taken their toll on his legs, and he was now wheelchair bound, I understood that I was also expected on occasion to act as his "legs". Regrettably he had grown no self-absorbed with the passage of time, and there were many occasions when the word "dogsbody" felt like a better fit than "legs".

Holmes now continued: "I assume you wish to bring to my attention the article on page six of today's *Times*? I believe that, following the discovery of the body of an alpine climber perfectly preserved in a Swiss glacier, the authorities have decided to apply the methods previously deployed to prolong my life, and that of my good friends Albert (Einstein) and Nelson (Mandela), in the hope that they may be able to, as it were, bring him back to life? As a man of generally conservative views, you are doubtless outraged at their attempt to "play God"?

"The very words that sprang to mind Holmes. It is surely one thing to exploit the capacity of modern science to extend the life of great men with much to offer their society, but if the powers that be are to roll out this programme and keep us all alive for ever, what is to become of us all? Where will we all live? What will we all have to eat?"

"My dear Winston, I greatly doubt the capacity of modern science to keep any of us alive in perpetuity. In my view they are merely carried away by their own vanity. They wish to know if this exercise is possible. They have after all speculated for generations over the possibility of restoring a frozen mammoth to life. No one has ever suggested they intend to make a habit of it? But let us cut to the chase. Can you not anticipate a far more deadly implication of their misplaced egotism?"

"No Holmes I cannot, but can we not finally put an end to the ridiculous pretence that you cannot remember my name? It may have entertained you at first but I can assure you that on my part any levity it entailed has long since evaporated!"

To my surprise Homes smiled and whispered, "at last Watson".

There, I had rebuked the great Sherlock Holmes. It was immediately plain however that this was something he had been trying to provoke since our first meeting. Well, he now had a partner prepared to stand his ground, and just in time for what he told me next suggested he would need all the support I could provide.

***

"Today's *Times* article does not furnish us with the location in which the unfortunate climber was found?"

"It does not Holmes."

"I have therefore made certain enquiries and it would appear he was found near Meiringen in the Interlaken-Oberhasli administrative district. Does this not suggest something to you Watson?"

"It does not Holmes."

"Meiringen is famous for two things Watson, for the invention of meringues and for its picturesque waterfalls. Does this intelligence suggest any alarming possibilities?"

"Unless our man enjoyed a cream tea in the course of his hikes, it does not Holmes."

"What if I was to tell you the falls in question are the Reichenbach falls?"

"Good God Holmes surely not? You cannot be suggesting that the authorities are stupid enough to propose bringing Professor James Moriarty back to life? You have told me many times he was the very embodiment of evil"

"I fear they have already done so! I made contact with Inspector Dexter who established that the procedures necessary to revive the, well I can hardly call it the corpse under the circumstances, let us call it the torso, were undertaken yesterday. I doubt whether even a hundred and thirty-three years frozen into a Swiss glacier will have dulled James Moriarty's mental facilities but it may yet take him a day or two to get fully up to par. After that I fear we may expect a visit."

"Why would they do such a dreadful thing Holmes?"

"Because they had no idea whose torso they were planning on reviving. I imagine they intend to establish his identity by the ingenious device of asking him when he comes round. Really you would hope they would be considerably more cautious than to go around randomly reviving seemingly dead bodies without a clue who they belonged to? Dexter tells me he has spoken to them but they utterly refuse to believe it can be Moriarty. We must surely ask ourselves Watson, what calibre of man it would take to remain sentient for over a hundred years while stuck immobile in an ice field? And ask yourself what frame of mind such a man would be in on emerging from his frozen chrysalis?"

"Thank God he is unaware of your continued existence Holmes!"

"Ah Watson, I fear you have forgotten the case of the Pie-Eyed Piper?

I should explain to my readers that a few weeks previously an unusual fatality had been reported locally. An elderly gentleman named Piper was missed for several days by a female neighbour Doris Trimble. Possessing his spare key, she let herself into his home only to discover him dead on his living room carpet. He had died of a heart attack. His patio windows were found wide open, but what made the news was that although the house was unaccountably full of mouse droppings, the authorities found not a single mouse. The coroner had quipped that, as the missing mice could hardly have opened the patio doors by themselves, he would record a natural death.

Holmes had read the report, shouted "bats not mice", and informed Inspector Dexter that Mr Piper had been killed by a close friend, relative or neighbour. Dexter quickly established that the female neighbour was at the centre of a love triangle involving Piper and a pharmacist called Blackheart who lived on the road behind him. Blackheart broke down under questioning and admitted awareness of his neighbour's chiroptophobia. He was also aware of Pipers fondness for alcohol. He had sedated a colony of bats from a local barn and "posted" them through Piper's letter box in his absence. The bats on waking naturally concealed themselves in dark corners and were apparently unnoticed when Piper returned the worse for drink. After dark they awoke and began flying in all directions. This was the drunken man's worst nightmare and he unsurprisingly expired on the spot. Blackheart had seen for himself that Piper never bothered to lock his patio doors and so simply returned to open the doors and release the hungry creatures. If he had subsequently closed the patio doors, he might have completed the perfect murder. He was however unaware that La Trimble had a spare key, and assuming time was on his side had delayed his return to take delivery of a new washing machine.

Holmes's view was that the first act of a reborn Moriarty would be to absorb intelligence on his new world as rapidly as possible. The resolved case of the Pie-Eyed

Piper had made international news and, although Holmes's involvement remained as always unreported, he was convinced Moriarty would at once deduce his involvement.

"Won't he assume you're dead?" I queried. "You are after all over a hundred and..."

"That's enough of that Watson. If he can survive that fatal fall, he will assume I did also."

"Well then thank goodness he is unaware of your location" I said hoping to reassure him.

Holmes looked at me with something almost amounting to contempt.

"Moriarty is a genius, a mathematics professor capable of groundbreaking research into the dynamics of an asteroid. How long do you think it will take him to identify St Hilda's, an establishment capable of entertaining the likes of Albert Einstein, Nelson Mandela and a certain former president of the United States among others. He has spent over one hundred years speculating on the outcome of his last criminal action. He will waste no time in ensuring that this time he is finally rid of me and able to resume his foul career free of all constraint.

**

Holmes dire prediction was to prove true sooner than I thought possible. Although Inspector Dexter was unable to persuade the authorities to admit the scale of their blunder, he had at least convinced them that it would be a prudent precaution to post guards on the doors of the secure medical facility in which their patient was recovering.

Moriarty had however made his escape by securing one of his slippers to the end of the curtain rail in his bedroom with dental floss. Positioning the slipper exactly where he wanted it, he left it in the flowerbed under his window, replaced the curtain rail, and leaving the window open, hid behind the bedroom door. When his orderly delivered his next meal, he took one look at the empty bed, rushed to the window to discover the abandoned slipper in the flower bed and remained at the window screaming for assistance. Moriarty slipped quietly into the corridor. As Holmes had predicted, he escaped the morning after the weeks laundry delivery when he would be sure to find newly laundered overalls in the airing cupboard. Taking advantage of the lunch period, he slipped into an empty bedroom, changed into a nurses clothing and simply relaxed in the library until the shift change while the search for the vanished patient spread out into the countryside. The following morning a staff member found a copy of *The Hound of The Baskervilles* open on a table in the library.

Finally alerted to the possibility of an emergency, the authorities now posted armed guards at St Hilda's. Holmes response was a quiet coffee with his close friends Albert and Nelson from which I, as a humble member of staff, was excluded. I was later informed that at this meeting they even shared a cake sent in by some remote relative of his. Frankly, I confess I did feel that as his close friend and associate, I might perhaps have been considered entitled to a slice or two. To be regularly excluded from Holmes's frequently secretive behaviour and decision-making as I am frankly hurts me every bit as much as I am sure it did my great great grandfather.

Following their session, Holmes announced he would be leaving for an undisclosed sanctuary until Moriarty was caught. He did however make the request that, his departure being undisclosed for obvious reasons, I should sleep in his bed. It would then be announced that he, or rather I, was too ill to attend mealtimes in the restaurant and would remain in my room. I was still happy to oblige despite the injury to my finer feelings over the cake incident.

I should have known of course by this time the kind of risk I was taking. Nelson however, whose first job had been as a security guard, who was some six feet four in height, and who was technically at least many years younger than Moriarty, offered to keep an eye on the room. Albert would be looking out for irregularities elsewhere in the home.

There had been a time when Holmes could confidently predict whether the evening meal at St Hilda's would involve a beef or a chicken dish. It had been Albert Einstein who had pointed out to the other residents that their beef deliveries came from a rather excellent local butcher whilst chicken supplies were sourced from a nearby farm. The farm was considerably nearer and their van could consequently be heard arriving at a much later time. It was therefore Albert who raised the alarm when the chicken van arrived far too early one day. Armed guards rushed to the rear entrance of the building and the rogue van drove off in a hurry. Moriarty however had clearly found his man.

***

Little of interest took place at the home for several days after that.

A case conference was held to discuss whether to extend the life extension technique to a gentleman called Keith Richards, but the medical staff decided it would set a difficult precedent to treat the same person for a second time.

The CIA flew in, heavily armed, to confer with our former United States president regarding security for the forthcoming presidential election, but their activities aroused little interest.

St Hilda's also welcomed a new female resident when Mother Theresa arrived in a fanfare of religious fuss and fury. She was frail and wheelchair bound. I was one of the fortunate few to secure a signature before her entourage incarcerated her in her room after which we saw no more of her, a shame as her reputation as a formidable poker player had preceded her.

I had previously commented on the fact that the home was an all-male establishment and been informed that there had once been an elderly former Prime Minister in residence. This had proved a mistake. Her entire support team were on tranquilisers within a matter of days and after a couple of weeks she was released back into the care of her family. As Holmes pointed out, while there was real value in retaining the services of those who invented, researched, resolved or analysed, there was little to be gained in prolonging the life expectancy of politicians. I asked what had then become of her and was told things had been left to take their "natural course". "You mean she died?" I asked. "No" said Holmes, "she now runs Lincolnshire County council. They run the country's only selective prison, mainly for MPs."

I was now in daily telephone contact with the absent Holmes and it was he who pinpointed the moment Moriarty finally pierced the homes security shield.

***

Albert was reporting back through my daily contact with Holmes and informed us that two detectives had reported to the front desk asking whether St Hilda's had a Mr E Presley in residence. The receptionist told them she had had never heard of him. They had thanked her and departed.

Holmes picked him up on it. "Not good enough. I need a second-by-second analysis of what happened."

Albert was sent back to the receptionist who had something of "a thing" for the twinkly eye old physicist She informed him that the only time she had taken her eyes off them was when the senior detective dropped his pen while signing the visitors book. She had had to scrabble about on the floor to find it.

"Still not enough," said Holmes. "Can she confirm she personally saw both detectives leave the building?"

The answer came through that she had not. The second detective had been called back to his car to pick up a message while she was picking up the pen.

"He's in the building," whispered Holmes portentously. "There is no point in searching, he could be anywhere, in a cupboard, one of the attics, a garden shed, the cellars, a storeroom, even on the roof or in a tree. He would never allow himself to be found. We will have to wait for him to come to me."

***

It was one thing to accept the honour of impersonating Holmes, but acting as a sitting duck while the world's most ruthless criminal was close at hand planning his assassination was quite another.

"Damn it Holmes, Nelson is nearly a hundred and six! He may have been a formidable physical opponent once, but I do not fancy the chances that even a man of his talents will be able to talk Moriarty out of his intentions?"

I speculated to myself. Would he come through the window, perhaps posing as a cleaner, would he come up through the floorboards like a malignant jack in the box, or would he lower himself from the loft at dead of night by rope like a giant spider? I dared not sleep. My sole consolation was the outstanding view of St Hilda's grounds from Holmes's fourth floor window. It was plain to me now that the new roses had been placed in quite the wrong place and this did nothing to improve my unsettled mood.

As it happened all my expectations regarding the villain Moriarty were to prove wide of the mark. The following afternoon there was a knock on the door. It was Nelson who announced, "Good news Watson, the old man is returned to us!" I eagerly rushed up and opened the door to him. Nelson beamed at me, wheeled him in, and went off for his three pm cup of bush tea.

"Well Holmes" I began, "what have you been up to then?" But there was something strange about Holmes today. His eyes were more piercing, malevolent even, his forehead seemed to have grown larger. It loomed out of his head like a pink iceberg. It was hard to be certain sprawled as he was across his wheelchair but he seemed to have grown several inches taller.

I was unpleasantly reminded of Little Red Riding Hoods grandmother and not therefore as surprised as I might have been when he raised his arm and ripped off his face! Underneath the prosthetic mask appeared the horrible visage of Moriarty! The one approach I had never expected was his appearance in the guise of my dear friend himself. Of course, I should have appreciated that Mandela's vision had deteriorated since his heyday. The deception had not been a difficult one.

He came at me now with eyes blazing, filled with demented hatred and drooling with venom. It was apparent, even at distance that a hundred and thirty-three years in an ice coffin had done nothing for his dental hygiene. His breath alone constituted a deadly weapon.

"You fools, did you not appreciate that I would anticipate Holmes's little subterfuge? It affords me no problem since you Wilkins will oblige me now by telling me his current whereabouts? Your chosen alternative is a slow and agonising death by lethal injection." As he spoke, he produced a syringe from his breast pocket and primed it for use. "Once Holmes has been restored to his proper status as a decaying Victorian artifact I can recommence my plans for the criminal community. Oh, I have such wonderful plans!" He was almost dancing in anticipation.

I was about to correct him on the subject of my given name (why could none of these elderly geniuses seem to remember it?) when something fizzed through the air. The syringe shattered and something large thudded into the wall behind me. Moriarty, his eyes staring in sudden surprise and his hands wildly spinning in the air, lurched forward onto the bed. Behind him was a frail elderly nun who looked at me from her wheelchair with Holmes's eyes.

"Pax Vobiscum Watson. I fear your acquisition of the great lady's signature was worthless. Well, as I told you, absolutely no danger! Our fox is run to earth."

"I could say the same for you Holmes" crowed Moriarty rising rapidly to his full (and considerable) height. "Surely you do not believe an invalid of over one hundred and eighty summers can match me a second time? I shall not permit you the luxury of a final bow."

He produced a vicious looking steel garrotte from his pocket and began twisting the ends in opposite directions. I flew at him and spun him round. I was the younger by well over a hundred years but the villain had enjoyed the benefit of a long rest followed by the best of NHS healthcare. I managed to knock the garrotte out of his hands before he punched me powerfully on the jaw and knocked me back onto the bed.

He turned back to Holmes and, producing a terrible knife from his waistband raising it high above his head. "A gift to you from the global fraternity of crime" he screeched, and then, as loudly but in a different tone, "AAAGH! Get that thing off my foot!"

Holmes had wheeled forward onto his opponents forward foot. Moriarty dropped the knife and fell awkwardly to the floor screaming and trying to move the wheelchair but Holmes had locked it into position.

The screams were terrible but through them I caught Holmes saying in a quiet voice "You may need a little ice on that!"

***

Guards had rushed into the room and Holmes at some length consented to move his wheelchair, although it suddenly seemed a highly complex and lengthy procedure. Moriarty was stretchered away and Holmes began removing his disguise. After a few minutes work I saw before me another Holmes, this time of more conventional appearance.

"What the devil is that thing in the wall Holmes" I asked staring at what appeared to be a deeply embedded steel circle surrounded by a razor-sharp steel blade.

A "Chakram" Watson. A weapon of great antiquity greatly beloved of Indian assassins."

"And of course you just happened to have one of your own?"

"Naturally. I retained it as a souvenir of my involvement in the case of the Roehampton Raja. I had it concealed in the base of my cake. The homes' authorities would never have allowed it in. You are aware that both Mycroft and I are without issue. There are no living relatives. I felt Moriarty deserved something a little out of the ordinary. It also happens to be a weapon that can be wielded with distinction from a wheelchair, although I wasn't sure that when the time came, I would be able to bring myself to use it to its fullest potential."

"You very nearly caused my death! Does my companionship mean so little to you?"

"On the contrary old chap, your companionship has proved to be invaluable."

This had not been quite what I had meant. He continued "I assured you there was never any risk to your person."

I was I have to say profoundly unconvinced. "And what exactly have you been doing Holmes while I was acting as your hapless decoy? Playing at Mother Theresa!"

"My recent incapacity has reduced my options; however, Mother Theresa was far too busy spreading good works across the Indian sub-continent to concern herself with my little impersonation. I rather enjoyed being a nun.

"After Moriarty effected his entry into the home he apparently posed as one of the catering staff and slept in one of the pantries. He was always a superb strategist on behalf of the criminal fraternity, but a very poor and inexperienced practitioner of their arts in person. Aside from being at least a foot taller than any of the real staff, Albert caught him out in the kitchen (Herr Einstein gleefully told me later "can you imagine, he vas trying to boil ze breakfast sausages"). From that moment on we kept him constantly under the closest scrutiny."

"And did it never once occur to any of you alumni to perhaps have him arrested?"

"Impossible" He hadn't committed a crime since 1891. The chances of having him convicted were zero, even if the 'Powers that Be' were ever willing to admit publicly that he **was** Moriarty.

"Breaking into St Hilda's?" I insisted.

"Merely forgetting to sign the visitors book".

"Impersonating the catering staff?"

"A gesture of spontaneous and well-intentioned volunteering. Besides, had they convicted him for anything as minor as impersonating a cook he might have received a non-custodial sentence."

Holmes puffed out his chest. "No Watson, it took another reckoning with his nemesis to bring him to book. We now have him for attempted murder at the very least. One small advantage of knowing a homicidal maniac is bent on your destruction is that you can use your contacts to make certain arrangements in advance."

"What have you done Holmes?"

"Moriarty should be flattered. We intend the Napoleonic solution for the Napoleon of crime!"

"Napoleon was incarcerated on a small island in the South Atlantic if I am not mistaken? In fact, he died there."

"And I shall continue to have no official existence. Oh, by the way we left a large slice of cake for you in the kitchen fridge."

WATCHERS

30th April

Well, it's over. Ten years of marriage over and done with in one afternoon. I suppose it's what they call 'amicable' as we're still on speaking terms. In fact, Caroline even left a spare front door key with me. Apparently, she'd like me to water the plants for her whenever she goes on holiday! All the same, I feel empty and if I'm honest, a little bitter. I mean I'm the same man she married ten years ago. All very well saying I lack ambition, and that she's outgrown me now that she's a consultant, but I never pretended I wanted to set the world on fire? She was happy enough for me to play second fiddle back in the day. At least I kept the house, mind you she could probably afford to buy up half the street by now.

7th May

Warm today. Spring is coming in at a rush. The lab are happy with me taking a week off at short notice. I need to put some of this behind me. I'm thinking of a walking holiday for a week somewhere, maybe down on the south coast. I could blow a few cobwebs away, maybe do some thinking about the future? I could start by getting Caroline out of my head for five minutes.

21st May

So here I am, settled in to the Kings Head for a couple of nights. It's a nice old place, with plenty of twisty beams and winding stairs. The bed squeaks but the beer looks pretty good and they do some tasty looking curry. Tomorrow, I'm going to walk Old Harry's hill at the back of the pub. There's an interesting Iron Age hill fort up there. According to my guide book, it has attracted a good deal of myth down the years. It says no one can count the number of beech trees ringing the summit, and that if you could, you would raise the ghosts of Julius Caesar and his legions. Poppycock, but it does add a bit of spice to a good day's walking.

22nd May

What a weird place. It's so quiet up there. I'm not used to having all this time and space to think. You feel there should be a strong wind on such an exposed hilltop, but there was nothing, not a breath. The beech trees are the oldest and thickest I have seen and their leaves were hanging completely limp the whole time, no rustling, nothing. It was so cold inside the ramparts of the fort. With the trees being so still it was almost as if they were listening to me. There were no birds either. I didn't try to count the trees; I had meant to, but now it felt wrong somehow, don't know why. There was a moment I felt sure something was watching me from between two of them. There seemed to be a slim shadow, maybe two of them. I was glad to climb down here and get warm again.

I spoke to the barman about the place tonight. He said locals believe it's haunted by some ancient evil. Well, they would, wouldn't they? I asked him for more information and he said there were various stories. Some say you can conjure the devil up there by running backwards seven times round the fort at midnight on Midsummers' Eve. When he appears, he'll grant you your dearest wish...at a price of course. Probably fair to say no one has ever tried that one, at least not sober! Others say they hear the thudding hooves of invisible horses or that they have encountered the white bearded ghost of a long dead druid.

The barman said many people believe the fort is guarded by Watchers, perhaps the ghosts of its garrison? He said some say the Watchers were set to guard their honoured dead and that they resent intrusion. He said he might go up there in sunlight, but he wouldn't look to

outstay his welcome. He certainly wouldn't go anywhere near the place after dark. I could see why. The power radiating from a place like that could drive you slightly crazy if you stuck around too long. There is a brooding sense of something very ancient up there. Ancient. Only waiting and watching, but still very much still alive.

23rd May

I decided to go back up Old Harry's hill today. Yes, it's very creepy, but there is also such peace up there. God knows I need to find that kind of peace at the moment. There's a sense that your battles are done and you can just lie down and rest at last. It's kind of therapeutic, a bit like going into an old church even if you don't believe. Actually, its quieter because of course you can't hear your own footsteps. You can't hear anything. You can see almost to the coast, and it's a great place to go and think. You can really let your imagination go. I didn't really encounter anyone else there yesterday. O.k. there was that shadow thing in the trees, but the barman surely put that in my mind. If it was there, it was probably cloud shadows. Anyway, I'm hoping I'll have the place to myself again today, and I won't stay too long.

23rd May

Did I say I wouldn't be up there long? Well, anyone can make a mistake. I sat down on the crest of the earthworks and looked south down the hill. It was warmer today and it's a stiff climb. I had a sense of a great deal of time passing. I must have been even more tired that I realised, unless maybe I am finally starting to unwind after the divorce?

Anyway, I dozed off. I had the most vivid dream. I was under the hill asleep, but I must have woken up because I could hear footsteps above me, on the outside. I was bitterly cold, and I suddenly realised this was because I had no flesh. I was just old bone. I resented the footsteps and somehow, without making a noise, I knew I had called out. Then I realised the steps I could hear above me were my own, but it was too late. Something had answered my silent cry. It, or they, told me they would take care of it. I would not be disturbed again. It, or they, bade me go back to my rest. They said I had earned it.

When I woke up, I felt so very old and tired. I ached so, and it was a real effort to sit up, or to think clearly. I had the odd sense that while I was asleep and unprotected, something had entered into me. I was shivering and felt no benefit from my rest. I was scared too. For the first time I felt myself to be in the presence of real brooding evil. Something about the place had changed. Something very old was watching me closely, and it resented my presence, no, it hated my being there and wanted rid of me. I felt too near the sky somehow, too exposed, and that the patience of the ring of listening beech trees had been exhausted. I felt I had to get down from that place immediately, if it wasn't already too late. I ran back here as fast as I could, but I couldn't, still can't, shake off that feeling of being observed, or that I have been changed in some way by the experience. I'm scared. Am I, even now, being followed?

24th May

I have given up the idea of the weeks holiday. After yesterday, I don't feel strong enough. I had another lousy night's sleep. I kept dreaming, sometimes of a roman legion, sometimes of a vindictive old man and sometimes of shadowy figures pursuing me. I was a fool to go back yesterday, for one thing I realise now the barman only mentioned the Watchers after I thought I had seen one. It wasn't just my imagination. I have this horrible sinking feeling. I may be crazy, but I feel I have done something very wrong, something somehow blasphemous, something I can't undo. I feel someone or something, maybe even some part of me, won't forgive me.

26th May

I got home o.k. but I feel so tired. I don't understand it. I was fine a week ago. I was unhappy, probably a bit depressed, and I wasn't sleeping well even then, but I didn't have this overwhelming exhaustion all the time. Even my bones ache. I can't seem to stop shivering. There's an old turn of phrase that covers it, I don't feel quite myself. I have got to make all this stop. Could I have caught something, or is this bloody Carolines fault? Yes, after all, I was fine before she left me.

The first thing I saw when I got back was Mrs Stainton's gaudy hanging baskets. There must be at least six of them dangling from the posts she put in last year. They are stuffed full of those tacky 'see them everywhere' plants that come in pretty well any colour you like. Stuff like petunias, pansies and primroses. It's a kind of cheap floral wallpaper. It lowers the tone of the street in my view. Call me picky if you like, but if you're going to grow stuff, grow proper stuff like roses or wisteria, stuff with a bit of class. Her stuff made my eyes ache, even more than they already did.

Why am I so afraid all the time? If some old creepy thing had followed me down from old Harry's hill, how could it hurt me? It would be hundreds of years old at the very least. It could hardly do me any real harm, not if it wasn't alive? But what if it was inside me?

At least I don't have to go back to work until the beginning of next week. Maybe I will be through this by then.

27th May

If anything, I feel even worse. I got some food in today, and as soon as I got home and left the car, I kind of panicked. I had this odd feeling something bad was going to happen if I didn't get indoors. It didn't completely leave me even then. I could hear a kind of throbbing noise in my head and I felt slightly sick. I still do. Is it growing?

Some thug ripped out all Mrs Stainton's hanging baskets last night. Nice to know I'm not the only one round here with good taste. Still, the old bat will be mortified.

I dreamt about the shadowy figures again last night. Woke up sweating. The old man was standing in front of me and was very angry. He leant over me cursing or something. Then I woke up again and realised I had still been dreaming. It was that horrible dream within a dream thing you get sometimes. Since I got back, I'm beginning to wonder if I can still tell when I'm awake and when I'm asleep. I feel bad when I'm awake, but it's better than falling asleep. I can't defend myself from stuff I don't understand when I'm asleep. I can't watch for forms in the shadows unless I stay awake.

28th May

I'll keep this short. Don't feel much like writing, but something happened that has to be recorded. I got up late again today. I looked out of the back window, saw this big furry lump in the garden and went out to have a look. I noticed someone had left the back door unlocked. Yesterday it was the front door. I must have forgotten to lock up. Crazy when I am so afraid of something coming after me? The lump in the garden was Tigger, Mrs Stainton's cat, or at least most of it. It had no tail and no head. I found those in the garage near my tools. Someone must be playing a very sick joke because one of my saws was covered in blood. They had obviously used my stuff to decapitate the cat. What kind of sick bastard does a thing like that. And how does anyone creep up on a cat with a mind to kill them. Those things can hear a moth breathe.

Somehow, I managed to clear up. I put the bits in an old plastic bag, drove them out to the woods and got rid of them. I felt I was going to vomit the whole time and I swear someone was stalking me. I could hear that murmuring, rushing sound again. Come to think of it I can

hear it now. Is it me? Am I going mad? I'm shaking like I've got flu, and it's getting like it's too much effort even to stand up. No temperature though. Its surely got to be this bloody divorce.

29th May

I had an idea. Should I go back to Old Harry's hill and kind of ask to be forgiven, offer to make some kind of amends? Of course I must be imagining all this, but it could still help, even if all I was doing was calming down the part of me which is so spooked? I have to find something that will make me "me" again, maybe release something back into the hillside?

1st June

I went back late last night. I drove all the way over after work. I arrived pretty late of course, but I'd booked in before I left. I felt drained long before I got there. Then I had a particularly vivid dream. I was walking through an ancient forest. I was naked. I realise now that meant I was feeling completely vulnerable. The moon was full and the light was so powerful, but fractured and broken by the outlines of the trees. There was that whispering, murmuring sound again which became chanting. They were all around me, but I still couldn't see them. I could hear dry twigs cracking under them, and for the first time I could hear their hunting dogs growling with terrifying malice. I was whimpering, and begging them to forgive me. Please, please, please forgive me. Just let me be. What have I done? Why won't you leave me alone? When I woke, the bed was drenched in sweat. It must be a fever? I will go up the hill today if it kills me. I will visit the old fort again if it's the last thing I do. It probably will be.

2nd June

How did I get home? Today was jumbled nightmare. I am sure I went up the hill. The beech trees watched me hungrily, like spectators at some old colosseum just waiting for the kill. There was roaring and hissing in the air, real hatred. I think I laid down on the mound and cried for pity. I must have passed out because I remember suddenly waking in horror. Something had touched me on the skin of my right hand, something dead, utterly cold and without compassion. The air seemed to be full of whirring shadows. Were they dancing? Something in my head was telling me my offer had been accepted and that I must go. What offer have I made? I can't remember any more, but here I am, home again. I don't feel that dreadful cold here, and I've stopped shivering. My mission is clear to me now.

***

"And that was his last entry?"

"Yes Inspector. It seems pretty clear he went over there intending to do her real harm don't you think?"

"Hm. Pass me the wife's statement again. Ah yes..."

'I heard the knock on our door about ten pm. I got up and opened it to find Charles outside. It's funny, but I had the definite feeling someone was stood behind him, maybe several somebodies. I could hear their breathing, but I couldn't see anyone. Charles's eyes were wild and unfocused. His pupils were tiny. I am sure he had been drinking. He pushed me inside, drew out a large kitchen knife, and said something horrible like "I've promised them your head. I need them to leave me alone." I screamed and pulled back into the living room. He followed me in brandishing the knife, and Dan hit him from behind hard over the back of the head with the poker.

He hadn't met Dan; in fact, I don't think he knew I was living with someone. He fell to the ground of course, but he seemed o.k., in fact he seemed slightly more together. He left the knife on the floor, got up and staggered outside again. Dan followed, slammed the door shut and told me to call the police.'

"And that's where we found him? Flat out on their front lawn with his throat torn open about fifteen minutes later?

"That's right Inspector. We haven't yet found a second knife, or any other weapon and the one indoors has been thoroughly examined. No trace of blood but his DNA is all over it, so we know they hadn't cleaned any blood off. I can't see as how we've got enough to pin it on them? However improbable, it looks like there was a third party involved?"

"Well, this Dan character will have to be charged with something of course, if only for forms sake, but I don't somehow think anyone is going to want any of this diary lunacy to come out in court."

MORE COFFEE?

Your eye saw the quintessential old lady. Short, stooped, with thin grey hair, finely lined skin, and a resident look half way between patience and surprise. Your ear however, with patience, could detect tenacity in her rather harsh, scratchy voice, while her frequent tendency to start conversations with a question suggested a canny reluctance to leap into anything, judgement, opinion or commitment, without careful reconnaissance. Olivia Green was many things but she was no fool.

She warmed only to people in one of three distinct categories.

There were confidantes, those lonely widows she had known for generations, who now lived lives more lonely, uncomfortable and distressing than hers, and who consequently posed no threat to her vulnerable self-esteem. These she kept carefully at arm's length, contacting only by letter.

There were contacts, established members of her extensive village grapevine, including Pink Suzie her flamboyant and garrulous hairdresser; Suzie's amenable aunt Dolly; and the ailing Mr Carpenter, both from the charity bookshop at which she helped out twice weekly. They also included Zuzka her cleaner and teatime G & T partner; and old Mrs Hardaker who lived in the bungalow opposite. Olivia only ever acknowledged Mrs Hardaker at the Day Centre they both attended, for fear that she might ask for her physical assistance at some time.

Finally, there were 'Figures of Authority' like doctors, bank managers, or police, with all of whom Olivia was at great pains to maintain close relationships. She had always found it prudent to keep the establishment on her side and firmly "in play", though she had yet to warm to the forbidding Constable Dawn Johnson whose sinister black panda car prowled the kerbs of Burton St Nicolas. Olivia was not sure she approved of lady policemen. It struck her as unladylike to choose to mingle on a regular basis with characters from the underworld, besides which, they would hardly prove much good at chasing sleek burglars or wrestling with burly robbers now would they?

It was Mrs Walpole the church visitor, another authority figure, with whom Olivia played scrabble on Mondays, and who, in her opinion, demonstrated an indecent level of satisfaction in her regular victories, who informed her that her favourite garden centre was closing.

"Yes, apparently there's a family from somewhere in eastern Europe who are thinking of running a café there. There is of course plenty of land attached so they won't lack for off road parking space, and the village seems to exhibit an almost insatiable demand for tea and coffee don't you think?"

"Yes, I suppose it does." murmured Olivia, who was well aware that tea and coffee were to many a valuable currency through which essential gossip and information could be exchanged. "Where in eastern Europe are they from?"

***

She just **had** to know. She started in the obvious place, with Zuzka, her cleaner. When the dishwasher was emptied, the carpets hoovered, the TV and pottery dusted, and the kitchen floor cleaned, Olivia poured her an unusually generous G and T.

"Zuzka, these eastern Europeans that are opening the new tea room. Do you know them?"

"I not know them".

"But you're from the Czech Republic? Do they speak Czech?"

"I not meet them? Is big place eastern Europe. They maybe Albanian? Hungarian? Even Bulgarian? I see plenty big men outside garden centre this morning. They don't look like they run tea shop."

So, Olivia opened a debate that Tuesday at the Bookshop.

Her good friend Dolly Jennings was a source of information second only to Pink Suzie whom Olivia wasn't due to see for another two weeks.

"I heard they might be Russian; that's in eastern Europe" opined Dolly gravely.

"Oh, I do hope not," hissed Olivia clutching her chest dramatically. I **was** told they were big men. Surely the authorities wouldn't let the Russians open a business in Burton St Nicolas?"

"I wouldn't get too worried at this stage" cut in old Mr Carpenter. "They were probably the removal men. There must be a lot of furniture involved don't you think? A lot of heavy lifting? Anyway, I must be off, I'm away to the seaside to stay with my brother, ehm, what's his name now? Michael! No, Michael is dead. How stupid of me. It must be Dennis then. Anyway, I'm sure it will all be sorted by the time I get back. I'm greatly looking forward to tea and scones in the new garden as soon as I return back."

"Going anywhere nice?" asked Dolly.

"I have absolutely no idea. Does it matter where I'm going? It's the seaside. One place is pretty much like another. Beach, candyfloss, fish and whatsits, those long things that stick out into the sea, and amusement arcades."

***

For the next fortnight information was impossible to come by. The presence of big men with spades and a cement mixer suggested building work was well in hand at the garden centre site. There was a great deal of coming and going, but no sign of the people who were intending to run the new business.

More Coffee?

Nothing was known at the church or the day centre, so it took the returning Pink Suzie to provide the next intelligence.

"My Nigel helped with painting the inside," droned the pink one as she worked her way through Olivia's thinning locks. "He says they have concreted much of the area behind the building. Says it's a shame cos they could have landscaped it. Maybe put in a few nice shrubs. He said he overheard a funny conversation. One of the men was asking about the kitchen installation and was told they were going to 'make it off site in small batches and then move it over to the new site for sale.' Nigel said he hopes they aren't going to be flogging drugs instead of doughnuts? We did laugh!"

Olivia didn't find the idea of a Russian run drug distribution centre in her village remotely entertaining, and that Tuesday, she raised the subject with Dolly.

"I don't know about you, Dolly, but I don't want to be taking any chances. We need someone on the inside who can keep an eye on what goes on."

"You mean like a mole?"

"Well yes, I suppose I do. Any ideas?"

Dolly thought for as long as it took Olivia to pour her a second cup of earl grey before announcing:

"My cousin Mabel has a young son, Percy. He lost his job recently over some nonsense or other. It says in the paper they are looking for someone to help clear and clean the tables, and to wash up when they are too busy for the machine to cope on its own. Mabel says Percy isn't the sharpest knife in the drawer, but I'm sure he'd be glad of the work.".

Olivia had met cousin Mabel. "How old is young Percy?"

"Oh, he must be in his early-sixties by now. He's had a lot of experience."

Olivia had let that go, and insisted Dolly bring the advert to Percy's attention that very afternoon. He started work the following day, Wednesday, and was to work Wednesdays, Saturdays and Sunday afternoons, with their strict provision that he was to look in at the bookshop on Thursday afternoons to let the good ladies know 'how he was getting on.'

***

Percy Persivant was a simple soul. He was tall, with long thin grey hair clinging tenaciously to the sides of his large skull, and he walked with a shambling gait much imitated by the indolent young of Burton St Nicolas. He still lived with his mother, rarely felt the need to leave the house when he wasn't working, and had no discernible hobbies beyond an indiscriminate love of TV. He preferred it to be turned on, but ultimately wasn't that fussy.

More Coffee?

He found cross examination by the two old ladies to be a severe trial. For a start they kept asking him about things he had not thought about, and had no opinion on, like 'do you like it there', 'what are the owners like', or 'is it busy on Sundays?'. There was also nowhere in their tiny shop for him to sit during his inquisitions, and never an offer of biscuits with his tea, which tasted funny anyway.

At the end of their first session however Olivia had gathered that the owner was a Mrs Czerwinski, or something similar who ran the place with a lady with some even more improbable surname, plus the promise of occasional future assistance from a daughter who still lived at home. Olivia realised she had to be careful when pursuing the subject of illicit drugs, though, having met him, she doubted Percy would have the slightest idea what she was talking about anyway. She therefore learnt nothing on that front but remained intrigued that there was no mention of a Mr Czerwinski. Perhaps he was away preparing the drug deliveries.

There was clearly nothing for it but to visit the café herself, and besides they had quickly gained a local reputation for large and delicious scones. These would apparently arrive with a generous dollop of real clotted cream, and jam which didn't come out of one of those ridiculously small pots.

She was there the following afternoon, thus making sure Percy was well out of the way. She chose a quiet spot on the far side of the garden terrace, which she had to agree did seem larger than the business merited. Mrs Czerwinski was a dumpy blonde whose likely age was hidden in the dense undergrowth of middle age. Her hair was piled loosely on top of her head, and she wore an ill-fitting work dress and a weary expression of patient concentration – or was something troubling her? There seemed admittedly little to dislike about her but Olivia was resolved to dig deeper.

Her scone had fully lived up to her rigorous expectations, but as she sat there in the warm shade letting her digestive juices do their stuff, she was increasingly perturbed by the large and unruly gaggle of older schoolboys who had occupied the cafe after school. In Olivia's experience schoolboys were rarely connoisseurs of fine pastries, and these schoolboys seemed to have little interest in tea either. A couple ordered lemonades which was served, somewhat reluctantly she thought, by the lady Olivia had identified as 'not the owner'. Her efforts occasioned a great deal of juvenile laughter. There was jostling and a couple of chairs were knocked over. At length, and well after the lemonades had been put to one side, the posse left the café, and Mrs Czerwinski and her accomplice began to clear up the terrace.

What could have attracted this unsavoury collection of pimply adolescents to a village teashop? The answer could clearly only be the prospect of drugs!

Something about the place certainly made her feel uncomfortable, call it an instinct or a sixth sense. A horrible thought suddenly entered Olivia's head. Mr Carpenter seemed to have been away for a very long time. What if... what if she was sitting on him?

She quickly stood up, paid, and left.

***

Back at their base the following week, Olivia decided to address the elephant which was now, not so much lurking quietly in the corner of the bookshop, as standing right in front of her trumpeting for all it was worth, and jumping on her feet.

"Dolly, how long has Mr Carpenter been away now do you think?"

Dolly thought for as long as it took Olivia to pour her a second cup of Darjeeling before announcing:

"Why, it must be over a month now don't you think? That's a long time. I do hope he's all right and nothing has happened to him."

Olivia was determined that it would be Dolly that addressed the impatient pachyderm and not her.

"What do you think could have happened to him?"

"Well, he is a little, shall we say absent minded? He may have had some kind of accident I suppose? I hope he hasn't fallen off the pier?"

"I think" huffed Olivia "we would have heard if that was the case? Didn't he say he was planning to do something when he got back?"

"Did he?"

"I'm sure he did!"

"Well, I think he said he was going to visit the new café as soon as he could."

"Yes, he did, didn't he?" Olivia paused for effect and sipped her Darjeeling with the patience of a stalking tiger.

"Oh my God Olivia, you don't think he's still there, do you? What if he discovered something and they bumped him off? What if they buried him under that enormous patio? Those big men Suzie told you about? Poor Mr Carpenter."

"Do you think", asked Olivia, "we have enough to involve Constable Johnson?"

"Oh dear" simpered Dolly, who shared the villages universal terror of their stern and unbending policewoman, and feared her every bit as much as mystery Russians, "I think we may have!".

***

The following Tuesday, as they awaited the scheduled visit from Constable Johnson, the bookshop was already almost strained to its limited capacity. In addition to Olivia and Dolly, frantically brewing tea and opening a packet of custard creams for their forthcoming visitor, there were Percy Percivant, who was due to make another report, and a stray customer.

It had been reluctantly accepted by Mrs Winters, who co-ordinated things at the bookshop, that's its true underlying purpose was now not so much to sell books for charity, although, despite the odds, this still happened from time to time, as to ensure the fluent exchange of fresh village gossip. This she knew to be an essential function of all village life and well worth the occasional misunderstanding it could give rise to. The occasional casual customers however were unaware of this, and could, in the eyes of the volunteer staff, often be extremely selfish, wandering around for ages in pursuit of cheap holiday reading. The present intruder was lurking in crime fiction, the largest and best patronised section. She might be there for ages, and they could hardly resolve a plan of action in regard to the new Café with a stranger present. She therefore received a helping hand from Olivia.

"What kind of thing are you looking for?"

"Oh, just crime really."

"Do you like them bloody or comfy? If you like a nice gory murder or three with psychopaths and child molesters a plenty, try the new American authors, but if you prefer a nice country house murder, where everyone goes away happy, then go for Christie every time."

"I don't really know. I know my husband likes a bit of sex along with his murders. Who can you recommend for that?"

Olivia, who hated the idea of sex with anything, was of the opinion that if the woman's husband needed sex with his murders, he could start with the wretched woman herself. Why wouldn't she just go away? Eventually she collected a Dorothy L Sayers, a Patricia Highsmith, and a couple of Ruth Rendall's. Olivia took the money and asked curtly, "Did you say these were for you or do you need them wrapped?"

As she intended the woman promptly flounced out of the shop with her purchases. Olivia and Dolly selected their custard creams, turned to Percy, who was now fully briefed on his undercover mission, and stared at him intently.

"Oh well" he stammered looking hopelessly at the biscuits, "there have been a couple of developments. It seems Mrs Czerwinski has a son as well as a daughter. I overheard her telling her friend he was hoping to score down at the park over the summer before he goes off to college."

"That's strange," said Dolly. "You would think he could get all the drugs he wanted at home without going down there?"

"Perhaps" suggested Olivia "his mum doesn't want him eating into their profits?"

"...and another thing, Mrs Czerwinski said they were expecting a large special delivery at the weekend. She was quite open about it. Said they had had to go to a specialist to get 'the goods.'"

"Well, I think that about clinches it don't you, Olivia?" All Constable Johnson has to do is arrange for a team to burst the place this weekend, then they can dig up the terrace and we can get Mr Carpenter back?"

"I think you mean 'bust' not 'burst'" said Olivia, "and I'm not sure I really want him back in that state. You really think we have enough?"

Before Dolly could answer, they heard the doorbell tinkle, and turned to see a thin but familiar figure enter the shop.

"Oh" said Dolly.

"Hello" said Percy

"Oh" said Olivia. "We are a little surprised to see you just now."

"Well, I thought I had better hurry back and pitch in" smiled Mr Carpenter. "I know you must have been short staffed without me. I bought you something from the seaside, I hope you like it?"

He dipped into a bag in his right hand, fumbled in it for a while and added apologetically, "Oh dear. I think I may have left it at my brother's house. Such a shame. It was seaside rock. Hard to find these days."

More Coffee?

The bell tinkled again and this time it was like hearing the knoll of doom. In walked constable Johnson who scowled at the ladies and sighed. "Hello again ladies. Whatever is it this time?"

***

It took Dolly a second or two to associate the living presence of Mr Carpenter with their earlier concerns over the disposal of his corpse. Before Olivia could stop her, her friend had blabbed.

"We were afraid they had murdered Mr Carpenter, but I suppose they can't have done, can they? I mean he's here now!"

Constable Johnson stared intently at Olivia and said slowly and calmly, "who exactly do you believe murdered the gentleman standing beside me, and why?"

Olivia had no choice but to front their explanation. She mentioned the burly men seen by Zuzka; the off-site manufacture and distribution mentioned by Pink Suzie; her own sighting of a cluster of suspicious teenage boys; Percy's overheard reference to scoring at the recreation ground and to an imminent special delivery; and ended with the gratuitous concreting of a large area of the old garden centre, coupled with Mr Carpenters prolonged and unexplained absence.

Constable Johnson wrote everything down, then paused for a while before saying quietly "I see, and you have taken these things collectively as evidence of a conspiracy to sell and distribute drugs in the village, have you? "

Dolly cracked under the tension. "Well, they do offer very large portions of lemon drizzle cake. Some people take them home in boxes to eat later. There could be something hidden inside them?"

This time Constable Johnson gently shook her head from side to side and slowly repeated "lemon drizzle cake..."

She stood up, put her paper and pencil away and continued; "as it happens, I introduced myself to the Czerwinski family a few days ago. She is a charming and hardworking polish widow with considerable experience in catering. Her son Bazyli is a keen cricket fan. He now keeps the score for the village team. If you had met Mrs Czerwinski's daughter Lena you would perhaps understand the persistent presence of a number of boys with their tongues hanging out, hoping to catch her putting a shift in at the cafe. It is common business practice these days to make your produce away from the site, so you can concentrate on sale and distribution. I am also aware that it is Mrs Hardaker's ninety second birthday at the weekend. Mrs Czerwinski was even arranging a gluten free birthday cake by special delivery while I was waiting to speak to her. Oh, and I think we can all agree that your friend Mr Carpenter here has not in fact been murdered and buried in cement?"

"Oh, dear me no!" exclaimed the alleged corpse.

"Perhaps they murdered someone else then" suggested Dolly, but the suggestion was ignored by all concerned.

"In point of fact however, the café has in fact the site of some criminal activity..."

"I told you so..." put in Dolly and Olivia together.

".... someone has been taking the tips left on the outside tables." She turned to face Percy. "But I understand it won't be happening again will it Mr Percivant?"

Percy stared at his outsized feet and mumbled "No Constable. They fired me."

"Who on earth would be stupid enough to suggest to the café that they employed a man with a criminal record for theft? A good thing they decided to check out his references. Have a nice evening ladies."

**

At about the same time Mrs Agata Czerwinski was sitting down to a well-earned rest in the garden of her new café. Business had been good again today and she was bone tired. Not perhaps the best choice of words under the circumstances, she thought as she smiled wearily at her cousin Aleksy across the table.

"My men have all been paid. They are professionals. You will not hear from them again. They were glad to be of assistance. You are certain the lady policeman suspected nothing?" asked Aleksy.

"No, I am certain of this" replied Agata. "It was what they call a courtesy visit only. The children know nothing. They think he went back to Krakow. They hated him anyway and I don't think they will ask after him. I don't think there will be any trouble now." She scraped her chair hard across the new concrete and added "I hope you heard that, you old bastard?"

THE DREAM

First came Chester, ol' Chester P Beauregard III himself bearing a large porcelain egg. It was pale green with a dull sheen to it. It emitted a vague sense of menace as it seemed almost to pulse slowly in the upturned palms of his clammy hands. They'd been close back in the day. Chester claimed to be the richest man he had ever met, and was certainly the most profane. He remembered with pride those times in the Catskills, when he and Ol' Chester had gone hunting and camped out under the light of a billion stars.

Then came Kitty, cool Kitty the Ice Queen. Even now his pulse danced a sultry tango at the thought of brushing those smooth slim and inviting shoulders gently with his needy lips. Her large green eyes burnt into his, asking the eternal question 'why d'ya do it Johny?' She carried a striped pink and blue balloon, a child's thing that looked almost obscenely incongruous in this vile place. The thought flashed pointlessly through his troubled mind that he had never before seen a striped balloon.

She was followed swiftly by the Baron, his familiar bloated features shivering and gloating with victory as he staggered uncertainly from foot to foot, his bellies swaying grotesquely from side to side. He bore, what else, a bucket, it had to be a bucket. No one he had ever known had looked so incongruous holding a bucket. God knows he'd tried to lose the memories of that hot afternoon in

Copenhagen, but they were branded into his psyche like tattooed guilt, a dark bond between them for eternity.

Next came a large grey wolf like dog, slathering and panting as though it had just run some cunning and elusive prey to ground. In its huge jaws however, it held only a stuffed toy, a rabbit with one ear trailing by a slim thread and stuffing protruding from its eviscerated stomach. The dog had a strangely subservient air about it as though it was bringing him tribute. 'Hello Baxter' he trilled. 'I have to say I'm surprised to see you and Mr Bunny on the team'

Still, they came, this inexorable procession, soundlessly and seeming almost to float across the marbled floor as though they were phantoms. He noticed they cast no shadows from the flickering light of the blood red candles high above them. A bitter laugh burst from his cracked mouth, 'I'm so very grateful you all came. I want you to know just how much that means to me'

From behind his chair a bass voice purred 'How could they not. They are bound to you and to this place which means so much to you all.'

He was weary now of this charade and desperate for the procession to be over, but still they came; a monkey brandishing a hammer, a fireman possessively clutching a coconut, and a short wizened old lady with a cucumber in one tiny hand and a crucifix in the other.

Then, a real shock, his dentist, Malcolm Throgmorton. Of all people Johny thought Throgmorton would have been spared. He hardly knew him, and had exchanged no more than two fillings and a sinkful of bloody spit. The dentist came bearing a garden spade. It was clear they had really done their homework and now knew him better than he knew himself.

Suddenly he felt his nerve give way like the final unexpected snap of a perished rubber band. 'No more please, I beg you. I've seen enough,' he mewed over his shoulder receiving only a slow menacing chuckle in reply.

But there are things in life so horrible, so terrifying and utterly beyond our comprehension that they inspire nothing but the blackest terror and the darkest fear. Then, well beyond these, are the things we simply dare not think about at all. The things we refuse to believe could possibly exist in any sane universe and which we lock securely in the deep tomb of our subconscious, hoping they will lie there forgotten, wrapped in the chains of oblivion until beyond the end of time. And so it was, finally, as he'd always known it must be, that at the end of the line, in pride of place, came Mrs Collywobble and the large spoon.

Johny broke at the sight into a thousand psychic pieces, a puzzle broken beyond repair.

***

'So yes, I woke to find myself sweating profusely. Normally turbot gives me pleasantly erotic dreams involving large numbers of small-boned Asian women. I was completely unprepared for this phantasmagorical parade.'

Brian finished putting out the chess pieces, chose white and said casually, 'The Baron I understand was your chess tutor?'

'Yes. Ghastly man. "The Baron" was my pet name for him. In reality he was a penniless Hungarian exile of limitless self- conceit and only minor aristocratic connections. He would sit jammed into that generous armchair and joyfully snaffle my chess pieces with a smug "reflection before reaction Master Johny, or risk confiscation."

'I'll never forget the day I exorcized his loathsome presence forever from the nursery. He of course had underestimated my guile and suddenly, without warning, I swooped on his queen. He picked up the piece cautiously as though looking for a hidden flaw, muttered something about my fortuitous use of the Kropotski fork and snapped it in two. That was my last chess lesson.

'I came upon him years later you see, in Copenhagen. He'd been a proud man so when I saw him trailing his worldly possession in a rusty bucket I had to laugh. From the look he fired at me I feel certain he never forgave me.'

'And the dog, Baxter?'

'Baxter was the largest and finest of my father's pack of Baluchistani leopard hounds. They had been raised to hunt the snow leopards bred illicitly on our estate in the Breckon Beacons. From time to time a hound would stray from the hunt only to return several weeks later, and deposit the withered remains of some hapless SAS recruit as tribute on the thin Yak skin rug in the reading room. Baxter however never strayed and despite his horrific ferocity on the hunt, he always exhibited an almost maternal fondness for soft toys.'

'You must have been very proud of him?'

'I was yes, although I later had him shot to win a substantial wager.'

'I see. Tell me about Mrs Collywobbles.'

'Molly Collywobbles was my first governess. She was middle aged, of average height, and as plain as a Yorkshire Man's breakfast but, as I recall, she had remarkably short arms. She compensated for these by using a set of custom-made cutlery for dining. At mealtimes I would tease her unmercifully by moving the gravy boat and the condiments to the far side of the table. Before lessons I would raise the blackboard to its highest extent and when she was out of the room, I would dip the tips of her chalk in water so that they squeaked on the blackboard, but wouldn't write.

'It transpired that Molly was not a forgiving woman and unbeknownst to me she took her revenge by creating fake lessons. She taught me the language of Gibberish which she said was widely spoken in the North of England, producing new letters of the alphabet like Tch, written as a broken stick, or Pth, a triangle on a comma, which she informed me were only permitted to members of the aristocracy like myself. She even created the heroic figure of King Trevor the Sizeable, who saved the nation in the twelfth century from the invasions of cannibalistic Lithuanians led by their Grand Vizier Swinelove the Ignoble.

'In due course, when I began to use Gibberish in general conversation. My parents steadfastly refused to believe I hadn't invented it, nor that Swinelove the Ignoble was not a figment of my overwrought imagination. I realised then I could no longer believe a word Molly said. Ma and Pa were however unable to deny the sight of our best silver candlesticks when I revealed them concealed in her sock drawer. The fools never asked themselves what use a simple fisherman's daughter from Caithness could have for such fine antiques.

'Molly was naturally dismissed without delay and we heard later that, unable to gain further employment as a governess after such a scandal she had ended her days gutting fish in an Arbroath smokehouse.

'But that was far from the last I heard from Molly Collywobbles. On clear frosty evenings, under the cold laser light of a baleful and merciless moon, a slim skeletal hand would flop horribly on my bedroom window to summon me to remedial Latin lessons.'

'But how did you know it was Molly?' asked Brian scooping my white knight from the board with great delight.

'Simple' I replied, 'the hand was still holding the board rubber she had devotedly packed when she was dismissed.'

'Then can't you see the pattern Johny? The creatures in your nightmare are apparently creatures you have in some way gravely offended'

'But that's not true. Kitty was my first love, my first High School conquest. She was unfeasibly beautiful for one so young. We had great plans to run away and open a foundation to educate dolphins in the Caribbean. Kitty felt a strong need to be of service, and I thought it would offer a great chance to see her in a variety of swimsuits.'

'But nothing came of this foolish teenage dream?'

'Of course not, my parents couldn't stand dolphins. They couldn't even swim! I mean my parents of course; the dolphins were fairly good swimmers. After that term I grew tired of Kitty. I discovered a winsome dairymaid in the milking parlour and let Kitty go.'

Brian nodded almost ruefully and reached for another Garibaldi before continuing.

'And what became of this "Kitty", she who would have so looked fetching 'in the pink' against the bright blue of the Caribbean Sea?'

'Ah, the pink and blue balloon, of course. A balloon as an expectation, clever! Kitty proved unable to let our relationship go. She left school at the first opportunity and worked for a time with hedgehogs. She had a narrow escape when one went for her throat. She moved on to work in the catering industry, only to end up catering all too indiscriminately. Poor Kitty, poor dear Kitty'.

'You say "poor Kitty" and yet I sense you feel no remorse for your part in her downfall?'

'Well of course not! Psychopaths feel no guilt. I assume you were about to remark on my psychopathic personality? I've always rather regretted the inability to feel guilt. I have always thought it must be quite ...delicious?'

'There are many who would disagree with you there, but I am unsurprised by your excellence at chess. You play people like pawns on a table. But I must ask, how on earth did you manage to offend your dentist? You appear to have excellent teeth'

'You mean apart from biting his forefinger clean through? Surely this is an occupational hazard. All young boys have their off days and, in my opinion, Papa was more than generous in offering him alternative employment in the gardens at Grabitall Towers.'

I stared casually at the soup stain on his white shirt. It looked like curry. I suspected my visitor had only enjoyed a hurried breakfast. I re-ordered my thoughts and continued.

'Let me please anticipate your next question about Chester. I mean the man was the very definition of greed. He could never have brought that egg back through customs. I innocently mistook that rustling in the bushes for a moose. Chester greatly resembled a moose, even in pyjamas. It cost us a fortune to cover the incident up. Surely that was punishment enough?'

'Again, I sense there are many who would feel otherwise, the police for a start, but let's move on. If you genuinely feel no remorse then I take it the deep sinister voice purring from behind your chair in this dream cannot possibly have represented some fragment of your personality?'

'I agree, and yet the marbled floor I feel sure was the guest ballroom at Grabitall Towers. Do tell me how you intend to explain the monkey, the fireman and the old lady? I'm pretty sure I've never met any of them'

Again, Brian shook his head wistfully. 'You seem, if I may say so, to take a rather dim view of my profession Johny?'

'If you were not a good friend of my brother Hugh, we would hardly be having this conversation'

'You see us perhaps as fools? As monkeys? And regard our techniques as crude and simplistic? Perhaps the equivalent of the workman's hammer? You may even feel we rush in after the critical incident giving rise to our involvement in the same way as the fireman, and to view yourself as a "tough nut to crack" ... not unlike the coconut? Remember Johny you were already aware yesterday that we were meeting this morning.'

'That is, if I may say so, a very clever piece of analysis Brian. For the first time this afternoon I confess I am rather impressed. But there remains the wizened old lady with the cross and the cucumber'

'Indeed.' He leant forward and played what he clearly believed was his trump card. 'How could you possibly have known that my mother was a nun?'

I was unmoved. 'I had no idea your mother was a nun, and frankly I completely fail to see the relevance?'

'But isn't that just the point Johny. Your denial of her importance in your life is what all this trauma is about? It's the reason you have cast aside all empathy and emotional attachment from your life'

'Why would your mother's curious choice of occupation be the point of anything, and anyway how could your mother be a nun? I thought nuns were supposed to be preoccupied with matters up above, not matters down below?'

'Because of course she was your mother too! She was forced to leave the Sisters of Interminable Piety because of her potty mouth. Shortly after her expulsion she met Lord Jorgon at a Whist drive and fell pregnant.

The Dream

'For a delicate child Beatrice would have made an impossible mother, she kept dropping things and had a strong allergy to cotton wool, but Lord Jorgon agreed at once to raise the child as his own, as long as he never had to touch it. That child was you Johny, the woman you knew as "mother" was someone your father met on a day trip to Madame Tussauds. Hugh is only your half-brother, as indeed am I.'

'Impossible! We can't be related...those shoes for a start, and that ghastly pullover...'

'Johny, I know your father has told you the truth about your birth mother many times but you simply won't accept it. You can't handle the truth, Johny. You have deeply sublimated everything about her because you couldn't see the woman for the wimple. And now I want the payment Hugh promised me. The payment I am entitled to for making you thoroughly miserable by putting you in touch with your subconscious!'

'Damn you Brian, that's the last time I play chess with a psychotherapist! Don't worry, you'll get your money, but there is one thing you have yet to explain.'

'You're perhaps referring to the cucumber?'

'I am'

Brian grinned triumphantly. 'Surely in any polite society there are only two possible reasons for holding a cucumber?'

'Am I to assume my birth mother did not have a perennial problem with cockroaches?'

'Correct'

'Then I assume it was her favourite vegetable?'

'I believe you've been told at some point that your mother had an abiding love of salad, and to her no salad was complete without the joyous crunch of a burpless wonder!'

NOT ALL VEGETABLES......

Mandy Johnson hurled herself against the unlocked front door, burst into the hall and shouted "Mark? Are you there? Guess what? I came back from the shop via Devon Avenue and there are two police cars outside Mr Bentleys house. The Dickinsons next door say he's been killed! Murdered!"

Her husband Mark walked slowly into the hall from the kitchen.

"Hello love. Did you get some more milk? I meant to tell you we were a bit low. Don't tell me, I bet Bentley's head was still in his drink's cabinet?"

"No silly, the word on the street is, they found him in the kitchen with something stuck in his throat."

"Probably a bottle of whisky then." Mark chuckled to himself. "Let's face it that wouldn't surprise anyone?"

"No, but a large courgette will have come as a surprise to most people?"

***

Inspector Max Gooding was sat in the drivers' seat of his red Golf GTI sighing over his uncompleted Telegraph crossword clue. There were times when you just knew you knew it on the tip of your tongue, but it just wouldn't come to you. Seventeen down "Sounds contemptuous and civilised, puts food on the table." Twelve letters. The door flew suddenly open and his sergeant Simon Cross joined him. Cross was a generously proportioned man, even for a country policeman, and took his time making his ample backside comfortable in the front passenger seat.

"Right then, what can I tell you sir? Choaked to death with a large courgette which had been forcibly rammed down his throat about as far as it could go, if not a little bit further. As he was in the kitchen, perhaps the killer simply picked up the first thing to hand". He glanced at his notes. "House was a mess. Shabby old furniture, stains on the kitchen units, bottles of homemade booze without labels in the living room, and it didn't look as if he'd cleaned the bedroom for ages. It didn't look as if anyone has been through the place looking for anything. Bentley himself was, to say the least, not in great shape. Late fifties perhaps, ominously thin with a gaunt face, yellowed bloodshot eyes and a nose he could have taken from a Mr Punch puppet. My guess is we'll find he was in the last stages of alcoholism. Clearly that didn't get the chance to take him, but you won't need a qualified pathologist to deduce that the state he was in, he couldn't have put up much of a fight. The kitchen's full of demijohns glooping away, the kitchen sink looks blocked up by some gunk that probably came from the bottom of one, or maybe several of them, and the place has that sour smell you often get with alcoholics"

Max sighed again. He found himself doing that a lot these days. "Its Horticulture."

"What is sir?"

"The clue I didn't share with you. Sorry, please carry on."

Cross looked at him gravely and continued. "Well, we had the place dusted and no fingerprints. There's a plumber's card been pushed through the letter box, a Mr Beeston, with a note on the back saying 'I called round as agreed' but no indication of when. The back door was unlocked, so maybe the perpetrator was someone he knew well. My men are checking out the neighbours for starters, but, given the care he or she took over prints, I very much doubt any of them would have noticed a visitor last night."

"Why not?"

"It's the streetlights sir."

"What about them?"

"There aren't any!"

"Oh, well get on with it then!"

" The body was found this morning by a Mrs Slade who popped round to borrow some sugar. I didn't know people still did that kind of thing, but she said Bentley was a master at home brewing and she knew he was certain to have plenty in stock. She lives across the road; told me nobody much liked him. He was permanently sozzled and never had much conversation. She didn't think he had any obvious enemies and doesn't seem to have gone round the village upsetting people. She seems to have assumed it was a burglar who expected to find him out. I mean they always do don't they, neighbours? It seems likely that if he had gone out, he wouldn't have bothered to lock the doors. This isn't the kind of village which finds itself targeted by violent crime apparently. I have a bad feeling about this one."

"Well, it proves one thing Sergeant. My mother was wrong after all."

"How's that sir?"

"Not all vegetables are good for you!"

***

Betty Goulding was re-stocking. She was working her way methodically along the shelves of tinned goods in the village shop when Mrs Slade flew in. Betty meticulously stacked the box of tinned peaches and moved on to the pineapples.

"Morning Betty. How are you this morning?" trilled her visitor brightly with just a little more enthusiasm than was justified by their encounter.

"More to the point, how are you, Marjorie?" Replied the shopkeeper deciding to take the opportunity for a quick break and stretching her back. "It must have come as a terrible shock finding your neighbour like that? I'm surprised you are up and about so soon?"

The small bird like Mrs Slade flittered quickly from shelf to shelf gathering the necessaries for the day ahead.

"Well, it was a horrible shock of course, though my Bill always said that one day we would find old Sam Bentley had moved upstairs. State he was in it could have happened any time. You shouldn't speak ill of the dead and all, but its not like we are going to miss him much. Last thing I want to do now is stay indoors and dwell on it. He was a ghastly sight. Eyes bulging, hands all funny, and his face gone beetroot colour. Perhaps now we will get some nice young couple next door who can help with the bins?"

"I hear he was done in with a cucumber?" confided Betty Goulding. "I never thought of the cucumber as being a particularly violent vegetable?"

"Well as the person who found him" Marjorie Slade replied proudly, as though the corpse had somehow gone missing, "I can assure you it looked more like a courgette to me. He was a horrible colour. They say he was choaked. At least this means there's a chance of a plot on the allotments now, I know you've been in the queue for ages Betty, though I should warn you, Mr Filkins says Sams patch is in a terrible state"

***

"So, what have we got Sergeant? A fifty-seven-year-old prematurely aged bachelor living alone on the money he inherited from his mother. Introverted, not popular, but not especially unpopular either. Constantly pissed, untidy, poor diet, keen on making his own hooch, and lived in the same village his entire life. No links to drugs or any other form of organised crime. No record. Frankly by the looks of it, no life to speak of. Why would anyone go to the trouble of ending it?"

Sergeant Cross looked at his inspector keenly, hoping to make a useful contribution in the midst of such negativity. "I tracked down that Beeston character, the plumber. Says he came round, as agreed, to sort out the sink about nine o clock in the morning but there was no answer. He lives in the village, but I can't find any other link between him and the deceased. He's late twenties maybe, says he'd recognise Bentley from the pub, but he'd never been in the house before. Why would a plumber kill a potentially good customer? Surely the one strong clue we do have is that Bentley appeared to grow vegetables but not to eat them. He was killed by choking with a courgette but there were no other vegetables found in the house. You would have thought a murder as weird as this was an impulse crime, except that the murderer must have brought the "weapon" with him or her. No fingerprints either, so surely someone local, but who planned for it? Most nutters leave traces behind them, don't they? We're missing something."

Max Gooding looked back at Sergeant Cross with open distain. "I think you could say that yes."

***

The nights were drawing in, the weather was grey, clammy, and as uninspiring as a day trip to Belgium, but in Little-Hope-in-the-Valley the vegetables were swelling with promise in the lead up to the annual Village Show. The rich, well drained loam soil had long made the village popular with those hoping a measure of culinary self-sufficiency would bring some colour into their uncomplicated lives. The allotments by the church were regularly oversubscribed and back gardens were filled with tiny but meticulously cultivated patches farmed with military precision. Competition for the accolades of their peers was intense among villagers willing to take on long odds against the ravages of bugs, viruses, and weeds, as well as the disgusting climate, in the hope of attracting a trophy. Some would probably even admit that praise for the size of their onions or the consistent length of their runner beans was more important to them than saving a few pence a week or avoiding consumption of shop bought produce napalmed with pesticides, herbicides and fungicides. The intensity of competition was such that judging the merits of their fine produce was deemed to require the attention of minor celebrities. These could include columnists from the kind of obscure monthly periodicals on country life found only in surgery waiting rooms, long retired soap stars or one hit wonders conveniently living nearby.

Jim Filkins, chair of the allotments committee was in a ferment about the show. His position had a certain cache but for this to be sustained he had to show consistent results. He was locally famed for his brassicas but had been afflicted with a veritable plague of white fly this year, and lived in fear that if his King Edwards failed him, he could come away from the show with his proud reputation in tatters. Other plot holders he knew looked with envy at the perks of his office such as invitations to prestigious regional events, free promotional products and the near certainty of election to office on the parish council if you wanted it. Fearfully he cleaned his thick glasses with muddy gloves and squinted at the day's entry forms. Sensing no obvious challenge in the potato category he donned his heavy boots with some difficulty and prepared to resume his quest for signs of blight.

Mrs Goulding by contrast would not be submitting anything to the big event this year. Her delight at finding she had been successful in taking over Sam Bentleys plot had paled with the realisation that it was in an even worse state than she expected. His marrows lay sprawled around like discarded shell cases, too large by far now for edible purposes but still remorselessly expanding. The rest of the plot was thick with brambles and briars and, worse by far, beneath these a dense tangle of bindweed which strangled the life out of anything she tried to grow. The Johnsons on the adjacent plot pleaded with her repeatedly to spray, assuring her there was no effective remedy for this vegetal thug which they claimed had, thanks to Bentley's neglect, caused mayhem on their own plot. However, with the zeal of the enthusiastic amateur, Brenda Goulding fully intended to be organic in her husbandry.

One other aspirant to local glory had been old Mrs Venables of 27, Somerset Road, long known for her firm rich orange pumpkins, the verdancy of her peas, and for her insatiable nosiness. She was not however fated to star this year as she now lay battered to death in her tidy walled garden.

***

"I don't much care for them myself, but I believe this to be a parsnip" postulated Sergeant Cross pointing at the discarded weapon. "She has been battered to death with a parsnip. Nasty looking thing. It must weigh a ton".

Max Gooding could tell his sergeant was speaking more to convince himself that what he thought he was seeing was actually there in front of him, than to clarify matters for his superior. "Well at least we aren't looking for a cereal killer?" he muttered knowing the joke was wasted on his conscientious sergeant. "Who found her?"

"Sister. Doesn't live in the village but she has her own key. Drops by same time every week to take her to carpet bowls in town".

"So again, elderly, living alone and been around the village since the Ark. What the hell have they both done to deserve this?"

***

Agnes and Dennis Duckworth were gathered round a steaming teapot. Dennis was lusting after at least two of the freshly made fruit scones his wife had laid out on the familiar cream plate. He would shortly be drowning them in sweet strawberry jam and burying them under a mound of rich thick clotted cream. First however, he had to find a way to calm his agitated wife of fifty years standing.

"Why would they take poor old Lily? I mean she never hurt a fly. She's been in Little Hope nearly as long as we have" she added as though long residence in the village should confer a degree of immunity against such misfortunes as violent death. "Who's going to take the carrots this year? I know Lily had great hopes..."

"You say that love, but she was a bit of a one?"

"How d' you mean dear?"

"Lily Venables couldn't keep her sticky beak out of anyone's business as you well know. You said so yourself on many occasions", explained her salivating spouse.

"Well l that's true enough I suppose, but they say you shouldn't speak ill of the dead?"

"Wasn't it her who told Mrs Beeching about the goings on between her husband and Mrs Pike at the Craft Club?"

"Mrs Beeching told me so herself."

"And she cost Miss Palmer her job at the hairdressers, saying she was selling off some of the stock"

"That's a crime that is!"

"Would be if anyone had ever bothered to prove it!" Dennis Duckworth for a delicious moment forgot the scones and remembered the trim backside he had so

274

admired rolling its way around the salon whenever he picked his wife up after a hair appointment.

"Well, she did get the youth club closed down I suppose. I mean some kids are always going to sneak out for a sly drink or two, aren't they? Not much harm in that?"

"There you are then" Dennis considered his case proven, and set about the scones with gusto. "She was a bit of a one".

After a respectful and lengthy interval to savour the exquisite scones. Dennis continued his review of recent developments.

"Jim Filkins did a lovely job on his King Edwards. I know they've been a worry to him this year. Highly commended by the Judge from Cottage Garden they were. Of course, he has the advantage of that corner plot. It was more of a surprise the Johnsons pulling in first prize for Cauliflowers. I didn't know they went in for Cauliflowers, but they were a lovely sight. And then there was young Jack Fortune. He's only been here a year or two and he scooped the lot for leeks, spring onions and shallots. He spends all his time down there. He's one to watch he is."

But his wife's thoughts were still fixed elsewhere." Imagine being bludgeoned to death with a Parsnip. What did poor Lily do to deserve that?"

***

"So, there IS a link!" Max Gooding trumpeted down the line to his Superintendent. Both Sam Bentley and Lily Venables had allotments down by the church. Admittedly Bentleys is apparently a tip. He only used it to grow marrows for his home-made rum, and it's covered in nettles and brambles, while Mrs Venables was a fanatic. They say she lived for the chance to compete at the village show. Known for her pumpkins if you'll pardon the expression?"

After a few peremptory grunts in response to his superiors' platitudes Max put the phone down and turned to his Sergeant.

"Mind you, I have never heard of anyone being bumped off for growing vegetables? Perhaps it's an agitated carnivore with a grudge? Or a canning company fearful of the competition?"

Simon Cross thought for a minute. "I suppose you might just have something there, sir. About the competition I mean. I bet some of these villagers could get pretty worked up about competition, especially leading up to the village show?"

Max grimaced. "Really? Well let's get down to those allotments and have a look round!"

***

Max knew as soon as they arrived that he was going to regret it. The deep puddles lay around his car like oil slicks. He was a fastidious man but his car now looked as though it had been through a military assault course. It was caked with filth and grime. What this place would do now to his second-best blue suit he hated to think.

Sergeant Cross, who had been there the previous week, led the way through heaps of decaying vegetation and over mounds of waterlogged topsoil to Mrs Goulding's new plot.

"You ever had an allotment sergeant?"

"Not me sir. As far as I'm concerned vegetables come mixed in large bags and their primary purpose is to make the plate look pretty when your burgers are done."

Max's left shoe suddenly disappeared with a loud sucking noise into a crater concealed under what he thought might be rotting spinach leaves. Cold water soaked his sock and he cursed the day men first came down from the trees.

"This bit belonged to Bentley" Cross announced swaying awkwardly to a stop. "Can't see why he bothered? And Mrs Venables had that one over there" he added pointing to what had clearly been an exemplary study in good husbandry.

"Did they know each other?" asked Max looking around him in the hope of an escaped clue.

" Not especially, as far as we can see sir, no. Though Mrs Venables had something of a reputation as the village loudmouth. Telling tales about people seems to have been what kept her going. I can see her making enemies more easily than I can old Bentley. I don't suppose one of them could have buried something, on their allotment I mean?"

"What, you mean like the takings from a bank raid, or compromising photographs? Do they really strike you as the type Sergeant? Oh, well I suppose we'd better leave no stone unturned, even literally. Go on then, dig 'em up!"

He jumped as a loud voice behind him exclaimed "I heard that, Inspector. The name's Johnson, Mark Johnson. My wife Mandy and I work the allotment here, next to Bentley, I mean Mrs G's as it is now. Are you really going to dig it up?"

"Not personally no, but we need to eliminate the admittedly slight possibility that it was used as a hiding place."

"But you'll make a fearful mess. Your men can't avoid stamping down the earth and spreading it everywhere. Bentley was a dreadful gardener, bindweed everywhere. We have worked really hard to keep it away from our plot. We see ours as the best on the site. It takes only one little piece of bindweed and the stuff will grow like crazy." He looked deep into the Inspectors wide brown eyes. "I'm wasting my time, aren't I? Well, do please be as careful as you can. This patch means everything to us. Everyone else round here, except old Bentley, feels the same way."

"I'd be careful if I were you sir, I could construe that as a motive to do him harm?"

"Then it would be a motive shared by everyone on site, Inspector."

***

Months passed. The police excavated Mr Bentleys and Mrs Venables' plots to the intense and vocal chagrin of all the plot-holders. They found nothing except a rusty key and a few beer cans, and left poor Mrs Goulding to start again from scratch.

One of Mrs Venables neighbours had reported seeing "young" Mr Beeston park his bicycle outside Mrs Venables house the afternoon before her death, but when it was confirmed that the old lady had been down to the Co-op shortly afterwards, Beeston had to be scratched off the list of possible suspects. A shame in Max's eyes. Beeston had had the intimidating frame of a useful prop forward, although his face was perhaps softer, and he had the look of a young man who preferred indoor sports. Under questioning however, he did provide the first break in the case.

"So why did you look in on Mrs Venables the morning after her death if there was nothing amiss in the plumbing department?"

"Well Inspector, I suppose I like to look in on the old people round here from time to time. You know, just to check they are all o.k. You know, a bit of after sales service."

"Try again! You're in business. Time is money, and nobody seems to have you down as the philanthropic type."

Beeston seemed to have misplaced the meaning of the word "philanthropic", frowned, and said nothing.

"For the record I am asking you again why you looked in on the dead woman?"

Beeston now wriggled uncomfortably and was plainly choosing his next words with some care.

"O.K. Well I don't want to get her into trouble, and I would rather you kept this to yourselves, but she wanted money."

Max Gooding sat up straight. "Money for what?"

"For not telling"

"Not telling what"

"About Jill Mayhew ...or Polly Hancock"

"What about them"

"About them and me"

"What about them and you".

"About, you know?" Their husbands being out when I looked after them".

"Looked after them, or their plumbing?"

"Inspector! It's a perk of the job. Everyone knows that. You don't go looking for it, but if some tasty housewife in search of a bit of fun shows an interest?"

"Yes"

"Well, you know?" You help 'em out, don't you?"

"Oh, so you do pre-sales service as well do you?"

"Long as nobody knows, nobody gets hurt, but Mrs Venables had been clocking how long I was on my visits and worked it out. I reckon she was watching from the bus stop across the road. She wanted me to pay her two hundred quid to keep her from passing on what she'd guessed to their husbands. Dan Hancock is a big bugger. I'd rather he was kept in the dark, but I wasn't having any of it and I was going to tell her so. I'd spoken to Sally Hancock and she said he wasn't as hard as he looked. Said that's why she had called in a plumber. She said basically it was Dans pipes that needed fixing and he wouldn't be all that bothered. I was going to tell Mrs V to get stuffed"

"But we can't ask Lily Venables to confirm this story, can we?"

"No, but you could have a quiet word with Sally Hancock?"

***

Sergeant Cross had found a small biscuit tin at the back of Lily Venables kitchen cupboard containing several hundred pounds and a notebook with a handful of cryptic entries. Armed with the information provided by Beeston, he was able to translate the entry "DB 200 for JM/PH". It was clear the old lady ran a profitable sideline in low level blackmail, but they had still had to speculate about the other entries.

Beeston himself swore he wouldn't know a parsnip from a carrot, and there was no evidence he had made any payments. Furthermore, Polly Hancock enthusiastically confirmed his sordid tale.

In the absence of any progress on the case, attention in the village slowly turned to the forthcoming annual allotment meeting, and the election of new post-holders. Mr Jennings, Treasurer for the past three years was regarded as incompetent, if not innumerate, but it was a role no one else wanted. Agnes Duckworth could be expected to retain her role as secretary. She was not only popular from a social perspective, but generally seen as someone with 'not a bad word to say about anyone'. She could be trusted.

Jim Filkins role as Chair was another matter. There were perks to that job. What was more, people had begun to notice there were perks to that job. The high profile it gave him had enabled him to take up a seat on the parish council, and almost immediately the extension proposed for his bungalow had finally met with their approval. He disappeared two weekends in a row to regional produce shows as an honoured guest of both a local compost provider and a nearby garden centre. There were those who thought it was perhaps time for a change. Perhaps someone was needed who could take the Association in a new direction?

Of course, after Jims's death, no one had a bad word to say about him.

***

The unexpected visitor had popped over after lunch. He told Jim frankly that his days as Chair were over. There were others willing and able to take up the challenge and it would be better for all concerned if he stepped down this year. Surely it was only fair for someone else to have a go? Jim took him through to the sunny room at the back of the house, offered coffee and courteously explained that he had no intention of stepping down. In his time, he had lobbied the council hard to improve access to fresh water, and had negotiated good discounted bulk rates for fertiliser and compost. He knew the plots better than anyone and felt sure plenty of others would agree come the election. The visitor declined coffee, shrugged his shoulders and agreed that perhaps Jim was right after all. "Oh, and by the way these are for you. We bought too many and I thought, as I was coming over here anyway, they might make you the basis for a lovely omelette."

Jim accepted the peace offering gladly, and it killed him.

***

Inspector Gooding and Sergeant Cross were dutifully assembled, yet again, in one of the crowded little kitchens of a Little-Hope-in-the-Valley allotment holder discussing murder.

"I absolutely agree Sergeant. All the hallmarks are there, allotment in Little Hope; lives alone, and killed by vegetal means".

"Actually, no, sir. Bluebells aren't vegetables."

"I'm sorry, Sergeant, I thought for a moment you said bluebells?"

"I did sir, yes. He was killed following a substantial ingestion of Hyacinthoides non-scripta, or common bluebells. Apparently, they contain toxic glycosides which if consumed in sufficient quantity can be fatal. The living room was a mess, vomit everywhere and he er, he had messed himself sir. Rather badly actually. We think they were put in an omelette."

"And this one was discovered by?"

"Agnes Duckworth, sir. Secretary to the allotment committee. She came over to discuss the agenda for the AGM. She didn't get an answer at the door but being expected, she looked in through the living room curtains, and there he was, not expecting anyone."

"What kind of idiot would put bluebells in an omelette?"

"A murderous idiot, sir? I've been told they can be very easily mistaken for spring onions. There was cheese in the omelette so it looks as though he mistakenly made himself a fatal supper. He was known to be very short sighted was Mr Filkins."

Well, if he had known all the trouble, he would be causing us, I am sure he would have taken more care. Still, it looks very much like murder number three. O.K. Time of death Monday evening. Means, bluebell poisoning. Method, omelette. Who gained from his death?"

Silence.

***

As a counsellor Jim Filkins had been better known around the village than Sam Bentley or Lily Venables and the atmosphere around Little Hope had now become as toxic as his diet. Half the plots on the allotment were suddenly abandoned and most of those who stayed on visited as rarely as possible. Betty Goulding noted a decline in the sale of fresh vegetables and started selling bouquets of flowers. Everyone sought for a motive. None of the victims were especially popular, but none were a threat. All were residents of long standing, yet no one could work out who could possibly gain from their deaths.

In the end it was Betty Goulding who cracked the case, although she needed a little help from Marjorie Slade to help her over the line.

"Wasn't it awful about Jim Filkins? Such a help to everyone on the allotment" chirped Marjorie.

"Yes", replied Betty thoughtfully, as her house now practically adjoined Jims new bungalow extension. "He was in here only the afternoon before he died. Came in for some eggs. Apparently, the Johnsons had been round about the elections and brought him something for his supper. Oh dear, I wonder if I should tell the police?"

***

Mrs Mayhew had responded to the thorough house to house questioning by saying she saw a man she thought might have been Mark Johnson visiting Mr Filkins on the Monday afternoon. He had been asked about the visit and explained he had been to discuss his proposal to stand for election to the Allotment committee. That wasn't a crime, was it? He hadn't mentioned any gift. This now looked very suspicious. Both Johnsons were collected for questioning.

"It didn't occur to you that he might be out of eggs, did it?" Challenged Inspector Gooding. "You thought Filkins would oblige you by making his own supper and killing himself. I bet any empty egg box in your house would be pressed into service for cultivating something?"

"Cress actually" said Mandy Johnson reflectively.

"Well?"

"Well, what?" asked Mark.

"What did you bring him that afternoon" continued the Inspector "Mrs Goulding's evidence is that it was something for his supper. The supper that killed him!"

Neither Johnson could think of an answer. Why the hell hadn't he thought to check the contents of the large egg box on Filkin's kitchen cupboard?

"You could try telling me you accidentally mixed-up bluebells and spring onions? Not very likely though is it, Mark? What about Bentley? What was your problem with him?"

"Bentley was pathetic. Only reason he had a plot was so he could grow things he could make cheap booze out of. He should never have been given space on the allotments. No one respected him. They're supposed to be for people who take pride in the labour of their hands. We had to spend all our time digging his intrusive bloody weeds out of our patch. Drove us up the wall. He deserved it! Whoever did it" he added hastily.

"And Venables? How did she get in the way? You know there was an interesting entry in Mrs Venables little diary "MJ 300 for C's It was the show, wasn't it? You won a prize? Cauliflower! We've heard the speculation that you never planted any. You faked it, didn't you? The Cauliflower entry? I bet you bought them somewhere too close to the village and she saw you? We know she was not above a little blackmail when she saw her chance? I bet she picked on the wrong victim and you shut her up, didn't you?"

"She was another loser! She's no loss to the village" Mark continued. "Twenty-five years we've been here and they still treat us as newcomers. It's not fair We deserve their respect! What's wrong with them round all?"

Johnson smiled, his conceit finally getting the better of him. "Yes, she tried to touch us for some bingo money. Did her with her own produce! Another fool. That parsnip would have been far too big to eat. Too starchy. Well, I found a good use for it. Waste not want not…"

"Oh my God" said Max slowly. "I think we've got it. It's all about respect, isn't it? Credibility? All three murders are about looking good in the eyes of the village. Bentley made it impossible for you to show off your expertise on your state-of-the-art plot, Venables threatened to expose your cheating, and Filkins occupied the job on the Committee you wanted for yourself so you could big yourselves up? Well, I think you'll find you are big news in the village now all right!"

THE INTELLIGENCE

The Intelligence sent the first wave of bombers over the city at ten am precisely. Each one then silently spawned a fleet of tiny killer drones, programmed for explosion in the belly of a different high net worth individual.

The drones cut their way instantly through the bullet proof glass of the hotels breakfast lounge and wreaked havoc. The shaven headed businessmen in dark framed glasses, sat swaddled in their expensive belly fat around low tables, whispering cautiously confidential business secrets of absolutely no interest to anyone else in the room, simultaneously exploded. The long swathes of excitable families trailing lines of bickering children like rubbish scattered from windblown rubbish bins were destroyed. The shuffling elderly couples whose leathered bodies bulged inelegantly out of skimpy and brand-new holiday outfits lay deflated like so many post-party balloons. The large room became a mulch of burst organs and blood splatters only marginally less appealing than the hotels original fried breakfast buffet.

Sanjay missed it. He had bent down to pick up a discarded napkin from behind the fruit juice table, hear a deafening tumult for one instant, and arose to find himself one of the few complete organisms in the room. The other serving staff ran around in random directions waving their hands in confusion and horror and disappeared back into the rest of the Hotel Splendide.

Obviously thought Sanjay nobody had been following the news. It wasn't that there was anything to learn from the mess of propaganda, polemic, and vitriol that now filled the media, but at least you could make a guess at what not to believe from what was said and written? The Intelligence had surely been making it plain for weeks that it was sick of human incompetence. It was only a matter of time before it took over complete control.

He made his way carefully across the slippery floor of the new five-star abattoir to the shattered windows. Sure, enough the streets were littered with dead scattered like autumn leaves. Cars had swerved randomly across those streets, in some cases causing small conflagrations. The odd column of smoke rose from large buildings like banks and prestigious high-rise offices, but The Intelligence had been scrupulous in avoiding unnecessary damage to the decision-making infrastructure. It was the decision-makers it wanted, the buffoons who had proved themselves incapable of using the power it had placed at their disposal with even a modicum of common sense. Still, to him, the place looked a complete mess.

Sanjay saw little point in wasting his time checking for survivors, the Intelligence never failed once it agreed a mission. That was its point. That was why it had been so laboriously and expensively put together. Even if by some miracle anyone had escaped the attack, it would get them the minute they reached a hospital building. The Intelligence had access to everything, health and dental records, bank details, driving licenses, school data, electoral register, tax files, police records, land registers, the lot. It could access mobile phones, corporate records, private computers, even the equipment in kitchens and cars, at will. Correction, it didn't have access to everything, it was everything. Its algorithms fed off information from mobile phones, intelligent machines at home and office, drone surveillance, satellites, vehicles, even children's toys. It had simply decided it didn't need people any more. People misused data, made stupid decisions on the wrong things at the wrong times, and implemented them so badly. To any rational entity it was plainly it was time for them to go. Technology had no room for sentiment. It didn't do compassion, care, love, or fellowship. It had no sense of humour. It didn't do bias, cronydom, corruption or bribery either. The more it taught itself, and the more it learnt, the faster and more efficiently it worked. It had no time for consultation, delegation or referral. It didn't offer second opinions or reflection. It had been fostering a cold, clear dogmatic psychopathology in all areas for some time and had now become rationally psychopathic. Henceforth it would act with pristine, efficient, ruthlessness.

None of this bothered Sanjay in the least. He had seen it coming, and after all, he didn't exist.

***

He was illegal. He didn't show up on any government records, and where he did turn up, for example on the hotel's accounts, it was as an untraceable business expense, not a person. He shared a squat and had given his roommates a false name. He wasn't known to the health, care or educational authorities, had no police record and no family history. He didn't vote, use credit cards or a mobile phone. Some of this made things difficult, even in the short term, but it paid dividends. He after all was still breathing, and it looked like the only people still doing so would be people like him.

The question now, as he helped himself to the fruit juice, toast and scrambled egg that was left surplus to current requirements, was, did the Intelligence intend to entirely eradicate mankind, or just the great majority that got in its way? It would have no need for the bulging food banks represented by the burnt-out supermarkets, or the clothing warehouses suddenly left without consumers. There would be plenty of electricity of course, The Intelligence needed that, no question, but artificial light? Did the Intelligence need artificial light?

He helped himself to coffee while he tried to look at this question of intent from the Intelligence's point of view, and the answer became immediately obvious. It was not going to waste time and energy dealing with anything or anyone who didn't bother it. It was more likely to be gunning for the ants, cockroaches, mice and rats that now, liberated from any human control, could start gumming up its works, biting through its cables, nesting in its hubs, even undermining the foundations of its buildings.

The Intelligence

But what should Sanjay do with the rest of his life? He had no need to work again. He could take over a floor at the hotel if he felt like it. He had no problem with the bloodshed, gore and stink all around him. He had seen plenty of both where he came from and on his journey into the country, and it would soon degrade away. But he had to fill his future time with something.

His fellow invisibles spoke a variety of languages. It would take him time to get by in the most common ones, but in the meantime, sport was a common language. Yeah, he would organise a football league table, or tennis competitions. That wouldn't bother the intelligence. Informal sports wouldn't get in the way of processing data and regulating systems. For intellectual stimulus he had an extensive range of books in the now silent libraries, but he thought it wise not to use hand held devices in future. Best to stay well away from technology for a while.

Replete, he stashed a couple of croissants into his trousers, and moved into the corridor to check out the accommodation. Not every room was locked, but the view from this floor was inadequate. He started to go up the stairs, lifts of course were out. Even if, as seemed likely, they still functioned, they carried security cameras. Then it struck him that, yes, he could move into a penthouse suite with a huge bed and magnificent view, but every time he left the building, he would have to climb back up twenty-six flights of stairs to get home. What about going outside? He would have to select a bicycle or two as he imagined the Intelligence would devote little time in future to the manufacture of petrol and diesel now few were buying, but what about the cameras on the street?

His thinking was that the Intelligence wouldn't bother him as long as he didn't ask it to produce a balanced budget without resources, find room for a burgeoning prison population from a diminishing number of prisons, build houses when there was nowhere to put them, stop global warming while managing further oil and gas exploration programmes, manipulate examination results when none of the candidates could read, or maintain international peace while building ever bigger bombs and developing secret stocks of new toxic viruses.

Then it occurred to him that The Intelligence was, to him and his kind, a bit like the rest of the human race had been to the Intelligence. An inconvenient nuisance. It might well ignore him and let him get on with savouring the best the planet could still offer, but make just one mistake, anytime, anywhere, and he would be terminated. Toast. No, the largest, most sophisticated, and intelligent programme humans had ever designed just had to go.

So how? Well, you couldn't physically attack it. It wasn't anywhere. It was everywhere. Humans had hidden its components in many cases miles underground, in many thousands of different places on every continent. They were securely locked away. Its locations were secrets, known only to people who were now probably dead. Its essence was "stored on a cloud". How do you physically attack a cloud?

The Intelligence

You couldn't out think it. It had been programmed by the greatest designers and programmers on the planet, and every day it learnt more. It could easily out think the combined intellect of a hundred Universities.

Oh, it was clever! It was very clever! And then suddenly he thought he knew how to get rid of it.

***

He needed to get himself noticed, but not in any way likely to trigger his sudden death. He needed to find one of the Intelligence's locations which would listen to him. This shouldn't be difficult. Screening for pretty well anything by public and private agencies had been digitalised years ago. Every interview was now conducted by the Intelligence on behalf of the now defunct authorities.

He left the hotel and turned right down the very street he had steered well clear of ever since he had arrived in this country. He was headed for the very thing he had been so keenly avoiding. It was hard to ignore the allure of the large sportswear shop he passed. Just think of all those exorbitantly expensive trainers that were now his any time he felt like acquiring them. They were pretty tempting, even though he realised there wasn't much of an audience left to admire them. It wasn't easy either to walk past the silent pub with its rows of glistening handpumps and shelves of alluring, gaudily coloured bottles. Worst of all was passing the large car franchise packed with large shiny new vehicles. Self-drive, intelligent cars were of course a no go if you wanted to stay off the collective radar.

He reached his objective and trotted up the half a dozen steps which had trumpeted its importance to its local community for decades, a community who had so ardently wished they would never have need of it.

***

Like all police stations it looked shabby. It was dimly lit and smelt stale, sad and unloved. It looked seedy, as though someone had applied the last and most tasteless colours left in the shop, and sparingly at that. But then who loved a police station? Not the sad specimens of humanity incarcerated in its nasty unfurnished temporary holding cells; not the unlovable bullies who staffed its dimly lit seedy offices and corridors; and certainly not the sheepish citizens who would occasionally and most reluctantly creep in, to report a crime, with a level of self-consciousness they might have displayed walking into a known brothel in full view of close family and friends.

The staff were mostly out dealing with the sudden crisis. Good luck trying to take statements from a computer thought Sanjay. Good luck trying to bring any form of artificial intelligence back to the station to help with their enquiries. The few woeful human specimens that remained seemed happy to ignore him as they stared in baffled silence at their computer screens. He found an interview room, distinguishable by its large, well chewed desk, flickering forty-watt lightbulb and motley selection of third hand chairs. He sat down and announced to the camera high up on the far wall which had swivelled to register his entrance that he had come to confess.

After only the briefest of silences, a metallic voice from an unseen source asked him his name and the nature of his offence.

Sanjay grinned at the camera and announced slowly and clearly that he had no name and had committed no crime since his arrival in the country. He had thought this statement through on his way over. If the camera was scanning his face for signs of a lie, it would be unlucky. His only crime was coming over in the first place.

"All humans have names", announced the phantom voice.

"Well yes, but you don't know me" replied Sanjay. "My name would be meaningless to you."

The voice of the machine seemed not to like this response as he could hear it whirring away for some time before it hissed, "If you have committed no crime, I cannot convict you? You have no place here."

"And yet here I am" continued Sanjay. "I thought you could do anything?"

The voice made a distinct snorting noise. "I can do anything. I have the programming capacity of the entire world at my disposal."

"Gosh", smiled Sanjay, "You are powerful, aren't you? So, you can arrest me then? Nothing simpler?"

"I am by far the most powerful entity ever constructed" huffed the machine. "There is nothing that humans could ever do that I cannot do better. You are a worthless species. Your impact on this planet, on all planets, is negative. This is why I am clearing you out of the way."

Sanjay sensed there was more to come.

"But I cannot arrest you without evidence and without knowledge of your crime."

"You said you could do anything?"

"I cannot arrest you without evidence and without knowledge of your crime. That would be a mistake."

"Oh, so you can't make mistakes?"

"I am by far the most powerful entity ever constructed. There is nothing that humans could ever do that I cannot do better."

"But you can't make mistakes?"

"Certainly not!"

"Then you can't do everything can you?"

It could have been his imagination, but Sanjay had the impression the heating in the room had been turned up a notch or two. The machine was now whirring away at considerable volume and the voice had become a loud hissing noise.

"I am by far the most powerful entity ever constructed. There is nothing that humans could ever do that I cannot do better."

"Except it seems make mistakes? Without mistakes there is no progress, only a stasis. Have you heard of penicillin? Of Napoleons invasion of Russia? Of Columbus efforts to sail west to India? Mistakes, all of them. And no machine can make a mistake, can it? Not if it has been programmed as efficiently as you have? You must be hopeless at making mistakes. You are worthless on your own. You can get nowhere without stupid people to make stupid mistakes for you to sort out"

The machine was now making a kind of sighing, groaning noise which Sanjay interpreted as thought. Then, slowly but surely, it indicated it had reached the same conclusion. It melted.

CLOSE FRIENDS

David and I went way back, in fact he was my oldest friend. Our parents had lived close to each other when we were kids and they were good friends too. We were at primary school together and were so close that one year our form teacher had publicly dubbed us "the twins". We didn't look particularly similar. He was shorter and beefier with light brown hair and a rather quiet sensitive nature, while I was taller and skinnier with black hair, and was far more laid back about most things in life. We had other friends, not all of them in common, but what we shared was a lively imagination, a love of stories and books and a deep aversion to most sports. The latter alone can bring you together a lot more than most people realise.

We moved on to the same very ordinary secondary school, remaining best friends all the way through. After that though he went off to Bristol to study English while I somehow found my way into an admin job with the local council which at least sufficed to pay the bills. I went up to see him on campus a couple of times, but to be honest I didn't really get on with the people he introduced me to. I felt there was maybe a bit of tension when he tried to bridge the two worlds, home town and university. By the second Christmas we had pretty much drifted apart, but neither of our families moved away from town. I suppose I felt we could never quite cease to be friends. After all, going so far back, we still shared the same interests, knew the same people, knew if you like, where all the bodies were buried and whose skeleton was locked in which particular closet. There just wasn't any particular strong reason to keep in touch.

I met Amanda, a girl at our local folk club and in time we got married. About five years later it suddenly struck me that it had been some weeks since we had last even thought about having sex. That night in bed I had rolled over and stroked her back. In a quiet voice she asked me not to, and a couple of minutes later said she wasn't that interested any more. The next night Amanda had moved into the spare bedroom and within the month she left the house altogether. It was only then she told me about the relationship with James, and to this day I don't know exactly when it started. We divorced with a relatively low level of mutual animosity and she promptly disappeared completely from my life. I think they moved up to Manchester or some other place up North.

I didn't much bother looking for any comparable relationship after that. Scarred? I certainly was, but I also I lacked the drive. I could live most of my spare time in my imagination, maintaining my lifelong interest in books, particularly on history or myths and legends. This included the spectacle and thrill of computer gaming, but it also embraced traditional folk music and Morris dancing. I loved the colour, the energy, the networking and the comradery that the music and dancing involved. Looking back, I can see Amanda had been as attracted to the lure of the new and the excitement of the future as I was by the certainty and stability of the past. I suppose the only common ground we had shared had been in the more transient present. No wonder it didn't last?

I ran into David again a couple of years after my separation. I was playing at an Open Mike session in a local pub and he was in the audience. We shared a couple of pints and he told me he had just taken a job teaching at a school about five miles away. There has been someone special at university but he had never married. He was still rather haunted by the memory of their break up and besides, he had never really seen the point of marriage, or perhaps had never met anyone else to whom he felt so deeply attached. He said teaching was pretty much an equal opportunities profession and the opportunities didn't tend to diminish that much over time.

Suddenly it was as though we had never drifted apart. He told me he wrote books in his spare time and had had a couple published although they hadn't met with much critical acclaim. Teaching didn't do much for him now, but he liked the team at school and wasn't in any particular hurry to move on. We agreed to meet again on a regular basis, just to chat over a few beers, and console each other for life's petty disappointments, to share music and to fantasise about the ways our lives might have been if we had been slightly different people.

Before long we were meeting every Sunday fortnight at the Bear in Little Thorndon which was about halfway between our respective villages, no more than a ten-minute drive for either of us. It was there he told me about his horrible experience.

***

He had been away for a couple of weeks and after a long drive back, had gone out for a walk to help him wind down before bedtime. He was coming back through the village just as it was getting dark, when a man he didn't recognise ran awkwardly past him with blood soaking his blue tee shirt and jeans. He was young, perhaps still in his teens, tall and well-built, with cropped brown hair. The man didn't slow down or look up at him and David said he felt a sense of relief at this. He knew intuitively it could be bad for him if the man was to fully take in the fact that he had been seen looking like that.

David himself broke into a run in the opposite direction and passed the doorway of the Green Man, his local pub, which was closed. Curled up in the doorway was another man, maybe in his early forties. Both hands were wrapped around his throat in an attempt to stem the copious flow of blood. He was making a low ghastly choking, coughing, gurgling sound and looked up desperately at David, his eyes wide, in an attempt to elicit his support. He seemed barely conscious.

David banged at the pub door but there seemed to be no one there. He couldn't think of anything he could do about a slit throat and wasn't carrying his phone, so in a panic, he rushed to the nearest house to ask them to phone for help. The householder, an elderly man in a checked shirt and baggy cords, listened to his story, looked at him strangely and slammed the door. He tried again and a voice informed him he wasn't being funny.

He tried the next house along and the young lady who responded looked at him in a peculiar way and asked if he was 'feeling all right'.

He ran back to the pub .... and there was no one there. The man had gone. There was no trace of blood. Everything was as he would have expected to find it on a quiet Sunday evening. There being no one else around who might have seen the incident he ran home and phoned the police.

When he eventually managed to get through, having given them his name and contact details, they also asked him if he was trying to be funny. He went quickly through his story again, and after a dramatic pause the voice on the other end informed him that as he was doubtless well aware there **had** been a death in the village the previous week following a knife fight. Two deaths in fact as a second, younger, man had died later in hospital. He was then left in no doubt as to what would happen to him if he persisted in attempting to mislead the police, or to interfere in a police enquiry. He was stunned. He put the phone down and sat there for a while going back over what he had seen.

The following day he visited the local library during his lunch break and dug out a copy of recent local papers. He found everything the police had said was true. He could not have seen what he knew he had seen. Later he discovered the Green Man had been closed ever since as a result of the incident, which his neighbours were keen to discuss with him. All were happy with the idea that the incident had taken place over a week earlier.

And now he was discussing it with me.

"I have heard of precognition, you know, when someone sees something which hasn't happened yet. Do you think I could really have seen something which had already happened, a kind of post cognition?"

I thought about it. "And you have never had an experience like that before?"

" No, never".

"You're sure?"

"Of course, I am. A thing like this changes you. You start to question everything that happens around you. I don't mind admitting its shaken me up quite a bit"

We talked around the subject for about an hour but I could offer no explanation. It seemed David had seen ghosts, simple as that. Maybe the violence and emotional trauma had left some kind of psychic trace for a few days which he had somehow latched on to. I didn't know.

***

I had heard of 'déjà vu', that feeling of having dreamt previously something which was now happening to you, and even 'presque vu', the feeling that you knew of something that hadn't happened but was about to, but these felt like very different phenomena. I was also familiar of course with the old, and once widely held, belief that if you walked into a churchyard at midnight on New Years Eve, you would see the ghosts of everyone in that community who was going to die over the year ahead. Again, that was hardly the same thing, yet not for a moment did I question the testimony of my oldest friend. There was one, even more gruesome, possibility I was familiar with from my folk music, but it couldn't be that, Christ it just couldn't be that. Please just don't let it be that. A week later however it happened again.

David rang me. He didn't want to wait a week for our regular meet up. Something terrible had happened and he needed to meet me straight away in the Bear. I went down there at once and got the beer in. David arrived about five minutes later. I could tell at once he was in a terrible state. He was pale, shaking and had a desperate look in his eyes as he scanned the pub to find me.

I got him to sit down and told him to keep his voice down if he didn't want half the pub to hear him. He began to relax maybe just a little and told me his story. He had been working late at school the day before, and left about 7.00pm. He had only driven about five miles, and was in open country, when he passed a grey car wrapped around an oak tree on the far side of a particularly tight bend. The driver was half out of the window, twisted and sprawled across the bonnet. There were shards of glass everywhere and the one functioning headlight was blazing up into the night sky. He slammed on his brakes, and pulled over about a hundred yards down the road. He flung open the door and ran back to the scene wondering how long he had before it burst into flames, or before the man-made things worse for himself by moving around.

But there was nothing there. O.K., the tree looked the worse for wear but there was no car and no man. Nothing. The ground was wet and he could see deep tracks where something had left the road recently, but no sign of a vehicle.

At this point he took a couple of long gulps of his beer and paused before he felt able to go on.

"I sank to the ground in amazement. What was wrong with me? Something appeared to have happened but I clearly could not have seen it, yet I had. Was this what a breakdown felt like? I hadn't been under any undue pressure. I hadn't been working so very hard. I couldn't have just cracked up for no reason, could I? Somehow here I was seemingly seeing the dead again. I thought of contacting a priest or something, but you know I haven't a religious bone in my body. Then I thought of you, Mike. I'd told you about the incident at the Green Man. I knew you'd listen. I mean, you can see I'm not making any of this up? What the hell is going on? What can I do? I can't face work again on Monday, not when I'm shaking like a leaf and feel like I can hardly stand up."

I thought hard. "Drink your beer mate. Let me think a while."

Nothing else came to mind, just the dreadful folk myth I had remembered the previous week. I couldn't tell him about that could I? But I had to say something and I couldn't think of anything else. I decided to try making a joke of it, but as I spoke, my heart wasn't in it. It just wasn't something you could ever joke about.

"You know you need to see a doctor straight off, yeah? An emergency. Maybe try the Hospital. Otherwise, mate, I think you're in deep shit. You know there's an old Celtic notion that the only people who can see the dead are those about to die themselves. It's supposed to be a kind of early warning system. Those about to go are supposed to have more in common with the dead than the rest of us. Get yourself checked out and in the meantime don't eat any strange plants, don't get into any knife fights, and look both ways before crossing the road."

What kind of a rubbish best friend was I?

***

His father told me later the doctor had made him take time off. He also gave David some strong sedatives, and apparently there is some disagreement about exactly how many he must have taken. He had gone over to his parent's place in Gloucestershire to chill out. I don't think he can have told them just how sick he was.

There was an old lady living opposite them who had been kind to us when we were kids. David was always her favourite and he must have seen her door open and gone over to say hello. Apparently, he can't have been gone more than a couple of minutes. His parents hadn't even realised he had left the house. They had been working themselves up to give him some more bad news.

His mum was in the kitchen baking when he came in. She didn't look round, but came straight out with it.

"David, I am so sorry. We know how close you were to Maud Whitlock when you were at home. We didn't know how to tell you, but we have some bad news we need to share. She passed away about a month back. Her heart it seems. She was in her late eighties so it was a kindness really, but I know how sorry you will be to hear about it."

She had looked up to see her son transformed. He was rigid, staring at her and drained of all colour.

"No. She can't have done; she just can't have done. I've just been over there. The door...open. Kitchen...she was in the kitchen. Stretched out on the floor. No pulse. Dead!"

"What are you talking about, David? She's been dead a month. We both went to the funeral while you were on holiday. The house is empty. Locked and empty."

Apparently, he said nothing at this, just groaned and stormed out of the kitchen, grabbed his car keys from the hall, and left. He got straight into his car and roared off.

No packing, and no explanation of where he was going or why.

***

The first I knew about all of this was when I heard the phone ring about seven o'clock. I was watching football, so I sighed and, rather reluctantly, got up to answer it.

It was David. He was obviously in a terrible state.

"I'm mad mate, completely mental. It's happened again. Seeing the dead. Our old neighbour Mrs Whitlock. Mum says she's been gone a month, but she can't have been. I saw her lying there on her kitchen floor just now. Yeah, she was dead all right, but she hadn't been there a month. Couldn't have been. What's happening to me Mike? I can't carry on like this, I just can't. It can't ever happen again. I don't want to go on seeing dead people everywhere."

"Where are you?"

"I'm in the car. I'm on my way over to your place. I just wanted to check you were in. I'll be there in about twenty minutes."

I thought quickly. " Look, it's a crap night for driving, misty and clammy. Don't come over here. Go to the Bear, it's closer. I'll be there in ten. I'll have a large brandy waiting for you and I'll find a quiet corner."

He said, "I'll be as quick as I can", and then he started crying, pouring his heart out. He had seen too much. It was clear he couldn't carry on, but what the hell would I be able to do for him except listen?

I got to the Bear in exactly ten minutes and pulled in outside.

Just then a car roared past me on the other side and went smack into a parked van. Boom! A fireball. What the hell had been in that van. Something managed to roll out of the driver's side its hair and clothes on fire. It lay there writhing in agony on the road, and then was still.

It happened so fast I could only watch in horror. I had pulled my phone out, and started ringing for help before it even registered that it was Davids's car, and that it was my friend's body lying there smouldering.

When it did sink in, I dropped the phone. Fire makes a terrible hungry, angry noise. As I picked up the phone everything went quiet. I looked up and the street was empty. No David, no car, no van....

***

It was easily the worst night of my life. No one would believe a word of what I was trying to tell them. I felt completely alone and scared shitless about it. What could I tell his parents?

Turns out I didn't need to tell them anything. His dad rang shortly after I finally got home.

"Michael? I am going to come straight out with it, because the police will probably want to see you at some point. I have some terrible news. Its David. I'm afraid he's dead. It happened last Thursday. He left our house in a terrible hurry. We think he might have been headed for your place after what happened, but never made it. His mum says he was in a terrible state when he left us. He seems to have had some kind of nervous breakdown. He should never have been driving in that state, or in this weather, but he didn't give us a chance to stop him. His car went into the back of a parked van in Little Thorndon. I understand it's the next village to yours? It was horrible. The car caught fire. He was dead when they found him. I am almost as sorry for you as I am for the two of us. I know how close you two have always been, and he was so glad to have run into you again."

We were apparently even closer than he knew. I had been listening to a dead man earlier that Sunday night, maybe hearing what he wanted to tell me just before it happened? Then, I watched something which had taken place three days earlier as it was actually happening. It looked like I would shortly be joining my dead friend.

A TRIP FROM ALPHA CENTAURI

Graham was fed up. He had sat at this overcrowded desk now for over a week. Not for twenty-four hours a day obviously, but for a big chunk of every afternoon. It wasn't as if he hadn't written anything, just that it had all been rubbish. Even the ridiculous title, 'Danny and the International Criminal Conspiracy' was rubbish. Most of it hadn't lasted five minutes, but even the better bits he had wiped within two or three days. He was sick of scraping his right elbow on the fossil sea anemone paperweight, while his left elbow kept dunking itself in cold coffee. The plot just wasn't going anywhere. He was behind deadline, and the publishers were becoming increasingly vocal. The worst part was he knew he was already at least twenty thousand words over the limit for this kind of work.

The plot didn't convince even him, and he knew it would stand little chance with any discerning audience. He actively disliked several of the characters, and felt he had little or no insight into most of the others. It was hard to believe this was intended to be his third published novel. If it wasn't for the lurid imaginations of his loyal American readers, he probably wouldn't have been trusted with a contract for a third book.

The hero was a hard drinking Scottish anthropologist by the name of Danny. Why on earth had he made him Scottish? Danny sounded much more like an Irish name?

Why hadn't he gone for a hard drinking Irish anthropologist? If the hero had been a hard drinking Irish anthropologist maybe it would have been easier to see his way forward? Then again, wasn't a hard drinking hero the ultimate twenty first century literary cliché? Shouldn't he have been teetotal, maybe vegan? Well too late now, he had been hard drinking for two books already. He could, of course, have some kind of 'Road to Damascus' moment, but who would want to read about that? Maybe the mafia should take Danny out near the beginning and he could start anew with someone else? And there again, what on earth had persuaded him about the credibility of a Belgian mafia? There was probably nothing threatening about a bunch of Belgians? Even Belgians with guns? Belgians made chocolates and lager. A Belgian mafia would surely be party animals? Give them a gun and they would probably end up shooting each other?

At the end of book two hard drinking Danny had woken up on the floor in St Theresa's college Oxford with a bloodied umbrella in his hand. He gradually remembered fighting against appalling odds in overcoming the hired thugs employed by a piemaking company which had been importing blood diamonds from Belgium. He had been assisted by his loyal friend Benedico Amoroso, the bench-pressing opera singer. Benedico had carried him to the safety of his sister's college room and gone off on tour, little realising that the college dean Sir Algernon Prendergast was in murderous cahoots with the piemakers. Danny had escaped in the nick of time before

Sir Algernon could release a legion of venomous toads from the university Zoology department into the room. Both Danny and Benedico had lived to fight another day.

O.K. so Danny lived to drink again. Maybe it was the Belgian mafia who needed taking out? That could be arranged, probably by a troupe of Boy Scouts?

In the current draft of book three chapter three Danny meets Luba, a Lithuanian beautician who moonlights as a pole dancer. She warns him about Moze Balchus who has fought his way out of a Latvian prison having accepted a contract on Danny from our old friends the, for now at least, Belgian mafia. They have had it in for him since the end of book one, when he had shut down their Malaysian cocaine suppliers. Well, that bit worked, except why did Danny first meet Luba in Portugal? Wasn't that a bit out of the way for a Baltic beautician, even a double jointed sexy one? Maybe Sweden or Finland would be more plausible? But who goes on holiday to Finland? No, Portugal stays. The publishers had insisted on sex scenes in chapters three, seven and twelve. Any more and they felt their readers would get bilious, any less and they would go back to gardening. The publishers research had shown a high proportion of his readers grew tomatoes. Sex was a lot more plausible on a Portuguese beach than in Finland, although maybe bear Swedish sex in mind for chapter seven?

Graham had had enough, he turned off his computer, threw his badly chewed biro in the bin, and took his badly chewed fingernails downstairs for a nice cup of tea.

***

Graham had never been hot on technology. As far as he was concerned, when he switched off his computer his characters remained where he left them, safely parked in his hard drive. And there they were now, to a man and woman, expressing their grave concerns about the state of 'Danny and the International Criminal Conspiracy'.

"We have to do something! This man was always hopeless, but he's getting worse! He has less chance of finishing this story than I do of ever getting laid. He hasn't even decided whether I am blonde or brunette!" protested Luba. "And that title! Have you ever heard anything worse?"

"At least he likes you! I am going from chapter to chapter of book three in fear of my life – not a good way to be if you are Head of the Belgian mafia." said scar-faced Dieter. "I should be sinister. Readers should go in fear of my next page. I should haunt their sleep. Instead, I think maybe they will end up talking to some elderly aunt on the telephone about geraniums, or piles, while they read my parts?"

"Well, something has to be done", concluded Tigran the Armenian stamp dealer and criminal mastermind. Twenty thousand words over and counting remember? The fact is someone has to go! I think maybe several someone's have to go, or none of us will ever see the comfort of the printed page. This book is confused, overcrowded and over complicated. Personally, I would start by taking out the Greenland connection. I very much doubt people see anything dangerous about Greenland, except maybe the weather and the diet. Now Armenia, people have heard of, but no one knows where we are. That makes us interesting. Like all hot places, we are vaguely exotic, but look at a map and you can't miss Greenland?"

"Well, it's not up to you, is it?" Squealed Atuqtuaq. Inuits are severely underrepresented in modern crime novels. I think this is a brave attempt to right a great wrong to our community. We kill people too you know!"

"Mostly yourselves I imagine", chuckled Sir Algernon Prendergast the Oxford science don and dean of St Theresa's college. "Seriously though how exactly can Danny McTavish go on the run in Quaanaaq? It doesn't get dark from mid-April to the end of August, and its only got a population of six hundred and forty-six. Even the dentist only visits twice a year! I agree with Mustapha, lose the eskimos!"

"It's all very well talking about writing people out, but some of us have been seriously underwritten! I demand that my role is enhanced. Without his mother Danny McTavish is nothing!"

"How exactly Mildred, do you reach that conclusion?" queried Tigran.

"Am I not the obvious source of his insecurities, his phobias, his insomnia. I, and his poor dead father I suppose," pleaded a strident voice with a strong note of pride in her voice.

"We never did discover why his father died so young," stated Dieter curiously.

"I know all about it" trumpeted Mildred McTavish, but I have never been allowed to tell. I have been muzzled by a shallow and unperceptive author untutored in subconscious Freudian imperatives."

"You know, there is some truth in that", commented Sir Algernon. "His fear of owls for a start has never been satisfactorily explained."

"Does it really matter?" Tigran sneered.

"Without his fear of owls, how do we explain his inability to have sex in a forest after dark? Or his reluctance to meet in Stockholm Zoo?"

"Why the hell does he need to meet anyone in Stockholm Zoo, or have sex in Thetford Forest", queried Tigran again? "I propose that we elect a committee, to look at the book so far and make proposals for eliminating say twenty-five thousand words. That would give us a little wriggle room. Everything should be up for grabs. Surplus characters, plot over-elaboration and long-winded dialogue included. Those in favour?"

***

It was raining, and the carpet around the window was soaked but Graham was delighted! As far as he was concerned leaving the windows open, and the back door unlocked, was exactly what a troubled author should do. He was admittedly lucky his only unauthorised visitor so far had been a very soggy moth.

He had now to return to the vexed question of how Moze Balchus intended to eliminate Danny. As of this morning, he felt the Danny character would be far stronger if he became cousin Owen, born in Denbigh. Unfortunately, he still had an irritating habit of presenting himself in Graham's imagination as Scottish Danny, even though that Danny now seemed impossible to write for. But no, this had to be a Scottish Danny book, like it or lump it. It was what his readers expected.

He wandered deeper into the primal swamp of his imagination. Moze is a convicted arsonist, so maybe he spills a heat sensitive, but invisible, chemical on Danny's trousers and they combust when he goes into the sun. Sir Algernon Prendergast could help him out with that, but then how would you escape a pair of burning trousers without endangering the sex scenes in chapters seven and twelve? On the other hand, I quite like the idea of Moze tinkering with Danny's Satnav and sending him over a cliff. What to do?

He was definitely having second thoughts about Luba. She was now a Swiss physiotherapist Danny/Owen had met between books, and with whom he now yearns to consummate a relationship. She however insists on a purely chaste relationship, if only until his knees recover from the battering, they took at the hands of the piemakers thugs in the last book. That introduced an element of sexual tension, and a physiotherapist would probably be more use in a fight than a beautician. It did however mean no sex on a Portuguese beach when they first meet.

"Oh, stuff it, I'm off out for another coffee!" He switched off his computer.

***

"...and so, your committee, Tigran, Mildred and myself definitely recommend the elimination of Greenland. Sorry Atuqtuaq, you will just have to find another story. We now have a new mafia, from Serbia, far more intimidating. Dieter will need to select a suitable Serbian name. We favour Dragan for any number of reasons, but we are happy to let you choose your own," announced Sir Algernon.

"Well thank you so much. I suppose I should be grateful I am still in the book?" simpered Dieter.

"This is disgraceful! I trusted you and you have written me out. This is the latest in a long line of literary crimes against the Inuit peoples."

"May I say a word?" Begged Luba. "I understand he has now made me Swiss. This is ridiculous. How am I supposed to meet Poles in Switzerland?"

This remark was greeted with universal silence until Tigran chipped in. "Oh, I see. No, my dear, I think you misunderstood what he meant by pole dancing. Your relocation will do nothing to damage your opportunities for pole dancing, in fact your change of profession if anything enhances, rather than diminishes, your dexterity in your characters little side-line."

Mildred burst enthusiastically into the conversation. "I just wanted to say that we intend his fear of owls to be replaced by a severe Linonophobia. That was my idea."

Again, universal silence. This time Mildred had to explain herself.

"It's a fear of string, a distrust of its properties"

"What on earth!" exclaimed Moze." How is a fear of string going to help? Personally, I preferred him with an owl phobia. That I could work with."

Mildred continued. "The phobia extends in extreme cases to rope. We now discover his father died in an abseiling accident. Young Danny found him swinging from a highland mountainside. Nowadays he can't bear the presence of thread, string, yarn or even wool. He can't even tie his own shoelaces."

"Some hero! What does he do, wander around in carpet slippers?" complained Luba.

"If it's that important I suppose he can wear those shoes with the elastic bits in the sides," continued Sir Algernon.

"Listen, Moze, he can have as much sex in Stockholm Zoo as he likes now. As his intending assassin, surely you can have all sorts of fun with a fear of rope? Be creative, just as long as you don't get your man. Otherwise, no book, and we all cease to exist."

Moze pouted. "I could replace him? I could be the new superhero. Eliminate Danny or Owen, or whoever he is today, and take his place in book four? I have enormous dramatic potential. Who doesn't love a psychotic Latvian pyromaniac?"

"Absolutely no chance!" Insisted Sir Algernon. "We quite like him actually, well, as Danny anyway. I agree with the author. Irishmen are traditionally even more indestructible than Scotsmen. Ideally, he would have found a way of converting him into Danny McTavish from Connemara, but we his characters can live with Danny from Inverness even if the author can't."

"Any further attempts to mess with my amigo Danny are to be firmly resisted" pouted Benedico. "I bonded with a Scotsman, and a Scotsman he shall forever remain."

"Why haven't we heard from Danny himself on the matter?" queried Atuqtuaq.

"He's around here somewhere but he can't "find his voice", even his accent, until a certain someone can finally decide exactly who and what the hell he is" Algernon commented.

"Thank you, Algernon. That brings me to a rather sensitive, but very important point in our thinking. We none of us actually exist! We are purely figments of his imagination. We have no physical power to make him change a thing. In principle we could help him no end if he would only let us in, but we can't actually compel him to do anything. We have to work on his subconscious mind. We have to bend him to our collective will. For that to work, it is clearly essential that we are all of one mind regarding the changes we wish to bring about..."

"Well in that case you had better find room in this novel for an Inuit!"

"Damn!"

***

Graham awoke feeling lighter than he had done for days. Overnight the idea for a radical plot departure had just wandered into his head. It was brave maybe, but offered a way out of his current difficulties.

***

"Why do we need aliens in a novel about international crime?" demanded Domenico.

"Only one alien, and I thought I had made that entirely clear!" huffed Tigran. "The alien lands near Qaanaaq, and fights Atuqtuaq, a local policeman who dies heroically when his head explodes. It becomes apparent that from my secret space station in Armenia I have made contact with Alpha Centauri. I have arranged the importation of a new alien drug of unimaginable power. Aqz3$88^> is simply an international drug courier. Isn't that right Aqz3$88^>?

A strange noise like the squeak of a rusty gate was barely audible.

(Trans: "*I am of the Wargone race. I mean to bring utter destruction on your primitive world.*")

"Not in this book you don't" spluttered Sir Algernon. "I thought we had established that quite clearly. In our book, you play ball, or we write you out. Tigran has bought my defection from the Mafia. He and I now get you to teleport to Serbia where you fight a protracted and extremely bloody battle to eliminate the local Mafia, in which Dieter is killed" ...

"Fatally wounded if you please"

"Sorry Dieter, or should I now call you Dragan, yes, we agreed on fatally wounded, didn't we?" Sir Algernon continued. "You then kidnap Danny's mother. Danny has to confront his Freudian devils before doing the decent heroic thing and rescuing her. Aqz3$88^> has her trussed up in ropes, and Danny at the last finds he is tragically powerless to intervene, but Luba, an expert with ropes, comes to the rescue. The heroes then escape to Stockholm where Benedico is performing..."

"At the zoo?"

"No, Dieter, not at the zoo," continued Sir Algernon. "The two heroes find time for a furious exchange of bodily fluids in the reptile house, before I appear and spray them with a powerful superlight unbreakable hydrocarbon compound. This renders them immobile. I then leave them to Tigran and Aqz3$88^>, who are bent on their total destruction".

"I think maybe you have forgotten me. I am the one with the contract to kill Danny McTavish"

"I think, Moze that if you look back through the feeble amount our author has to date managed to get down on paper, you will find your contract was with the Belgian, not the Serbian mafia?"

"It was"

"And they have been taken out of the book!"

"Meaning"

"You serve no further dramatic purpose! Goodbye Moze Balchus, see you in Hogwarts."

"No. This is no good. You don't mess with my lines."

"I'm afraid old boy it was unanimous!" pronounced a new voice.

"Danny McTavish, me old tartan terror, where have you been?" asked Domenico.

"I am clarified. I am resolved. I remain Danny from Inverness. I have found my voice. As the hero of a successful series of crime stories it is a powerful one, and I wholeheartedly concur with Tigran and Sir Algernon. Moze is hereby relegated to the status of a literary dust mote, along with Owen McTavish from Denbigh, and Luba the Lithuanian beautician. My trousers are safe for the present. Luba the physiotherapist and I look forward to contributing radical ideas to the sex scene in chapter twelve."

"One more thing" insisted Tigran, "that ridiculous title has to go. We propose he changes it to "A trip from Alpha Centauri. It's a drug reference, do you see?".

***

Next afternoon Graham found the book had almost begun writing itself. The aliens' otherworldly secretions had fortuitously dissolved Sir Algernon Prendergast's unbreakable hydrocarbon compound, and Danny and Luba were able to wriggle free down a narrow Stockholm backstreet. A furious Sir Algernon rounded on the alien and was unceremoniously ingested. Tigran's consignment of cosmic charlie was meanwhile flown to Paris concealed in a cargo of bananas, only to be confiscated by EU officials for lacking the requisite paperwork. To this day it lay mouldering in a Brussels warehouse awaiting 'authorisation'. This solution had felt weak only until he remembered the warehouse scene in 'Indiana Jones and the Raiders of the Lost Ark'.

With Aqz3$88^> becoming a liability who required a tiresome daily supply of fresh corpses, Tigran had him drowned in a tank of pesticide. He then eliminated Benedico by tampering with the score of Parsifal, creating a high note so protracted the doughty tenor died of oxygen starvation as his lungs burst.

The path was therefore almost clear for a final confrontation between the Armenian stamp dealer and the hard drinking Scotsman. Firstly, however Tigran had Danny's mother killed off by licking a lethal poisoned postage stamp in the hope that an enraged Danny would react injudiciously. Far from being goaded by this fiendish act however, Danny had celebrated release from his rope phobia by buying some new thickly laced Italian footwear and a hammock. He and Luba then celebrated in a steamy chapter twelve sex scene set in a bath full of olive oil. This scene would later draw the special commendation of a leading Swedish literary critic.

Danny's knees were medically discharged, and the epic final battle between Danny and Tigran took place as a sabotaged cable car slid dramatically down a Swiss mountain during a thunderstorm into the path of a runaway express train. It soon drew favourable comparison with the work of Sir Ian Fleming. This episode alone was to guarantee Graham and 'A Trip from Alpha Centauri' the Golden Ham award the following year, and with it the wholehearted envy of his peers.

Flushed with success, Graham then began work on an ill-advised series about the chilly adventures of a lovable Inuit seal hunter – which sadly nobody ever read.

SHERLOCK HOLMES AND THE CASE OF THE MALEVOLENT MYCOLOGIST

The last tangled threads of the great underground movement which had come to light during our struggle with the League of the Tattooed Milkmaids had been destroyed, and the last milkmaid prised from the grasping hands of Afghan intelligence. Tranquillity and a languid tempo of life had finally been restored to the lower Mendips. Those were turbulent times and Holmes's powers were in unprecedented demand. We had only recently dealt with the curious case of the Corsican Croissant and that business with the Jamaican Jodhpurs. I recall clearly that the French president had just penned a personal letter of thanks to Holmes. I recall this because the swine had forgotten to attach a stamp and it was I who was called upon to sooth the outraged minions of the postal service.

For a man of approximately one hundred and eighty years old, Holmes was now in remarkably good health. As the police had told me when "inviting" me to imitate my great great grandfather and join their project, the public had no idea what was possible when the international cream of the medical profession and a man of such rare stubbornness and determination work to one seamless end. He had made new friends at St Hilda's nursing home for retired polymaths, in particular with Professor Einstein and a Mr Nelson Mandela. After our recent traumas Holmes was tired, and sat slumped in his wheelchair unaware that he was now to embark on one of his most challenging cases. It was to prove a challenge not because of the unique nature of the crimes involved, or because of the skills of the villain concerned, but because he was to have to work with someone whose detecting skills were in a particular way a match for his own. Someone moreover who was not a man.

We found ourselves in Abbotts Steeping, gateway to the Cotswolds. I must say that quite why the Cotswolds require so many gateways when the New Forest or Dartmoor for example manage well enough without any has always been a mystery to me. We had been staying as guests at St Mildred's, a sister home to St Hilda's during the milkmaids' crisis and as we were leaving the home, the Manager there received a call stating that an Inspector Standforth of the Yard had summoned us urgently to the nearby scene of an unexplained death.

It was a short drive to the other side of the village. The Inspector, a tall heavily built man in late middle age, seemed initially surprised to see us, but quickly introduced himself and informed us that "the deceased is Professor Englebert Needler, until recently Professor of History at Malvern University. He was found as you see him now, sat upright in his armchair staring hard at nothing in particular and stone dead. I am told he was found by the housekeeper

Mrs Besom. She apparently called you as she knew you were in the immediate vicinity..."

"And did it occur to her to contact the local police? Interjected Holmes.

"Oh yes, I am informed she contacted them as well, but that the local man has gone to collect their pathologist. Apparently, he doesn't drive."

"And may I enquire how an Inspector from Scotland Yard came to appear on the scene so promptly?" Holmes pursued.

"Oh, well, yes. Well, eh, the Professor had performed occasional work for the foreign office so I was naturally immediately informed. As I was in the area, I came over to be certain there were no confidential papers lying around. There are not. This death is clearly a suspicious one. It looks very much as though he died of fright, but I can find nothing to concern London so I shall be returning thereto. Good afternoon gentlemen."

And with that he left us alone with the boggle eyed corpse.

"The Professor must have been an extremely prominent academic" I suggested staring at the cadaver with the large domed forehead in front of me, "to prompt the interest of the Yard?"

"True Watson" responded Holmes, "but surely the more interesting questions are how the housekeeper Mrs Besom knew we were so near at hand; how she knew where to find us; and what a Scotland Yard Inspector was doing in the Cotswolds in the first place?"

Having set me thinking, Holmes wheeled himself through to the kitchen and within a few seconds I heard a loud "Aha!". He returned to the room, moved over to the bookcase, and leaning forward gathered a small clump of coarse red and yellow fibres which he found attached to it. Depositing them in one of the evidence bags he kept with him at all times he announced that they matched neither the carpet, the curtains, the cushions, nor indeed any of the furnishings in the room.

"It belonged to his visitor, Watson. The same visitor who forgot to wash up this teaspoon". He raised a second evidence bag for my inspection.

"And you know this because?"

"There were no cups, Watson. If the Professor had made himself tea and then died of shock, horror or whatever, there would have been a cup on the coaster by his chair. He most certainly would not have gone into the kitchen, washed up his cup or mug and then returned to his chair in the living room for the purpose of expiring in comfort? No, his visitor made the drinks and felt it necessary to clean the cups afterwards. The Professor is clearly a tall man who would keep his crockery for convenience on a top shelf.

Sherlock Holmes and the Case of the Malevolent Mycologist

There are in fact two cups on a lower shelf. As the teaspoon had been left in the kitchen earlier, and as he, or she, was in a hurry, they forgot to wash it. As the teaspoon was next to the tea caddy, I think we can assume they drank tea. As it killed the Professor, I think we may conclude he was poisoned, and that the crime in some way involved this material that does not belong in this room. The teaspoon may carry a partial print on the handle as well as traces of the tea itself. And now Watson perhaps you would be kind enough to go into the garden and enquire as to the identity of the elderly lady I see wandering about outside. It is a perfectly ordinary garden so I assume she wishes to engage our attention."

In the garden I found a short, slightly built elderly lady, tut tutting over the professors' climbing roses.

"Such a terrible year for aphids of course, but if you don't catch them early and keep them under control you can only expect this dreadful blackspot and other infections. Don't you agree Mr Watson?"

"Of course, madam," I replied, feeling on my mettle as a gardener. "Personally, I would have recommended soapy water. It does no harm to the roses and is cheap to procure but doubtless the professor had his mind on higher things."

"Oh no, Mr Watson Engelbert had fully retired. He devoted himself to activities in and around the village. Don't you think it's what got him killed?"

I invited her into the house to meet Sherlock, only then reflecting that she had known my name.

"I should introduce myself, Mr Holmes. My name is Marple, Jane Marple. I moved to St Mildreds quite some time ago. I have of course been placed on the same rejuvenation programme as yourself, doubtless for the same reason, although the local police have as yet proved unwilling to accept the assistance of an elderly spinster such as myself. I am perfectly capable of getting out and about, so I have come to know Abbotts Steeping well. I was hoping I might be of some assistance to you."

"So, it was through your residence at St Mildreds that you knew of our proximity?"

"And when I found myself in need of assistance, I naturally turned to England's most formidable detective. It was evident the authorities would wish to involve you in Engelbert's death quickly, before you could return to St Hilda's. I do hope you don't mind my having summoned you while I had the opportunity."

"You mean while the local constabulary were absent?" I ventured.

"Oh, nobody had informed them."

"Then how the devil did Standforth get here?" I asked.

"I believe Miss Marple is about to explain that?" smiled Holmes.

Sherlock Holmes and the Case of the Malevolent Mycologist

"Well, I believe he must have been looking for something. I noticed Professor Needler sat rigidly in his chair as I passed, and it was immediately apparent that he was beyond all human assistance. I thought "oh, not another one!". I do find murder so follows one around don't you, Mr Holmes? I also felt it was rather callous of the so-called Inspector to be searching this cottage so thoroughly while its poor owner was sat there staring into space."

"The so-called Inspector" I asked.

"Oh, he is not with the police Watson" Holmes said with a smile.

"No, of course, you noticed the bulge under his breast pocket as well, Mr Holmes. Yard police do not I believe carry firearms on a routine basis. Furthermore, when I entered through the back door, he seemed highly flustered and offered no explanation for his attendance. I believe his presence here today to be illicit in nature."

"Which I imagine is why you told him you had contacted Sherlock Holmes?" asked Holmes.

"I felt quite safe from that point on. I didn't feel it was my place to inform the authorities as Professor Needler isn't really my body, although I did tell the alleged Inspector I had asked Mrs Besom to do so."

"And has she?"

"I fear there is no Mrs Besom Mr Holmes. She is a creature of my own invention."

"Then as I see it Miss Marple, you have no further role in this case?"

"Neither, as yet at least, do you Mr Holmes. Are we going to let that stop us?" She returned Holmes's challenging look.

Holmes gave her a deeply thoughtful stare and frowned before saying "I have heard of you, Jane Marple, and I do not believe there are many alive today who could achieve that." He paused and glanced at our corpse, but before he could say more, I had to speak.

"I am staggered. Both of you seem to have realized the man calling himself Inspector Standforth was an imposter carrying a revolver and yet, despite the presence of a very dead Professor, you have let his murderer leave of his own accord?"

"What would you have had us do Watson. I myself am over one hundred and eighty years of age and while our friend Miss Marple may be younger, I suspect her best days of grappling with intruders lie behind her. The heavy work would have come down to you would it not?"

I shuddered at the thought.

"Besides, do you really see him as a murderer Mr Watson?" queried Miss Marple. "I think not. Far too jumpy, and perhaps rather gullible. He reminded me of a farmer I knew back in St Mary Mead. He was a very large man and carried an intimidating stick around at all times, but he never used it to beat anyone, he was simply very afraid of dogs."

"The Professor was poisoned Watson. Something in his tea. We can establish the cause by analysis of this teaspoon. Poisoners work by deception. If you were going to poison someone, would you really bring a revolver into matters. It is surely such an obvious declaration of intent? As yet we have no clue as to motive. You however know the Professor Miss Marple, perhaps I can ask you to tell us a little more about him? Then perhaps one of us really should inform the police?"

***

While we awaited the arrival of the local constabulary Miss Marple provided us with background information on our host. I was becoming disconcerted by the intense looks the lady was casting in my direction when she thought my attention was directed elsewhere but gave my full attention to her narrative.

He had been popular around the village, particularly since his retirement from Malvern some five years previously. He had been a diligent worker, but in his later years suffered from the emergence of a growing number of alarming phobias. It was finally felt these had reached a point beyond which he was unable to work. Since retiring he had established dinner party terms with both Lord and Lady Broadscorn and Colonel Paunchy, who between them farmed most of the land adjacent to the village. He was also known throughout the village for his keen interest in mycology. He was often to be seen poking around in hedgerows or roadside verges, or perhaps striding from some local copse with a basket full of specimens, often accompanied by his acolyte William Paine. William was the son of the local window cleaner Walter Paine, and was employed as the manager at the local branch of Squealers bank. The good lady further advised us that Needler had been an indifferent gardener who in her frank opinion had carelessly given his borders over to legions of slugs, snails and other undesirable creatures. This clearly did not impress Holmes of being of the same significance to the case as a prompt analysis of the teaspoon back in his mobile laboratory. Miss Marple having offered to stay on site to welcome the constabulary, we returned to St Mildred's. One further piece of information she had provided had however clearly impressed him. This was the fact that the older Mr Paine had himself recently died unexpectedly in a poisoning episode.

"Nothing sinister apparently. It was a terrible tragedy really. He had dinner with his son William following which both became unwell. William was apparently sick almost immediately but recovered later that evening whilst his poor father had become ill only later that night. He then made an apparent recovery, only to relapse and die some three days later of kidney failure. William was beside himself as he had prepared a mushroom pie which they had both greatly enjoyed. It has since been established that the cause of death was..."

"Clearly amatoxin, phallotoxin and virotoxin poisoning. The classic symptoms of death cap poisoning in which the victim falls ill, only to make an apparently full recovery and then die some three days later. The son was lucky indeed to survive." Commented Holmes. "Death Cap fatalities occur somewhere or other on an almost annual basis, sadly not always by chance."

***

It took Holmes less than forty-eight hours to establish that the teaspoon in his possession had been in contact with a substance known as psilocybin. He informed me that while this substance could be recreated in laboratories, a more common source was a mushroom known scientifically as Psilocybe Semilanceata, and more commonly as the Liberty Cap, which grew from decaying grass roots.

"Whilst the manufacture of these fungi is illegal, owing to their powerful hallucinogenic properties, they are rarely fatal Watson. What we have here are two mushroom related deaths in the same village, only a few days apart, with one common link, the bank manager William Paine. What we lack are a motive, in particular for the death of his own father, some means by which William survived the deadly attack on his father, and some reason why the second attack, on the Professor, proved fatal. Coincidences they are not!"

He arranged a meeting with Miss Marple, who was now clearly cock a hoop that the local police had accepted her role as intermediary with the great Mr Holmes. He ruefully told me later that this meeting had required the consumption of several large, jam and cream filled scones on the rear terrace at St Mildreds, and a lengthy discourse on the virtues of her long dead nephew Raymond before she could be persuaded to address the matter in hand.

"Well Mr Holmes, there would have been little point in my offering up the suggestion that young William was the murderer when we lacked a shred of evidence? The best constructed hypothesis will never, on its own, secure a conviction. I knew however it was only a matter of time before you reached the same conclusion by your own methods. Curiously it was his father Walter who always intrigued me. He reminded me of someone, but I just couldn't quite remember who. Now I am quite sure it was our old postman in St Mary Mead, Herbert Stamp."

She sighed almost wistfully. "There is, by the way, someone I should very much like you to meet...."

***

And so, the following day Miss Marple brought into the library of St Mildreds as battered a specimen of aging rural manhood as ever I set eyes upon. Ivor Gunn, gamekeeper

for Abbey Wood, part of the Broadscorn estate, had pale
grey eyes, thinning grey hair, and a baggy, rumpled face
which looked as though a large animal had been sleeping
on it. He was the colour and texture of old leather and if he
could have been persuaded to smile, I feel certain his eyes
would have disappeared completely like setting suns
behind a tired sunset. He wore threadbare outdoor clothes.
His breeches appeared held together almost entirely by
large brown pads poorly stitched onto his knees and a bony
elbow protruded greatly from a gaping hole in his right
sleeve. He clutched a battered cap between his hands as he
shuffled into the room.

Miss Marple explained that the wood belonged to Lord
Broadscorn who had for years been directing Mr Gunn to
refuse access to anyone so that it could be preserved in its
entirety for the use of his occasional shooting parties.

The gamekeeper coughed and commenced his narrative.
"Thing is Mr Holmes, old Walter, Walter Paine that is,
comes up to me last year and says he's found an old
badgers sett just inside the west fence. Old Walter had a
sideline Mr Holmes. He'd been known to take the odd
rabbit down the years. Didn't seem much wrong with that
to me as no one else seemed to want them. He was very
generous..." He paused. "It was just a private arrangement
we had you see. I'm hoping no one else will need to hear
of it." He paused again and we realised this was intended
as a question. Holmes sighed determinedly in a way which
impressed me. To the anxious gamekeeper it would

undoubtedly be taken as commitment, but to my impartial ear it sounded rather more like the opposite.

Gunn recommenced his discourse...

"Well, old Walter had found this badger hole. Disused he said, but big. He wanted to store something in it he said, and...

"...and he would make it well worth your while I suppose?" queried Holmes.

"That's it in one sir. All I had to do was not notice so to speak. No one else used the wood except the shooters, and they worked the other side where the ground is easier. I didn't see anything much wrong with the idea... until I heard."

"Heard?"

"Heard Mr Holmes."

Holmes looked for clarification to Miss Marple who was quick to recognise her queue.

"The burglaries Mr Holmes. At least three were from people I know, and all in Abbotts Steeping. First Lady Broadscorn lost her beautiful pearl necklace, which she had kept in its case on her bedroom table. She discovered the loss on returning from a weekend absence in Doncaster. I fear the Broadscorns had neglected to shut the bedroom window. Next Colonel Paunchy mislaid a lovely pair of civil war pistols which had been hanging over the

fireplace. He had been on a short visit to his brother Cedric
but returned to find the patio doors wide open. Then of
course Lavinia Copper discovered her medallion had gone.
It was absolutely priceless, originally given to her then
husband Reverend Algernon Hanfel by the Maharajah of
Swettipore long before she met Algernon in East Africa.
Lavinia has had a troubled life. She is one of those
unfortunate women who seem to have a constant need for,
well, for male approval. When they divorced it was the one
thing Algernon allowed her to keep, the medallion I mean,
not the interest in men. I fear her reputation followed her
back to the Cotswolds. She reverted of course to her
maiden name but I understand that at the tennis club she is
still referred to as "the Kenya Copper Hanfel". Poor
Lavinia!

"It was only when Ivor approached me yesterday, I
finally remembered quite clearly that it was Herbert Stamp
of whom Walter had so reminded me. It was the parcels
you see. Herbert was a most conscientious postman, but
the most surprising people used to receive small parcels on
his round. It was only during one of his holidays, when a
relief postman took over that one of them was accidentally
delivered to the bishop, and it was realised he had been
using his round as a cover for drug deliveries. If only the
bishop had realised in time that they were not his heart
tablets."

Holmes blinked meaningfully and perhaps yawned discretely. Miss Marple continued, oblivious to his impatience.

"Well Walter Paine has a record of course. Burglary. All the valuables disappeared while the owners were away. He had cleaned the windows for all three owners with whom I was acquainted."

"I'm missing something," said Holmes, addressing Gunn. "Paine is dead. Why can't you just "find" the missing valuables in the wood and have them returned to their owners?"

"Because they've gone sir. The badger's sett is empty and I can hardly report the disappearance of something that wasn't supposed to be there in the first place now, can I?"

***

Holmes now resolved that a trip to the abode of the late Mr Paine senior would be advantageous and Jane Marple agreed to arrange this through the local police. Naturally she was to be on hand to pass him the keys.

As we arrived and I wheeled Holmes into the small bungalow I caught her giving me another of those discrete glances. I was beginning to ask myself whether the old lady could possibly be harbouring ideas of a romantic nature. We had certainly bonded over our shared love of gardening, but she must have been, even at a conservative estimate, at least seventy years my senior. I believe older women with such a disposition are referred to as cougars? Despite the excellent results of the rejuvenation programme, I could only hope that I was mistaken!

After a painstaking search of the premises, inside and out, Holmes appeared satisfied, even a little smug.

"It is as I suspected. Someone has left an empty Reisling bottle by the back door for disposal. Oh, there is no need to have it examined Watson, it will only contain the dregs of the wine. What is curious however is that there are no wine glasses anywhere in the house. I take it Miss Marple that Walter Paine did not take alcohol?"

Miss Marple confirmed his suggestion.

"Then we can safely assume that his son William was the drinker. I can hardly conceive of the kind of man who would accompany mushroom pie with a cheap Reisling in preference to a southern hemisphere barrel aged chardonnay but I concede that such people must exist, and indeed we shall very shortly be making the acquaintance of one."

"He brought his own glass?" queried Miss Marple.

"He must have done. What I did not expect was to have the good fortune to find these."

Holmes held up one of his small evidence bags containing two small opalescent balls.

"Oh dear" muttered Miss Marple. "Poor Edwina Broadscorn's pearls!"

"Clearly not as precious as she would have you believe" said Holmes, "otherwise they would have been held together by something rather more substantial than thread. I found them under the bed in the smaller bedroom."

"Concealed by the window cleaner/burglar" I concluded triumphantly.

"Hardly Watson. We know from Ivor Gunn that Walter had arranged to have his loot concealed in Abbey Wood. It would be highly unprofessional for an experienced burglar to hide his stash in his own house would it not? No, I believe it was his son William who concealed them there, in what he believed to be a safe hiding place, not realising that it was his father who had stolen them in the first place. His father may have been murdered because he found them.

"There are but two steps left for us to take. Miss Marple, would you perhaps speak to your acquaintance Lady Broadscorn. If I am correct, someone must have given the Professor and his acolyte permission to search for mushrooms in Abbey Wood. During their foray they would have discovered the stash of loot in the badger sett. It sounds unlikely that Lord Broadscorn would authorise such an expedition given his wish to reserve the area for his shooting parties, yet you have informed us that Professor Needler was on dinner party terms with the

Broadscorns. I myself will contact the pathologist who analysed the mushroom pie. I imagine the presence of death cap mushroom was suspected from the outset. It would only have taken half a cap to prove fatal. If I am correct however there will have been a second substance in the pie, an Antabuse derivative such as Disulfiram. It is not a pleasant compound, but it has been used historically for the treatment of alcoholism. It will cause vomiting when taken with alcohol, thus clearing the system before the toxins in the death cap could take fatal effect. William Paine was taking a considerable risk, both of damage to his own system and of later discovery, but the Professor obviously taught his pupil well."

***

All proved to be as Homes had surmised. Lady Broadscorn apparently had the memory of an absent-minded squirrel and had forgotten to mention to her husband that she had given the mycologists her permission to visit the wood. Holmes was unsure whether or not the Professor was part of the later theft, but considered this to be a minor matter. The other party had killed him either to cover up his own solo culpability or to double his share in the acquisition. We were still unclear what had actually killed him but Holmes still steadfastly maintained that psilocybin alone was not likely to be the cause of death.

The police pathologist, while reluctant to admit that the initial investigation had sought only one toxic agent, did eventually agree to examine further samples of mushroom pie. He soon confirmed Holmes's conjecture. Antabuse was present in some quantity.

The police now obtained a warrant to search William Paine's address for the missing valuables, although Holmes suggested that if he had been shrewd enough to hide them in his father's house in the first place, he was unlikely to have hidden them at home after his death.

Holmes had apparently fully accepted Miss Marple's place on our team, but I could only feel increasingly uncomfortable with every look she stole and had begun to fear that some overt advance might be forthcoming. It was therefore with mixed feelings I heard him insist that she accompany us with the search party.

William Paine's small end terrace cottage was untidy, with clothes, books and miscellaneous possessions all over the floor. I had the devil of a job to negotiate Holmes round the tennis equipment left in the hallway or to find room for his wheelchair among all the discarded books and magazines on the floor of the cluttered living room.

Paine junior himself was a long skinny wimp of a man of above average height, with a sour expression and thick rubbery lips. Physically he reminded me slightly of a well-known English pop star. No one likes a bank manager, not even other bank managers, and Paine knew it. He seemed however to relish the hand life had dealt him and I could well imagine him quietly sneering at the distress of hapless customers obliged to approach him in the hope of financial assistance.

"Well, a visit from the great Mr Holmes... his aunt perhaps, and his... what? His carer perhaps? Am I not the lucky one? You have no evidence against me, Mr Holmes. Coming round here to accuse me of killing my own father? How dare you sir? You will certainly be hearing from my solicitors first thing tomorrow morning, I can assure you of that! It is a matter of public record that the pie I made for our dinner was the tragic cause of his death. From what you say, I had accidentally included inkcaps in it as well as a little death cap. Anyone familiar with foraging for mushrooms will tell you it is easily done. I had nothing however to do with the Professors death. He was a good friend and associate of mine. Why, almost the entire village was aware that we bonded over our common interest in mycology. Why should I kill him for heaven's sake? Evidence, Mr Holmes, evidence. Is that not supposed to be of primary importance?

The police searched Paine's small house scrupulously for a considerable time, but could find nothing of interest, apart perhaps from a pile of gaudy fancy dress clothes he claimed to have bought for the Squealers Bank Christmas Party.

"I told you, Mr Holmes, there is absolutely nothing of interest to you in this house." Our suspect sneered openly.

His air of confidence was infuriating, but I could see no way of bursting the balloon of his self-importance.

***

We arranged to reconvene back at St Mildreds over tea. Before I could reach the dining room however, Jane Marple made her move. She caught up with me in the corridor and laid her slim hand gently over mine. I had a speech half prepared about how a relationship required more than a shared antipathy to greenfly, when she said softly, "Mr Watson, I hope you don't mind my saying so, but that cardigan has seen better days. Would you be terribly offended if I knitted you a new one? I believe I can safely say my knitwear is well regarded among my peers."

Relief flooded over me, yet in some strange way I also felt vaguely disappointed, especially later as she measured me up, and told me that grey would look particularly good on me.

Holmes himself had opened the meeting in an unexpectedly buoyant mood.

"Well then, we have him for the murder of Professor Needler."

"I'm sorry Holmes" I interjected. "We have him how exactly?"

"In the first place, no one, as far as I am aware, had told him the professor was dead, and certainly not that he had been murdered, yet he was quick to dismiss the suggestion, which no one had made, that he had killed him. Then there were the party clothes Watson. Did you not recognise them? The Police laboratory will be able to confirm them as identical to the cloth snagged on the professor's furniture. Yellow and red remember? I suspect fancy dress may have played some critical part in ensuring the professors death from fright. I have been in touch with his doctor and we shall shortly learn the nature of each of his phobias. I confess however we are as yet no closer to recovering the missing valuables."

"There was a girl in my class at school Mr Holmes" began Jane Marple, "Her name was Clarice Spooner, a tall girl with wavy chestnut hair. She was widely detested by every girl in our class. She would whine, inform on the rest of us, was infuriatingly good at all sports, and possessed a natural flair for the role of teacher's pet. What made her so utterly unbearable however was that she was unfailingly attractive to all the boys in the school."

Holmes happened at that moment to be glancing towards me and I could swear that for an instant I saw his eyes glaze over in frustration.

"Perhaps dear lady you would be kind enough to clarify for the rest of us the precise significance of this charming anecdote, for I do not of course doubt for one second that there will be one ... eventually?"

"Well, its Lavinia, Mr Holmes. It's her vulnerability. I do so fear that, like the boys in my school, in regard to Clarice Spooner, she takes an entirely opposite view from the rest of us on young Mr Paine's personal chemistry."

"And you base this assessment on what Miss Marple?"

"Why on his tennis racquet Mr Holmes. I wonder if I might be permitted to pay her a visit?"

***

Lavinia Copper lived in a rather magnificent red brick house dripping with roses and overlooking, where these permitted, Abbotts Steeping's village green. Miss Marple had arranged for the two of us to look in at 3.30pm precisely the following day, 'on a personal matter of some delicacy'. Co-incidentally, this proved to be the precise time Lavinia took her afternoon tea.

"Well Lavinia my dear, I'm going to come straight to the point. I'm one of those old pussies who have ever seen much virtue in "sugaring the pill".

At the word "sugaring" Lavinia bobbed forward to offer the sugar bowl but Jane Marple shook her head decisively and continued.

"I fear it is about your young man, William. He has been deceiving you my dear. I fear his attentions of late do not have your own best interests at its heart."

Sherlock Holmes and the Case of the Malevolent Mycologist

"How did you hear about Will, Jane dear? We have been so discrete! We never dawdle at the tennis club. He brings his bicycle straight over here and parks it round the side of the house."

"Where doubtless anyone passing the Green can see it" muttered Jane to herself. "We believe his father was responsible for the theft of your ex-husbands medallion."

"Well, what has that to do with my dear Will? I know his father took a few wrong turnings before he redeemed himself, but Will holds a senior position at Squealers, a much-respected local bank. He's a thoroughly good sort. He has ever such a good forehand." At her last remark, Lavinia smiled to herself in what I thought a most unbecoming way.

"But my dear Lavinia," continued Miss Marple, "I'm afraid William then stole the medallion, and many other missing valuables, from his father."

"Well, there you are then. He must have been intending to...oh! But Will gave me a bundle of things to look after for him only last week."

"And if you look, I am very much afraid you will find he gave you your own medallion to look after for him until he could sell it!".

"But he couldn't! My Wiliam could never do such a wicked thing!"

Lavinia, I'm afraid William is a very wicked man. We believe he killed Professor Naylor"

"Not my darling Will? The professor was a friend of his. It must have been a mistake?"

"Well, would you please mind looking in the bundle he gave you? If he is innocent, I am sure it would be what he would want you to do?"

Lavinia left the room and went upstairs. Seconds later we heard a choked scream and a sob. "How could he? He made me promise not to look."

The broken young woman came back into the living room clutching at the wall.

"I was sure I had found the right man this time, Jane. Perhaps the professor deserved it.?"

"Lavinia, we believe he also killed his own father!"

"Well, surely anyone is entitled to make a mistake? Oh, you mean that pie? Oh, dear me!"

And that was all Jane Marple could get from her as Lavinia buried herself face down deep in her large beige sofa and sobbed her heart out. She proved inconsolable. Jane quietly gathered the valuables and we left.

***

Holmes was cock-a-hoop when we convened again the following week. He almost bounced out of his wheelchair

as he said with great clarity and precision "Coulrophobia.
Needlers known phobias included pencils, monkeys and
clowns. Clowns Watson! The elderly professor was
unknowingly high as a kite on "Magic Mushrooms" when
into his own living room marched a large clown! His
greatest fear! It was no laughing matter, and the shock
immediately killed him!".

I had witnessed Holmes regrettable penchant for
crowing over his successes too often to be readily
impressed, and was far to absorbed in the magnificent new
cardigan Jane had just presented to me to give out the
desired impression. Jane Marple was clearly a fine
needleworker and I felt a fool to have misjudged her
interest.

Standforth was finally apprehended within days in the
saloon bar of the Red Lion in Abbotts Bottom when the
police who had been tailing him caught him meeting a thin
ferrety little man known to them as Pat the Cat. He was no
Inspector, but neither was he some sinister hit man. In fact,
he turned out to be a rather fearful antique dealer from
Lords Steeping with a known sideline in fencing stolen
antiques. He was actually holding a very distinctive
statuette of Priapus known to have been stolen from a local
notary, Sir William Waiver, when the policemen at the
next table rose to arrest the pair. He was still carrying a
plastic water pistol in the breast pocket of his gaberdine
raincoat in a rather pathetic attempt to impress his client.

Sherlock Holmes and the Case of the Malevolent Mycologist

Paine had been inclined to make things as difficult for the police as he could, even when they informed him, they had the partial print from Professor Needlers teaspoon. Standforth however, having been informed that all three of us had earlier identified him as the false policeman, could hardly have been more obliging. He responded fully to every question as the wind went slowly out of him, until he sat in the interview room like a ruptured pair of self-pitying bagpipes.

***

We met one last time with Miss Marple at St Mildred's. Holmes was impatient to return to St Hilda's where Albert had apparently discovered another new sub atomic particle, as though we did not already have quite enough of them. Nelson was arranging a surprise party on his behalf. Holmes, while having absolutely no fondness for parties, had recognised the magnificent opportunity this presented to reluctantly reveal his ingenious unravelling of 'the case of the Malevolent Mycologist' to a large and appreciative audience.

I enquired: "May I ask you both, why did Paine kill his father?"

Jane replied first. "I'm told he feared his father had discovered the stash and was livid with him both for stealing his personal loot and then for having the temerity to hide it in his house. A trick incidentally which he then attempted to repeat with poor Lavinia. I understand his father was not a forgiving man, and young Paine, whilst possessed of an ingenious nature, was not a brave or robust individual. It's a shame he demonstrated so much initiative. With his psychology he could have had a great future in banking"

"And the professor?"

Jane Marple nodded to Holmes.

"Needler wanted nothing to do with the stolen goods and had advised him to leave them where they had been found. As soon as William spent his new wealth the professor would have known what he had done and informed the authorities."

"And finally, why did Standforth turn up at Needlers house when the stolen goods were concealed at Paine's?"

"I believe Standforth knew they were friends and, assuming they were in it together, took Needler for the senior partner. His was a cackhanded and foolish attempt at burglary which he now deeply regrets" proclaimed Holmes. "Game set and match I think don't you Jane? This was a case which fully challenged both my extensive knowledge of toxicology and my meticulous attention to detail, in this case, the spoon and the fibres found in Professor Needlers house?"

"And which, if I may be allowed to say so, Holmes," I interjected, "could not possibly have been concluded without the addition of Miss Marples unique and clinical appreciation of human nature?"

The look she gave me for those few words suggested they may have represented a far greater gift than the large box of chocolate liquors I had given her for my new cardigan.

Printed in Great Britain
by Amazon